I0823963

THE UNINVITED

THE UNINVITED

NANCY BANKS

DELACORTE PRESS

Delacorte Press
An imprint of Random House Children's Books
A division of Penguin Random House LLC
1745 Broadway, New York, NY 10019
penguinrandomhouse.com
GetUnderlined.com

Text copyright © 2025 by Nancy Banks
Jacket art: iron gate by Jamroen_Photo Background/Shutterstock.com,
rose by Sasha Chornyi/Shutterstock.com, ornaments by Joygul/Shutterstock.com
Eiffel Tower chapter opener art by Nikolai Tito/stock.adobe.com

Penguin Random House values and supports copyright. Copyright fuels creativity, encourages diverse voices, promotes free speech, and creates a vibrant culture. Thank you for buying an authorized edition of this book and for complying with copyright laws by not reproducing, scanning, or distributing any part of it in any form without permission. You are supporting writers and allowing Penguin Random House to continue to publish books for every reader. Please note that no part of this book may be used or reproduced in any manner for the purpose of training artificial intelligence technologies or systems.

Delacorte Press is a registered trademark and the colophon is a trademark of Penguin Random House LLC.

Editor: Alison Romig
Cover Designers: Trisha Previte and Tatiana Guel
Interior Designer: Michelle Canoni
Production Editor: Colleen Fellingham
Managing Editor: Tamar Schwartz
Production Manager: Liz Sutton

Library of Congress Cataloging-in-Publication Data is available upon request.
ISBN 978-0-593-90029-1 (trade) — ISBN 978-0-593-90031-4 (ebook)

The text of this book is set in 11.25-point Calluna.

Manufactured in the United States of America
10 9 8 7 6 5 4 3 2 1

The authorized representative in the EU for product safety and compliance is Penguin Random House Ireland, Morrison Chambers, 32 Nassau Street, Dublin D02 YH68, Ireland, https://eu-contact.penguin.ie.

Random House Children's Books supports the First Amendment
and celebrates the right to read.

This book is dedicated, with love,
to Kevin,
who gave me France.

Arrête!
C'est ici l'empire de la Mort
(Halt! This is the empire of Death)

—Inscription over the entrance to the Paris Catacombs

PROLOGUE

SIX WEEKS AGO

I was twenty-some meters under Paris in a room hacked out of limestone, huddled against the farthest wall, shivering. I didn't know what to do next. A frantic voice in the back of my head kept shrieking, *Run!* Like that was a solution. Where would I go? I didn't have any money with me. I didn't have my passport. I didn't have a plan. What I did have: My phone. A pack of cigarettes. Some matches. A set of lockpicks. Also shame. And guilt. And blood soaking my shirt and stiffening my hair.

Besides, running was what had gotten me here, to the farthest dark corner of this sour-smelling room in the cellar of a forgotten church. I'd been running, and I didn't see its steps rising out of the sidewalk until I went sprawling. As I got to my feet, I noticed the church's weather-beaten door with its clumsy medieval lock that I could have picked with a damp twist of paper. It looked like a good place to hide.

Inside, soot-crusted stained glass held the dark in. Dust coated the floor so thickly that my steps threw up little puffs. Automatically, I looked for the votive stand, but it held no candles, just a few blackened wicks trapped in grimy pools of wax. The tiny nave contained several disorderly rows of chairs and a thirdhand table, bearded with dust, that must have been the altar. The place was as dead as last year's leaves. Near the altar in a grubby little grotto stood the only saint in the place, leaning casually on his club. His specialty was lost causes, but the dour look on his face said my troubles were beyond his powers. In the space before the ambulatory, the floor opened, and a wide stair descended into the dark. I followed it down and found myself in the crypt. Another set of steps took me down again, to a room that harbored a sad little regiment of rush-bottomed chairs—amputees all, too damaged to repair and return to the nave. I needed to make a plan, but I was too weary to think or even to cry. I sank to the floor, pulled my knees close to my chest, and rested my head on them.

CHAPTER 1

TWELVE WEEKS AGO

Three days before we were supposed to move to Paris, Dad's company had a major supply-chain disaster, and he had to fly to London to meet with a new supplier to make sure its waterproof fabric was up to Great Outdoors' specs. It was kind of ironic. He'd started working for GO part-time in college because one of the perks was a discount on hiking boots, and now he spent half his time flying to places where a hike meant walking to the subway station.

"I can't believe this," he said, scheduling his Uber. "You know I'd send someone else out to deal with it if I could, right?"

"It's okay, Dad. I know how airports work." I'd flown to meet him for long weekends when he'd had business in fun cities—Barcelona, London, Prague, Ljubljana.

"I know, but I was looking forward to starting this adventure together."

"Me too. But I'll be fine."

"Nina"—our Portland housekeeper—"will take you to the airport, and I've scheduled a car in Paris to pick you up. Our new housekeeper, Madame Dupuy, will be at the apartment when you arrive, so you'll be fine." He sighed. "But I didn't want you to do this by yourself."

I smiled at him. "I'm really okay."

He gave me a quick hug. "I hate that my work means I have to leave you like this."

I hugged him back. "On the other hand, your work means we get to live in Paris."

On the flight to Chicago, I had a row all to myself, and I hoped I'd have the same kind of luck on the Paris leg. But not long after I settled into my new seat, texting Dad that I was on the right flight and that it was on time, a guy in a business suit put his laptop down onto the seat next to me. I sighed. Business Guy shucked off his jacket and looked around for a flight attendant to hang it up for him. I went cold. He was wearing the same blue-and-gold-striped tie my debate partner, Cole, wore to meets. That stupid lucky tie. Business Guy handed off his jacket, then did the tie-flapping thing that guys do—why? What is the purpose of it?—and all I could see was Cole, smoothing his tie before a round, almost petting it, attributing every win of the season to its magical lucky powers instead of my research skills. I tried to reassure myself that hundreds, maybe thousands, of people wore that tie. It was probably the third-most-common tie in all of menswear, and of course I'd see it. It didn't disappear from the world just because I was putting a whole country and an ocean between me and Cole. I was stupid to let it make me miserable. But I felt the way I felt.

I fumbled my earbuds into my ears, hoping Business Guy would ignore me. I'd been looking forward to getting some sleep on this flight. The past few weeks had been exhausting—finals, packing, saying goodbye to Lily and Mina. But I wasn't falling asleep next to someone wearing that tie. I concentrated on my phone's screen, stress-watching Buffy kick vampire butt until Business Guy closed his laptop, reclined his seat, and went to sleep. I pulled my legs up close to me and turned so I could keep an eye on him, the armrest digging into the small of my back.

By the time we landed in Paris, half an hour before our scheduled arrival, I'd been awake for twenty hours straight. My body said it should have been the middle of the night, but the morning sun glowed confusingly through every window. The floor bobbed under me as I walked through customs, and my eyes slipped in and out of focus. People zoomed their luggage-laden trolleys by, buffeting me as they passed. Signs morphed as I tried to decipher them, so that Contrôle de Passeports became Controversial Parrots and Arrivées turned into Archrivals. And it was so loud. The PA system kept up a nonstop "bargle bargle bargle" of important unintelligible announcements, while people meeting passengers called out names, little kids collapsed onto the floor and screamed, and strained-looking travelers scouted for restrooms.

I finally made it to the "archrivals" area. Just like Dad had promised, a bunch of dark-suited car-service guys stood there, holding up signs with people's last names on them. I found my driver and followed him to the car. He put my bag into the trunk and held the door open for me, then waited calmly while I fumbled with my phone so I could tell him the address. I really, really needed coffee, but I didn't know if I could ask him to pull off the autoroute at the nearest Starbucks. I didn't know if there *was* a nearest Starbucks, or what the French equivalent was.

After almost an hour on the autoroute, we exited into Paris; dodged through an enormous, chaotic roundabout; and finally turned into a narrow street lined with straight-edged, modern-looking apartment buildings and crammed with parked cars. Dad and I'd traded postcard-Paris architecture for a light-drenched apartment in a plain, six-story box in a redeveloped area three blocks from the Eiffel Tower. We chose it for the large park in the center of the block, an almost unheard-of amenity in the city. The view on Google Maps showed a long rectangle of green—the park—which took up almost half the area. Surrounding it like walls surrounding a medieval city were four apartment buildings. Six openings between the buildings gave you street access on all sides from the interior while maintaining the peaceful feel of a sanctuary.

The driver got my bags out of his trunk, wished me good day, and drove off. I looked around, blinking hard, because the street kept going out of focus. I wanted to lie down right there on the sidewalk and go to sleep. Instead, I pulled my phone out and found the text Dad had sent with our address, the apartment number, the two security codes I'd need to get into the building, and Madame Dupuy's cell number. I'd never lived in an apartment before, so I wasn't sure how to work the codes. My head felt like eighty pounds of wet cardboard, and things were blurring at the edges. But I found the code box, so yay me. I punched in the first code. Nothing. I punched it in again. Nope. I squinted at the keypad until the numbers were in focus and then punched them in, slowly, consulting my phone for each one. Nothing happened again.

There was a button on the box marked Guardian, so I pressed that, thinking somebody would come. Somebody didn't. I tried the second code. Dad could have gotten them reversed, right? But that didn't work, either. I didn't have a French SIM card for my phone yet, so I couldn't call our new housekeeper or Dad, and he wouldn't be back for three more days in any case. Madame Dupuy should have already been there, but when I pressed the buzzer for our apartment, nobody answered. I didn't know anyone in Paris. I had an emergency credit card, but I didn't know where to find a hotel. I told myself I didn't need to cry yet; maybe Dad had just typed the numbers in backward. I punched in a different combination. It didn't work. Tears filled my eyes and slid down my face.

"It's fine," I muttered to myself, wiping my eyes with the back of my hand. I'd just failed again with the codes when Nick walked up with his little sister, Sophie. I didn't know he was Nick then, of course. He was just a random boy with a cute little sister.

She pointed at me and said something in French that I didn't understand.

"Mademoiselle?" he said.

Oh, God, I thought. *I'm going to have to talk to an actual*

French person, and I can barely remember how to speak English. I would have pretended that I was leaving if he'd been alone, but the gap-toothed six-year-old smiling tentatively at me made me decide it was safe to ask him for help. I tried frantically to remember the words for "door" and "It doesn't work." I didn't even know what you'd call the code box in English, let alone French. In the end I failed to say anything at all.

"Je peux vous aider?" he asked, and through the fog of exhaustion and frustration and anxiety, I realized he'd asked if he could help me.

I took a deep breath and gestured at the code box. "It's broken," I said. I'd meant to say it in French; I did remember the word for "broken." But I opened my mouth and English came out, which was humiliating. I was still crying, too. I felt like such a loser.

"You speak English?" he said in a very friendly sounding American accent. I nodded.

"Hi!" the little girl said. "Don't cry. We'll help you."

I gave her a weak smile. "Thanks."

"You're American?" he asked.

"Yes," I said.

"Us too," she said. "You look like Princess Merida."

"Thank you," I said, smiling bigger. "I love her."

"Me too!" she said, bouncing in excitement.

He noticed my suitcase and backpack sitting on the sidewalk. "Did you just get in?"

"Nick!" She pulled on his arm. "Help her open the door."

"Oh. Yeah, of course." He smiled at me, and I noticed his eyes were chestnut brown with glints of amber in their depths. He punched in some numbers. The door buzzed, the latch released, and he took my suitcase in one hand, opened the door with the other, and said, "After you."

"The code is three-six-one-nine," she informed me as she led us across the lobby to the second security door.

"Oh, that explains it," I said. "My dad added a zero when he texted the codes. Big thumbs. Thanks for helping me."

"You're welcome. This one is two-two-two-three," she said, reaching up to punch in the code. Nick held the door open again. We walked through, and she pressed the elevator call button. Then she took my hand, and I felt a burden lift. I already knew two people in Paris. I wasn't alone.

"What floor?" Nick said when we were on the elevator.

"I'm on four," I said. "Four-oh-one."

He smiled at me. "Five-seventeen. I'm Nick, by the way. And this is my sister, Sophie."

I smiled back. "I'm Tosh."

"Do you have any brothers or sisters?" Sophie asked.

I shook my head. "It's just me and my dad."

"Don't you have a mom?" she said.

"That's kind of personal, Soph," Nick said.

"It's okay." I smiled at her so she'd know I wasn't mad. "She had cancer. She died when I was six."

"Oh, I'm sorry," Nick said. He looked uncomfortable.

Sophie's eyes were wide. "Six is how old I am."

"It was a long time ago. I still miss her, but she's always in my heart." I squeezed Sophie's hand, and she squeezed back. The elevator doors opened. Nick took my suitcase for me because Sophie hadn't let go of my hand.

"You should come meet our mom," she said. "If you get lonely. She's really nice."

"I'd like to do that. Thanks for helping me get in."

"You're welcome."

Nick smiled at me. "Remember," he said, "we're in five-seventeen if you have any more problems with locks."

The strangest things can change your life. If Dad hadn't been in a hurry when he sent me the codes, I might not have met Nick. If I hadn't met Nick, I wouldn't have seen the Paris that lives underground. I wouldn't have climbed the Eiffel Tower and seen it sparkle in the twilight. I wouldn't have fallen in love. I wouldn't have killed somebody.

CHAPTER 2

TWELVE WEEKS AGO

Nick and Sophie rang our buzzer the next morning while I was scavenging a breakfast of jam and a leftover baguette. I'd thought I'd be by myself for the two days until Dad got back, but our new housekeeper had shown up half an hour after my adventure with the code box, just when Dad had asked her to. If I hadn't been so jet-lagged, I'd have remembered that my flight had arrived early and not panicked about her not being there.

"Hi!" Sophie said when I opened the door. Nick grinned and waved. In the fog of yesterday, all I'd really noticed about him were his eyes, his skill with a code box, and his friendliness. Now I took in his height—almost a foot above my five feet and three inches—his adorably messy dark hair, and the warm smile that made his eyes crinkle at the corners. And then I remembered what I was wearing. Dad went to U of

Oregon—go Ducks!—and I have a large and embarrassing collection of duck-themed clothing.

"Hi," I said, hiding as much of my yellow-and-green T-shirt as I could behind the door and trying to keep my mouth closed because I hadn't brushed my teeth yet.

"Mom said we could invite you and your dad over for dinner. Can you come tonight?" Like Nick, Sophie was dark-haired and brown-eyed, but her hair was straight, cut in a chin-length bob, and pushed back with a yellow-and-black polka-dot headband that matched her capris.

I smiled at her enthusiasm. "My dad doesn't get here till tomorrow. Can I tell you what day would work for us when he gets home?"

She made a "tchu" sound. "Just text him, silly, and you can tell us now."

"That's rude," Nick told her. She frowned at him.

"I don't have a French SIM card for my phone yet or I would," I said.

"We can help you get one. Right, Nick?"

He nodded. "Absolutely."

"Wow, that'd be excellent," I said. "I can't do anything without my phone. I'm about to lose my mind."

"Okay, but we have to go to school now." Sophie took Nick's hand and pulled him toward the elevator.

"Hang on," Nick told her, turning back to me.

"You have school?" I stepped out from behind the door. Sophie giggled.

Nick gave me a smile and an eye roll. "The French believe in the maximum-torture method of education. We've got three more weeks."

"Ouch."

"We can help you after school," Sophie said. She leaned close to me and stage-whispered, "Do you have a shirt that doesn't have ducks on it that you can wear?"

"*Sophie*," Nick said. "That's rude."

I laughed. "It's okay. This is just for at home. I would never go out into Paris looking like this. There's probably a law against it."

One corner of Nick's mouth quirked upward. "Decree number 177 of 22 April 1693. It is forbidden upon pain of death to go forth into the streets, avenues, boulevards, passages, alleys, byways, or other ways paved or unpaved wearing clothing upon which humorous waterfowl are emblazoned."

I snorted out a laugh, and he grinned at me.

Sophie tugged his hand. "We're gonna be late."

"Just a sec," he told her. Then, to me: "Is after school today okay? Like a little after five?"

"They make you go to school till five p.m.?"

Nick's face went tired and serious for a moment. "Like I said, torture is a curriculum component here."

"Wow. Okay. Yeah, a little after five sounds great."

AT SIX p.m., we were having Cokes in a sidewalk café with a red awning on a busy, tree-lined boulevard. My phone worked, I had a booklet of Métro tickets, and Nick and Sophie had shown me how to navigate the closest station. I took a photo of them and texted it to Dad over the caption, "Nick and Sophie—our neighbors who helped me get my phone working and figure out the Métro."

"I can't wait to meet them," he texted back. I told him we were invited for dinner with their family as soon as he got home, and then Sophie wanted to know what he looked like, so he texted a very dadly selfie of himself in an office.

"He's got a big nose," she said when I handed her my phone.

"Rude again," Nick said.

"Dad's terrible at selfies. His nose is fine in real life," I assured her.

"Tell him I think he looks . . . friendly," she said, handing my phone back.

"Good save," Nick told her. She smirked at him.

AND THE first thing she said when we walked through their door Friday night for dinner was "Tosh was right. Your nose is fine."

"Thank you," he said solemnly. "I've always felt that way about it."

"We're having un apéro," she informed him. We followed her into the living room and discovered that it was French for "an appetizer." Nick's mom handed around the olives and charcuterie, which Sophie translated for us as "salami and stuff," while his dad poured wine for the adults and Orangina for Nick, Sophie, and me.

"What's your favorite thing about Paris so far?" Mr. Wallace asked as he handed me the glass.

I thought for a minute. I'd barely arrived, but Paris had

already embraced me. "It feels like a city that really likes its people."

"Intriguing," Ms. Wallace said, putting her arm around Sophie, who snuggled next to her. "What is it that makes it feel that way to you?"

"It's really easy to get around on foot." She nodded. "And it's built on a human scale. Buildings don't tower over you looking down their noses at you because they're immense and you're not. I haven't seen a building yet that was over six stories. And so many of them have pretty details—carvings or wrought iron work or doors—just so people have something nice to look at. There are so many street trees. There are unexpected tiny parks. The best thing, though, is the light. The buildings seem to glow."

Dad and I had come to Paris in March to find an apartment. We'd left sodden, dreary Portland and arrived in rain-soaked Paris, and the first thing I'd noticed was how bright it was despite the rain. Unlike in Portland, the gloomy sky didn't hang a foot over my head leaking an endless drool of rain. We didn't need streetlights at noon. When I pointed this out to Dad, he gestured to the cream-colored stone buildings that surrounded us. "Paris is built of limestone," he said. "And the pale color reflects light." Portland was made of wood and brick and glass and metal, and they all seemed to get darker in the interminable winter rains. Maybe it was the way moss and mildew crept across their surfaces. Decay was a constant in Portland.

Nick grinned at me. "I have a friend who talks about buildings like that. It's one of the reasons we're friends."

"Paris just seems so alive and vital." I sipped my Orangina, which was so fizzy it made my head bubble.

"It is alive," Nick agreed. "That's why it's such an incredible city." I smiled at him, feeling a tug of connection between us.

The Wallaces were from Minneapolis, and they'd been in Paris for three years. Nick's dad was some kind of manager for 3M, and his mom did freelance tech support for small businesses. Dad told them about how Great Outdoors had just acquired a French recreational gear company and had sent him here to manage the European supply chain.

Ms. Wallace turned to me. "Where will you be going to school, Tosh?"

"École Jarret." I jiggled the ice cubes around in my glass.

"Oh, Nick goes there. It's a great school; I'm sure you'll enjoy it."

"My school's just down the street," Sophie volunteered, "but Nick has to walk twenty whole minutes to go to school."

"So you speak French already, if you're going to EJ," Ms. Wallace said.

"Well, I thought I did. I took the entrance exam remotely, back in Portland, and they told me that I'd have to take an accelerated French class over the summer so I could keep up when school starts."

Nick grimaced. "Ouch."

"Yeah. I had totally different plans for this summer."

"Like what?" Sophie asked.

"Oh, you know," I told her. "Frenchy stuff like sit in cafés and buy glamorous shoes and eat all the pastries. See the Louvre. Get a beret." Nick made a choking sound.

"Only tourists wear berets," Sophie informed me, her face serious.

"I see," I said, matching her solemnity. "Well, I'm going to be in class for half the day and studying for the other half, so I wouldn't have time to go buy one even if I wanted to look like a tourist."

"I could help you with your homework," Nick volunteered. "And if you want to see the Louvre, I could take you tomorrow." He smiled, and my insides went fluttery.

I smiled back at him. "I'd love that. Thank you."

"The Nick Wallace Tour Company is at your disposal."

"You're not a tour company," Sophie said.

"I am if Tosh wants me to be."

"I'd love to tour the Louvre with the Nick Wallace Tour Company," I said, and we arranged to meet next morning just as Ms. Wallace announced that dinner was ready.

The adults talked about work and the exchange rate and where to find kitchen cabinets over the salmon in butter sauce while Sophie told me about visiting the Astérix theme park. We'd read some Astérix comics in French class this year, but I didn't know there was a whole park. I asked her what her favorite ride was.

"Les petits chars," she said. "I smashed everyone."

Nick saw my blank look and translated. "Bumper cars. She's a demon in those things." She told me about her bumper-car strategy, which was to bang furiously into another car until she scared the driver away, as Ms. Wallace brought dessert out.

"Yum," Sophie said, and looked at me with a sly smile. "Do you know what this is?" She pointed to the plate in front of me, which held a slice of chocolate cake surrounded by a ruby-colored pool of sauce.

"Looks like chocolate cake?"

"In *blood sauce*." She widened her eyes at me, smiled, and nodded hard. Nick groaned.

"It's your fault," Mr. Wallace told him.

"It was *Halloween*," Nick said. "I was just trying to make it festive for her."

"Yes, and now every time we have raspberry coulis with anything, it's blood sauce."

"It looks like a vampire bit it," Sophie said around a mouthful of cake. "Did you know that there's a vampire in Paris?"

Mr. and Ms. Wallace looked at each other. "Where did you hear that?" Mr. Wallace asked.

"Clémence said. She said he bites people on the neck and makes them bleed, and it looks like blood sauce." She had a ring of chocolate and raspberry around her mouth.

"Clémence is exaggerating, sweetie," Ms. Wallace said. She looked uncomfortable. To me and my dad, she explained, "Somebody with a mental illness bit some people recently, although he seems to have stopped now. He's not a vampire, and the police will find him and help him get treatment so he doesn't do it again." She addressed the last bit to Sophie, who said, "Can I go watch Princess Merida now?"

"Yes," the Wallaces said in unison, looking relieved.

"Who wants coffee?" Ms. Wallace asked, getting up and starting to clear away plates. Nick and I rose to help.

"Sorry about that," Mr. Wallace said in a quiet voice. "We had no idea Sophie knew about the attacks."

Nick and I followed his mom into the kitchen, carrying

glasses and silverware. “I’m sorry my sister was annoying,” he said.

I shrugged. “It’s okay. I like cake with blood sauce.”

He grinned. “Next time you come over for dinner, we’ll have ice cream and blood sauce. It’s even better.”

CHAPTER 3

TWELVE WEEKS AGO

Saturday morning, as I was battling my hair into a braid, Nick rang our buzzer. Madame Dupuy invited him in, and their voices receded down the hall to the living room. I wrapped an elastic around the end of my hair, slipped on my baby-blue platform Vans, found my phone and purse under my bed, and trotted down the hall, ready for the Louvre.

I felt like I'd stepped into a job interview when I entered the living room. Madame Dupuy sat in Dad's chair, looking polished and professional in her crisp white blouse, slim black ankle pants, and gleaming black loafers. A scarf in Starbursts colors knotted casually around her neck relieved the severity of the outfit. Her dark hair fell around her face in a stylish shoulder-length layered cut that emphasized her gray eyes. She looked both intimidating and striking. And amazingly, she looked like that every day, cooking and cleaning in outfits like the ones my friends' moms wore to work and leaving every evening looking just as spotless as when she'd arrived. I mean, aprons were involved, but still. Our Portland housekeeper dressed like a grad student, in old logo tees from the brewery where her boyfriend worked, faded chinos, and sneakers. She was also a potter, so her clothes were usually dusty and often spattered with clay. I didn't think Madame Dupuy would so much as go down to get her mail in anything less than business casual.

Nick perched on the edge of the couch, moving his hands up and down his thighs like he wasn't sure what to do with them. He wore the cornered look of an interviewee who'd forgotten his résumé, and he was dictating a phone number to Madame Dupuy as she typed it into her phone.

"I'm ready," I said brightly, and Nick looked up, relieved. Madame Dupuy raised an eyebrow at me, and now *I* felt like the one who'd forgotten her résumé. I repeated myself in French. She nodded and got up, satisfied with my pronunciation for once, as well as the fact that I'd remembered to use the feminine form of "ready." She told us to have a good time, glaring at Nick to imply *But not* too *good a time*, and we left as quickly as we could without actually running.

"Wow," Nick said as we waited for the elevator. "Your housekeeper is really old-school."

I nodded. "She's a little scary. She's been nice to me, though."

"She made me give her my number, tell her both my parents' names, their cell numbers, where they worked, and their work numbers. I thought she might ask to see my passport next."

"I think she takes her job seriously." We got off the elevator and crossed the lobby.

"*I* think she used to work for the French secret police. She's probably calling an old colleague right now, asking them to run a background check on me." He held the door open for me, and we started toward the Métro station. I laughed at the thought of Madame Dupuy as a spy. She didn't look like someone with a secret identity.

"Is there anything special you'd like to see when we get to the Louvre?"

"The *Mona Lisa*," I said immediately. He groaned like I'd just tightened the thumbscrews.

"What?" I asked.

"It's . . . kind of meh. She looks like she's listening to a geometry lecture. Take my advice and don't bother."

I stopped in the middle of the sidewalk and put my hands on my hips. "I don't care. I've never lived in a city with a must-see painting before. I promised my friends I'd send them a selfie with it. Plus, I have to spend the rest of the summer conjugating the subjunctive plus-que-parfait, so you have to treat me nice today and do what I say."

He stroked his chin, pretending to think it over. "Okay, but then you have to let me show you the stuff that's worth seeing."

I nodded. "Sure. But first, the *Mona Lisa*."

He sighed. "Yes, mademoiselle."

I'd just gotten my Navigo card so I didn't have to keep buying Métro tickets, and I was super excited when I passed it over the scanner at the station and the gates opened and let me through. I waved it at Nick. "It worked!" He smiled at my enthusiasm and scanned himself through like it was not a thing at all. We climbed the stairs to the platform, whose walls were covered in giant ads for Galeries Lafayette, Club Med vacations, and mobile phone companies. Across the tracks on the opposite wall, somebody'd graffitied a pigeon riding a skateboard onto a Visit the Parthenon travel poster.

"I love that pigeon," I said, pointing.

"That's new," Nick said. "I know the guy who did it."

"Really?" I was impressed. The pigeon looked so alive that I started to imagine a life for it—where it hung out and what its favorite sandwich was and how it lived with its grandma and dreamed of competing in the X Games.

"Yeah. He's kind of a friend. Nice that he's doing new work; I haven't seen him around for a while."

"Wow, you have impressive friends." The train pulled in, and we got on, settling into seats near the doors.

Part of the Métro line in our neighborhood ran on elevated tracks. As we rode above Boulevard de Grenelle toward the river, we got a wonderful view of belle epoque apartment buildings decorated with carved-stone flowers. Every building had a different pattern of wrought iron railing for the windows and tiny balconies, some sinuous and viny, some geometric. Planters filled with trailing geraniums hung from their railings, adding splashes of red, orange, and lavender to the tawny limestone buildings.

We had to change lines to get to the Louvre, which I hadn't done before. "Just remember the end point of the line you want to be on," Nick explained, "and follow the signs. It's easy."

I stuck close to him, though, because I had no idea where

we were going in the bewildering maze of hallways crammed with people. I dodged a woman headed straight at me, and we got separated, the stream of people pushing me farther and farther away. I could see him, parting the crowd as he went, but the mass of people flooding between us wouldn't let me close the gap. I was afraid I'd lose him and be stuck down there forever. He finally noticed I wasn't beside him and scanned the corridor, but short people in crowds equals invisible. He didn't see me, so he stopped. People flowed around him like a river flows around a boulder. I thought for the billionth time that it must be nice to be tall. Battling my way to him, I said, "Sorry I lost you, but people kept trying to run me down. Is walking a contact sport here?"

He smiled. "If you don't yield to them, mademoiselle, they'll get out of your way."

"It's just, I have this super-big personal bubble, and I don't like people getting in it uninvited." Cole was always doing that, standing so close he almost touched me. If I moved away, he'd just move closer. I shivered and reminded myself that he was in Portland, and I was here.

I turned my attention back to Nick, who was nodding. "I get that. When we first moved here, I hated how people get right into your space, and they're like, 'Excuse *you*.' What you do is, you think of your bubble as impenetrable and use it like a tank. Aim it straight at people, and they'll go around."

That seemed unlikely, but then I remembered how our debate coach had told us to stand when we were debating. Straight. With our shoulders back and our feet apart. "Take up space," he'd told us, practice after practice. "People who take up space are intimidating. Intimidating debaters win." He said it so often that Cole turned it into a joke. "You're taking up too much space," he'd say when I'd pause outside our round to make sure I was standing straight and had my shoulders pulled back. It worked, though. At one meet, Lily told me about overhearing one of the guys from Eugene talking about this scary Portland debater and realizing they were describing me.

I looked at Nick and put my shoulders back, spaced my feet apart, and stood straighter.

"Nice," he said. "You look badass. Now, the next person who comes at you, aim your bubble-tank straight at them and imagine flattening them. Ready?" I took a breath, then nodded.

We eased back into the tide of people, me muttering, "Take up space. Be a tank." The first time someone headed straight at me, I flinched and stepped aside.

"You're a tank," Nick encouraged. "You will squish them if they get in your way." I squared my shoulders again and headed straight at a burly guy with a beard who saw me but didn't try to avoid me. I fought the urge to dodge. At almost the last minute, he veered out of my path.

I turned to Nick, jubilant. "It worked!"

He smiled back. "Of course it worked. You are invincible."

We barged through the crowd, me giddy with my newfound superpower. There were so many people that Nick jostled against me a couple of times. "Sorry," he apologized as we emerged onto the platform. "I'm being all French and invading your space."

With Nick, though, it didn't seem like invading. More like politely sharing. I bowed, flourishing my arm out. "Consider this your engraved invitation into my bubble."

He laughed. "I accept, mademoiselle." Then he stepped closer, bumping my shoulder with his.

We got off the Métro a couple of stops early so we could walk to the Louvre his favorite way, through the most human-made park I'd ever seen. I was used to the slightly wild parks at home, the ones that looked like they'd just randomly grown that way and someone had said, "Hey, let's make that a park." This one had been planned, from the pristine rectangles of obsessively clipped lawn to the trees and shrubs spaced with military precision around the perimeter and pruned to exacting specifications. The flowers looked like they'd been placed with the aid of a ruler and compass. They looked like little ranks of infantry.

Back home, people flopped all over the grass in parks. But here, in a park filled with people, signs warned you that the grass was "forbidden," like some exotic treasure that you were supposed to enjoy only with your eyes. Instead, everyone promenaded on the gravel walkways under the shade trees or sat primly on metal chairs at the outdoor cafés. We continued down the wide walkway, and shrubbery replaced the trees, politely but firmly fencing off the lawns from anyone who might be tempted to step on them. Ahead of us stood an enormous buff-colored building as stiff and regimented as the plants in the park. Not even the tiniest sprig of green showed against the unrelenting expanse of architecture. "The Louvre," Nick said, gesturing like a salesperson. It bordered three sides of a paved space the size of two or three city blocks. Arched openings marched along the ground-floor facade. Smaller rectangular windows, centered above the arches, pierced the floor above. Triangular hat-looking details crowned the windows. Youssef would tell me later, after he quit laughing about "hat-looking," that they were called pediments. The next floor had even plainer, smaller windows, capped by a gray roof. It wasn't an exciting building, or a pretty one. It looked like it had planted its feet and pulled its shoulders back and was standing up straight. Taking up space. Intimidating the opponent.

The main entrance, a big glass pyramid crouched in the center of the plaza, clashed hard with the old-fashioned stone. It didn't belong, yet when I tried to imagine the space without it, the palace looked smaller and weaker. I guess the tension between them kept both strong. "I feel like we're looking at a standoff," I told Nick.

"My friend Youssef says pretty much the same thing. He thinks the architect was a genius to build something that fights the existing building so hard. Old versus new. Modern versus historical. Triangle versus rectangle." We crossed the street and entered the courtyard, where a student tour group engulfed us. They wore matching yellow neckerchiefs and followed a guide holding a giant yellow sunflower on a long staff. She was not quite shouting, and her voice had that weighty cadence you hear from teachers that says, *This is an important fact; it will be on the quiz*. I shivered. If I'd been in that group, I would have gone AWOL at the first opportunity, even if I'd had to crawl out a window. "Never fear, mademoiselle," Nick said, noticing my reaction. "You are seeing Paris with the Nick Wallace Tour Company. We offer personalized, neckerchief-free, off-the-beaten-track adventures, with no annoying tour-group members, the flexibility to stop for a snack whenever you want, and no stinky bus bathrooms. In fact, no buses at all. Also, the Nick Wallace Tour Company believes that any cultural outing must first be preceded by dumb fun. Or replaced by. This way, please."

He steered us toward a golden King Tut figure standing nearby. When we got closer, I realized it wasn't a mannequin advertising a special exhibition, like I'd thought, but an actual person, encased in stretchy gold fabric, wearing a King Tut mask and standing as still as a column. Nick dug a coin out of his pocket and tossed it into a little pot sitting on the ground next to the immobile pharaoh. As the coin chinked against the others, the pharaoh bowed very, very slowly from the waist. Then he straightened up again very, very slowly.

I looked at Nick, grinning. "That was spectacular!"

He grinned back. "Dumb fun, at your service." He took out his phone. "Go stand next to him." I stood beside the pharaoh and tried to imitate his serene poise. Nick took a photo, and I looked at the pharaoh and said, "Merci," dropping another coin into his bowl. He nodded once, gravely. I trotted back to Nick and looked at the photo. My hair looked cute, which made me happy. Portland's humidity usually made it look feral.

"Send that to me, okay? Mina and Lily'll love it."

He texted it over. "Mina and Lily?"

"My best friends from Portland. We were on debate team together." I was just about to tap Send when I noticed a red-clad figure behind me in the photo. His hooded cape hid his face, and he seemed to be pointing at me. "Look at cosplay dude," I said.

Nick stared. "That's weird. I didn't see him when I took the picture."

"Ooh, spooky." I grinned at him. "Maybe it's a ghost. Do you have that new phone with the special paranormal camera?"

Nick laughed. "Maybe it's the famous Red Man of the Louvre."

"Who's that?"

"Some queen had her own personal assassin. The story is, he enjoyed his job so much that he turned into a vampire after he died. If you see him, it's supposed to mean that somebody's going to die."

"Another vampire? I did not realize Paris was the City of Vampires, Nick Wallace Tour Company."

He smiled reassuringly. "It was probably just another busker. They dress up as all sorts of things."

"Okay, but now you double have to show me the *Mona Lisa*, in case a vampire bites me and I die." Nick shepherded us through the line standing and the ticket buying while I concentrated on not letting the crush of tourists separate us. Once we got into the galleries, it wasn't as crowded, but then we had to walk for miles. You'd think they would put their star attractions closer to the entrance.

"Here it is." He ushered me into a large room just off a hall filled with endless portraits of saints. People crammed in, pointing phones at a surprisingly small painting. My heart beat faster. This was it. The painting that everyone went to see when they visited Paris—even people who didn't like art. We nudged our way through the crowd until we stood in front of her. We were the only people who didn't have our backs to her, holding up phones for the iconic selfie. The title plaque called her *La Joconde* rather than the *Mona Lisa*, but it was her, all right: the famous smiling woman. I examined every crackled inch, expecting at any minute to see the magic. Mona appeared entirely ordinary, just a woman in a three-quarters pose, her long hair parted down the middle, her hands folded gracefully on her lap, looking like she was trying to remember where she left her car keys. I turned to Nick, trying to work out why I was so disappointed. "I'm not getting anything here."

He shrugged. "Don't look at me. I like Renaissance paintings, and I've never gotten why this is *the* one. It's okay, but I don't think it's worth special status."

I considered it again, looking for anything I might have missed. "It's smaller than I thought it would be," I said. "And it looks just like the T-shirts." I stuck my phone into my pocket without taking a photo. I'd just get postcards at the gift shop.

"Yeah, it moves me deeply, too," Nick said. We turned away. He led me back down the hall of saints, pointing out the funny ones, like a very annoyed Saint Peter, apparently because of the cartoony cleaver stuck in his head. Then he navigated us to a ginormous room of ginormous sculptures, which were so perfect they were lifeless. He watched my meh response, nodded to himself like I'd passed a test, and took me to a different part of the museum to see a pair of immense winged bulls with men's heads. I fell in love with their serenely amused expressions and elf ears.

"Can one of these guys please be my emotional-support statue?" I asked. "I feel I need one by my side at all times."

Nick chuckled. "Deal. One for you and one for me. What would you like to see next, mademoiselle?"

I thought for a minute. "I want to see your favorite thing in this museum."

He didn't stop to think but led me to a room in a different wing and pointed to a small painting of an old man sitting behind a desk in a room full of wiggly kids. It was called *The Schoolmaster*. A couple of the kids were playing on the floor, and one little guy was trying to climb out the window. Some of the others might have been doing schoolwork. Or running a preschool numbers racket. It was that kind of chaotic.

"Okay, why?" I asked, trying to discern any Art-with-a-capital-*A* aspect to it. "It's cute, but isn't it a little, I don't know, minor?"

"It's a view straight into the past," he said. "This is how schools used to look. Can you imagine how hard it must have been to learn anything in a roomful of kids presided over by one exhausted old man? They didn't even have books or enough tables and chairs. Things like this make the past a real place. I think that's magic."

I loved that he'd trust me enough to show me a funny little painting and tell me the truth about why he loved it instead of picking something famous and safe and blathering about composition or artistic whatever.

As we rode the escalator under the pyramid up to the exit, Nick said, "Well? What do you think? Did you like it?"

I gave him my biggest smile. "You're definitely getting a five-star review on Yelp."

CHAPTER 4

ELEVEN WEEKS AGO

"N'oubliez pas que vos exposés doivent être prêts à présenter lundi," Professeur Joubert admonished us before he dismissed us from immersion class. I sighed as I loaded my books into my pack. Class had started only yesterday, and we already had a reading assignment and a huge report due Monday that we were supposed to memorize and present in front of the class, as well as handing in a written copy. Mine was barely started. I'd already discovered that I couldn't just write it in English and run it through Google Translate. Madame Dupuy had been quite sarcastic when she'd proofread that version. I'd admitted about Google, and she'd told me I had to rewrite the whole report without using the internet. I was only partway through because I had to look up every third word, and I still also had the reading to do, so there went all my free time.

I clomped down the stairs of the school building, feeling like a prisoner. Outside, Paris waited for me to sample its pastries, walk its neighborhoods, and linger in its parks, but instead I had an appointment with a Bescherelle guide to verb conjugations, a French-English dictionary, and Victor Hugo.

I crossed the lobby heading for the front doors, wishing Nick weren't in school all day. It would be fun to get lunch with him in a café where we could sit outside and people-watch. I reminded myself that I'd get to see him later, after his classes got out. That was my reward for doing my homework. I'd find a bench in the little park that was the heart of our block, the one he walked through on his way home, and he'd join me for a couple of hours before we both had to go in for dinner. The way he grinned when he caught sight of me waiting gave me tingles.

I waded diligently through my homework, taking a break late in the afternoon to go to the boulangerie with Madame Dupuy to get a baguette. She always bought me a snack, too, one of the pastries they made in addition to bread. "You need un goûter," she'd tell me. "Dinner is still far away." Every time we went there I got a different kind of pastry because I had this idea that I'd try all the pastries in the shop. So far my favorite was pain au chocolat. When we got back from the boulangerie, I finished up my homework, then changed into my flirty green tank dress. I told Madame Dupuy where I'd be, and she raised an eyebrow, then smiled. I trotted down to the park and found a bench with a view of the gate Nick would be coming through. I wondered why more people didn't cross the interior of our block on their way to wherever they were going. It was such a refuge from the noise and people. The wide walkways between the park and the buildings never had more than a few people on them, even though the street-side walkways were always crammed. At night, the gate to the park was locked, but there were benches right outside its fence. They were the perfect place to sit on a summer evening after dusk.

Nick pushed through the gate, and I waved. His face lit up, and he hurried over.

"Hi." I smiled.

"Bonjour, mademoiselle." He flopped beside me on the bench, dropping his enormous pack. "How were les dieux de la grammaire today?"

"The grammar gods were random and capricious, as always. I mean, why is 'solde' both masculine and feminine? That's just mean and unnecessary."

He put on a heavy French accent. "Eet ees zee jobe of zee grammair gods to be mean, mademoiselle."

"Tell me it gets better."

"It gets . . . different. I felt like I had a new superpower when I could finally swear in French without making people laugh." I sighed, wondering if I would ever be able to achieve that. "Let's go get a Coca," he said. "I'm parched."

The café was starting to fill up, but we found a good table under the shade of the awning. "What's your curfew tomorrow night?" he asked as we sat down.

"I don't have a curfew. Dad trusts me. And he's in the UK till Friday, anyway." He'd called me from the Eurostar just before it went into the Chunnel, all excited about crossing the English Channel in a train. Dad loved train travel. He geeked on trains like I geeked on research.

"You may not have a curfew from your dad, but I bet you do from Madame Dupuy. She came over and talked to my mom after I took you to the Louvre, basically doing a background check on my whole family. She told Mom she was responsible for you when your dad was out of town, and she wanted you to be safe."

"She what?" I was mortified. But also kind of touched. If my mom were alive, I knew I'd have a curfew. So it was really nice that Madame Dupuy cared enough about me to intrude on my privacy. I mean, she seemed to like me; she took me shopping with her and praised me when I said things correctly. Sometimes when I was helping her in the kitchen, she told me stories about growing up in Croatia and what it was like to move here when she was seventeen. But she wouldn't go to the trouble of talking to Nick's parents if I didn't really mean something to her. It made me kind of love her, to be honest. I told Nick I'd ask about the curfew.

AFTER DINNER, I flopped onto the couch with my phone.

Me: You were right. I do have a curfew. But she says it depends on what we're doing

Nick: There's this great club over in the 11th arrondissement. You like to dance?

Me: I'm the queen of awkward dancing

Me: But don't we have to be 18 to get in?

Nick: Nope. 16. They'll only card you if you try to drink

I told Madame Dupuy we were going to a club called Le Shopping. She shook her head when she heard the name. "I do not know this club, but the neighborhood is safe. I will investigate."

While I waited, I googled the club. The name made me think it would look like a department store: shiny surfaces and angular furniture in gray and black and white. Instead, the pictures on the website looked like Portland Saturday Market meets Mardi Gras in an architectural-salvage yard. It looked like a wonderland. I hoped she'd let me go. I sent the link to Mina and Lily.

Me: Nick asked me to go dancing at this club tomorrow

Mina: Cute upstairs Nick?

Me: 😊

Lily: OMG SO JEALOUS

Lily: Tomorrow I will be glamorously hosing out dog kennels

Mina: I'll be scrubbing dried Play-Doh out of the rug. Again

Mina nannied for her neighbor during the summer, and Lily volunteered at the animal shelter. I felt a little twinge of guilt sending them amazing Paris club pics when they were stuck in Portland cleaning up after dogs and kids.

Lily: Send pics of your fabulous club experience so we can see how Paris Tosh lives

Me: 

A couple of hours later, Madame Dupuy finally okayed the club. Nobody'd ever spent that much time figuring out whether somewhere I wanted to go was safe. Dad trusted me to be sensible and didn't set many boundaries, and the housekeepers we'd had in Portland had taken their cues from him. I knew he loved me, but sometimes it would have been nice if he'd shown it by holding me close instead of encouraging me to get out of the nest. Lily and Mina had always envied his relaxed approach, but once, one of them was arguing with her mom about going to a concert in one of the old warehouses near the river, and her mom said, "I just don't think it's a safe space, and I want to keep you safe." In that moment I was pierced by a longing for my mom so sudden and brutal that I had to go shut myself in their bathroom so they wouldn't see me cry.

With Madame Dupuy's approval secured, I took stock of my closet and panicked. Nothing I had looked sophisticated enough to go out dancing in Paris, so I raced out to Zara after class the next day to try on every dress they had. I finally found a sleeveless sea-blue frock with a swirly skirt. When I got back to the apartment, Madame Dupuy eyed the shopping bag, smiled slightly, and said, "Be home by one a.m."

I smiled back at her. "Thank you." I would have preferred three a.m., but I was pretty sure that was an argument I'd lose if I tried it.

"And," she continued, "if you are late this time, you will not be allowed to go out with Monsieur Nick again. You will call me when you return home to tell me you are safe. If you try to deceive me, I will know. Do you understand?"

"Yes," I said, wondering how she would know that I was really home unless she stayed at our apartment all night.

"Bon. This place where you are going, it is safe, but the arrondissement next to it is not so nice. Two women were attacked there last year. You should be . . . vigilant." I nodded, a little worried. Dad had made me take self-defense classes, and until the thing with Cole, I'd been confident I could defend myself. I was still ashamed that instead, I'd frozen.

"Also, I am asking you to wear this." Madame Dupuy unclasped the silver filigree heart pendant she wore, and before I could say anything, she fastened it around my neck.

"Um, thank you?" I didn't mean it to come out as a question. It sounded sarcastic, which wasn't my intention. I was just startled by the intimacy of her gesture.

"It is superstitious of me, but what can it hurt?" she said, as much to herself as to me.

I touched it. It was warm. "Is this like a good-luck charm?"

She nodded. "For protection from misfortune. My great-grandmother was wearing it when a vampire attacked, and it saved her. Silver burns vampires." I raised my eyebrows. A vampire? Really? She flicked her hand like she was brushing off a fly, gave me a brief smile, and said, "This is what my mother told me when she gave it to me. People are superstitious where I come from."

"Well . . . thank you." It was both nice and odd, but I liked that she wanted to protect me.

When Nick knocked on our door that evening, I was still trying to figure out what shoes to wear. I stood in front of the mirror playing "heels or flats," afraid that choosing the wrong footwear would doom the entire evening. When Madame Dupuy tapped on my door to tell me Nick was in the living room, I squeaked, "Can you help me?"

She came into my room, shutting the door behind her. "You look very pretty," she said.

I smiled weakly and gestured at my feet. "Which shoes?"

She pointed to my right foot. "You will be dancing, so the flats."

"Thank you." I'd been leaning toward the heels, but since I'd asked for her opinion, it felt rude to ignore it.

"Do you remember what I told you about your curfew?" I nodded and picked up my clutch. She surveyed me, which felt nice. Lily's and Mina's moms used to do the same thing before we all went out, and I'd always felt the emptiness of not having a mom to perform that ritual. She nodded. "The blue suits you. Bon, you are ready."

I walked into the living room, and Nick's eyes lit up. "You look gorgeous," he said.

I smiled, the warmth of his compliment driving away my jitters. "Thank you."

He looked gorgeous, too. Most guys I knew back home with shoulders that wide wore their shirts too big, ballooning over their pants. Even debate guys, who had to wear suits to meets, tended to go oversized. But Nick's trimly cut shirt fit like it loved him. He'd rolled the sleeves up to just below the elbow, and the crisp white fabric glowed against the honey color of his skin. The shirt rode neatly over a pair of slim black trousers. Nobody I knew back in Portland wore trousers. They wore pants. Trousers were stylish and adult; pants were . . . comfy. I looked up at him and regretted choosing the flats. I could have used the extra inches.

"One a.m.," Madame Dupuy told Nick, giving him her best glare.

THE CLUB had a main level with an enormous dark wood dance floor. In the center, a DJ spun tunes from the middle of an antique carousel. On the walls, gilt-framed mirrors reflected the warm red-and-purple lighting and the still-sparse crowd. Nick steered us toward a wide, curving staircase with sinuous wrought iron railings. On the second-floor mezzanine, mismatched vintage tables and chairs jostled together. Wrought iron gates hung on the red wall to our right. Chandeliers dripped from the ceiling like a rainstorm of sparkles. Pillars and garden statuary covered the opposite wall, which was turquoise blue, and a giant Buddha presided over the zinc-topped bar. I spun, taking in the room, the people, the fantastic artifacts. Then I turned to Nick, my eyes wide.

"It's like an enchanted carnival. I've never seen anything so amazing."

He smiled and held his hand out. "Would mademoiselle like to dance?"

I nodded like a bobblehead. It was Latin night, and the speakers thumped with a cha-cha. Nick swung me into a dance hold, and I shook my head, embarrassed. "I don't know how to partner dance."

"No worries, mademoiselle. The Nick Wallace School of Dance is at your service." He raised his arm and twirled me under it so that I stood at his side, surprised, exhilarated, and pleased with myself for not stumbling or kicking him. He walked me slowly through the steps, his arm around my waist so I could feel how he moved. I could barely focus, though. The warmth of him so close made me tingle all over. He took us through the pattern again and again until I felt comfortable with it. Then he swung me into a dance hold, making me giggle with pleasure. He smiled with his whole face. A current of electricity sizzled up my backbone as we started the push-pull of the dance. We advanced and retreated, spun away and came together, our eyes only on each other. When the song ended, he twirled me into an embrace and held me so close I felt his heart beating to the same rhythm as mine. Then he twirled me back out, facing him. We balanced on the moment, glowing and exhilarated.

"Nick!" a girl's voice called, breaking the spell.

He looked around. "Martine! Youssef!" He waved a girl and a guy over. "How are you?"

A dark-haired, doe-eyed Amazon in a sleeveless black shift dress accessorized with a thick silver rope-braid necklace and large diamond stud earrings model-walked up to us, arm in arm with a dark-haired guy wearing an improbably stylish combo of a purple checked shirt and ochre-colored jeans. The girl kiss-kiss-kissed Nick on the cheeks. Jealousy stabbed me. She was gorgeous, she'd stolen our moment, and now she was kissing Nick. But then the boy she was with kissed him, too, and I thought, *Oh. Right. I'm in France.*

The Amazon towered over me, her height augmented by skyscraper heels. She wore her hair swept back into a complicated-looking twist. I ran my hands over my curls, trying to smooth down the sproingy mass, feeling unsophisticated and really, *really* regretting my shoes.

"Tosh, this is Martine," Nick said. Martine bent and did kiss-kiss with me. "And Youssef, her boyfriend," Nick continued. Youssef also kissed me on each cheek. Given the way I felt about people in my personal space, I was surprised not to feel weird and uncomfortable, but the way they did it was as matter-of-fact as a handshake. We moved off the dance floor and found a table.

"Tosh just moved here from the US," Nick told them as we sat down. "She's from Oregon."

"I am not familiar with this city," Martine said.

"It's a state," I told them. "The city I'm from is Portland."

I got out my phone to show them a map. Martine looked and said, "Oh, it is near California."

"Just five hours and a million miles from the border."

"A *million* miles?" Youssef frowned. "I do not understand."

"Metaphorically. It's like they're two different countries," I said. "California is the fifth-largest economy in the *world*—bigger than France's." They looked shocked that their country's economy was outclassed by a mere American state's. "Oregon, on the other hand, is the twenty-fourth-largest economy in the US, which is good, and better than it used to be when we just logged and ranched, but it's like a kids' soccer—sorry, football—team playing France in the World Cup. Very not in the same league. California's economy influences Oregon in almost every way, and we don't really benefit— What?"

Nick and Youssef were staring at me like I'd just said I liked to sacrifice kittens to my alien overlords. "Wow," Nick said. "Are you the expatriate arm of the Oregon Chamber of Commerce?"

I died a little. I was at a *club*. In *Paris*. With cosmopolitan French people. *Say something normal*, I scolded myself.

"Sorry." I grimaced. "Debate-team flashback. One of our research topics last year was about the economic dis—" I stopped myself and shook my head like, *Yes, I'm a complete nerd*. "I get excited about this stuff," I said. "I really, really love research. Like an unnatural amount. I'll stop now."

I put my hands over my face, feeling awkward times ten.

"Debate team?" Martine said, her tone bright. "Have you ever done Model UN?"

I took my hands down and smiled at her. "I went to a session once, and it looked interesting." I'd been looking for a debate-type event that didn't require a partner, but Mr. Donnelly wouldn't let me change events that close to State. "Is that your event?"

"Yes. You should try it. It is very fun."

I turned to Nick, thrilled about meeting a fellow debate nerd. "You have excellent friends."

He did a little bow. "Thank you, mademoiselle. I think so, too."

Martine pulled her chair closer to me, and I asked her how

she prepped for Model UN. We were deep into a comparison of research strategies when I remembered I was on a date. I looked at Nick, who was talking with Youssef. "I'm so sorry," I told him, blushing.

He smiled. "Nobody *ever* wants to talk Model UN with Martine. You just did us all a huge favor."

She nodded, beaming. "I will look forward to seeing you at tournaments. What school are you going to?"

"École Jarret."

"Formidable! It is where Youssef and I go also. You should join our team."

"I'd love to." It would be nice to do a new event, something that didn't have any bad memories associated with it. An event where I didn't have to rely on a partner to do well.

Nick grinned at me like, *Well done, you*, and sparks of happiness ran up my arms. I'd passed the friend test. And bonus for me, I now knew two more people in Paris. This was going to be such a great year.

"Can I get a photo with you all?" I asked. "My friends in Portland demanded pics of clubbing in Paris."

"Is there not clubbing in Portland?" Youssef asked, slipping his arms around Martine.

"Well, yeah, but it's just Portland. People wear flannels to clubs." Martine raised an eyebrow. "It's not . . . elegant. It's not special."

Youssef smiled. "Bon. If we are elegant and special, we must of course take a photo."

I sent the pic to the girls, then tucked my phone into my purse. I wanted to focus on Nick and this night. A guy so California-handsome he could have been Barbie's dream date sauntered up to our table, said hello, and asked Martine to dance. His teeth glowed when he smiled, which unnerved me a little.

"Yann," Martine said as she shook her head, "you know I am here with Youssef."

Yann mimed being shot through the heart with an arrow of love. "What can I do but try?"

"You can listen to me when I say no." Her expression remained friendly, but her voice had an edge. Yann shrugged one shoulder, like, *Ah, well, life is sad*—and his eyes shifted to me. I edged closer to Nick, shaking my head, and he didn't even bother with the arrow of love business. He just moved his gaze to a nearby table, all, *But wait! There are more girls over there*. He drifted off to see if he could charm one of them onto the dance floor, and Martine and I shared an eye roll.

"How long have you been in Paris?" Youssef asked me.

"About a week. Nick's been showing me around." I told them about our trip to the Louvre, and Martine said, "Nick, why are you not taking her to do things real people do? Fun things. Museums are where you go because your professeur makes you."

Nick smiled and shrugged. "I'm only the tour guide. I take mademoiselle where she asks to go."

I looked at Martine and Youssef and smiled apologetically. "I mean, I really did like the Louvre. But what else should I see?"

"Flea markets," Martine said at the same time that Youssef said, "Zombie escape room."

Nick nodded enthusiastically. "Oh yeah. I'm putting that on the itinerary."

"Zombie escape room?" I repeated.

"You have to evade a horde of zombies. It's not really a room; you're supposed to get from one part of Paris to another without having your brains eaten," Nick explained. "It's perfect dumb fun."

Martine was shaking her head. "You did not hear? It has been stopped. A girl was attacked and bitten last week during a game."

"By one of the zombie actors?" I said. Some people get way too far into role-playing.

She shook her head. "No, it was the man who is biting all these women."

"Did she—" Nick didn't finish the question.

"She lived," Martine said.

"Okay, good." Nick looked relieved. We didn't say anything for a few moments.

"Is this the 'vampire' Sophie was talking about the other night?" I asked finally. Nick nodded. "Our housekeeper mentioned vampires, too. Like she thought they were a real thing." I touched the heart pendant she'd given me. "She gave me this necklace and told me I should wear it tonight to protect against them. Which was odd, but it's a pretty necklace, so." I shrugged.

"Madame Dupuy thinks there are vampires?" Nick asked.

I shrugged again. "She was all, *Great-Gram fought off a vampire with this necklace, so wear it*, but then she said she comes from a superstitious country, so who knows."

"Hé, mes amis."

We looked up. Yann was back at our table, blinding us with his teeth. "Come over. Join us." He nodded toward a nearby group of about ten people, crowded around three tables. "We are celebrating, and also"—he indicated Nick with his chin—"Clément and Bastien said they want to talk to you about an expedition."

"Celebrating what?" Martine said as Nick nodded okay.

"Le Bec finished his piece on Le Mur."

"Le Mur Oberkampf?" Nick said. Yann nodded, and Youssef whistled, impressed.

We got up and joined the other group, squeezing in where we could. Everyone was focused on a pale, skinny-but-muscular guy our age gripping a Champagne bottle. I guessed he was an artist; the grubby, paint-spattered hoodie and jeans yelled, *Ask me about my latest painting*. They also said, *I'm famous enough to get into a nice club even though I dress like I sleep in doorways*. The fact that he looked like a debauched KJ Apa probably helped, too.

"Bonsoir, mes amis," he crowed, climbing up onto his chair and waving the bottle. We bonsoir-ed and started a round of kiss-kiss with his friends. He jumped off the chair, landed right in my space, pulled me way too close, and kiss-kiss-kissed me. I didn't like the way this guy did bisous. Too personal. He grinned, showing his teeth, then stepped away and embraced Nick much less ardently.

"Hé, mec," Nick said. "I haven't seen you around for a couple of months."

"I was here and there," Le Bec replied.

"Anywhere interesting?" Nick asked.

Le Bec smiled. "Where I am is always somewhere interesting." He moved on, finishing his hellos, and I sat down between Nick and a girl wearing a fuchsia tunic and a close-fitting black headscarf with large fuchsia-and-orange flowers printed on it. The scarf hung down under her chin in soft, loose folds, skimming back over her shoulders. She had a wary air, but she flashed me a quick smile as more bottles of Champagne appeared.

Le Bec opened them and filled glasses. Then he stood on his chair again, holding his glass high. "To Le Mur!" he said.

"To Le Mur!" we toasted. The girl in the headscarf raised her glass and put it down without drinking.

I leaned into Nick. "What is this wall?"

"It's a group that invites street artists to paint the side of a building here in the eleventh arrondissement. It's a fairly big deal."

"So this guy did a piece on this wall?" I felt sophisticated. I was hanging out at a club in Paris with an artist. Drinking Champagne. I took a tiny sip from my glass. Nobody jumped up and yelled, "Put that down; you're not legal yet!" I felt bold enough to chance another sip. It tickled my nose.

Nick nodded. "Remember the pigeon we saw in the Métro station? He's the guy who did that."

"Oh, wow." I grinned. "You have *excellent* friends. I've never met a street artist before."

Nick smiled. "Would you like to go see the new piece?"

I grinned bigger. *I would go see an exhibition of quadratic equations with you*, I thought as I said, "I'd love to."

A guy farther down the table called out a question that I didn't catch, and Nick turned to answer. I settled back into my chair, happy to watch everybody and try to remember what name went with which face. Conversations in French and English flowed around me as I sipped my Champagne.

The French ones were challenging; by the time I'd figured out what people were talking about, the conversation had turned in another direction. And listening to English conversations surrounded by French disoriented me so much that I couldn't anchor myself in either language.

After a while, my brain clocked out, and all the words turned to radio static. Nick, Youssef, Martine, and a guy down the table who was probably Bastien were leaning toward each other, talking intently. Bastien pulled out his phone and showed them a video of some guys maybe caving? It was all shadows, jitters, and blinding headlamp flare. In reply, Youssef showed one of his own caving videos—much better filmed. I recognized Nick, Martine, the girl in the scarf, and Le Bec. Were there caves somewhere near Paris?

A voice next to me redirected my attention. "That is a beautiful pendant."

I turned to see the girl with the scarf. She spoke in English, which was kind. I brushed my fingers over the pendant. "Thank you. I love your scarf. The flowers are great—so bold."

"Bold. I like that." She smiled. "I am Noor."

"I'm Tosh."

"So you are a friend of Le Bec?" she said.

I shrugged, shaking my head. "Nick knows him. I just moved here, so I don't really know anybody yet. I only met Martine and Youssef tonight. How about you? Are you one of his friends?"

She glanced over to where he was acting out a story for three listeners, his gestures extravagant. "We used to paint together. You know—street art. He was a taggeur when we met, and now he is going to be famous."

"Wow," I said. "That's so great."

She smiled, small and tight. "Yes."

"So you're a street artist too?" When she nodded, I said, "That's amazing. I've never met a girl street artist. I mean, I've never met any street artists at all until you and him." I inclined my head at Le Bec. "The city I'm from has some excellent art, though."

"Where are you from?"

I told her and was amazed to learn that she'd heard of Portland. She said she followed several Portland artists on TikTok.

"So what kind of things do you do?" I asked.

She picked up her phone, thumbed through a couple of screens, and handed it to me. The image sent a shock of recognition through me. I looked up, excited.

"You totally nailed this. That's what I wanted to do when I saw her."

Noor nodded, her eyes bright. "She is too powerful to be vulnerable like that."

"Exactly," I agreed. Noor's photo showed a black-and-white Banksy-style stencil of the Venus de Milo on the side of a building. When Nick and I had seen Venus in the Louvre, beautiful but off-kilter and powerless because her arms had been broken off, I'd wanted to make her new arms. Seeing her so vulnerable distressed me. She could have been someone I knew. She could have been me.

In the photo, a girl wearing a spring-green headscarf that matched her coveralls stood on a ladder next to the painted Venus, attaching her left arm. The right one was already on—you could see the jagged line where it joined, and you could also see that, in contrast to the black and white of the rest of her, it was the warm color of living flesh.

"It's perfect," I said. "She looks strong."

The girl helping Venus was rendered with a simple, graphic vibe, and her lively colors contrasted with the black and white of the statue.

Noor's smile took over her face. She nodded toward Le Bec. "When he saw it, he said, 'Why are you ruining his art?'"

I shook my head. "Not ruining," I said. "You made her whole."

She nodded. "That is what I said, but he could not understand why that was important." I made a disbelieving noise. "I know," she agreed. "This artist—Uno—paints stencils of the Venus de Milo all over the city. That is all he does; he is famous for it. I wonder if he knows what it means to girls, seeing this damaged body everywhere, as if it were normal." She looked down. "One time, somebody put my face on one of his stencils, and all the guys I used to paint with thought it was very funny. They said they preferred the version of me with no arms."

"That's a creepy thing to say. Why did they think that?"

"Because I am a better artist than they are." She shrugged. "One day, I saw one of the Venuses that Uno makes in my neighborhood—in *my* neighborhood—and I just got so angry, you know? I thought, *What could she do if she had the full use of herself?* So I gave her arms. Now she can do anything she wants."

"I love that," I said. "You saw a problem, and you solved it with art."

She smiled, delighted. "That is exactly it—that is what I do."

"I'd love to see some more."

When she showed me the next piece, I laughed in recognition. It was the *Mona Lisa*. Same subdued palette as the original, same pensive expression. But she was wearing a headscarf.

"I just saw her at the Louvre," I said.

She smiled wryly. "That one is certainly more popular. Mine has been painted over many times, but I always put her back."

"Why does she get painted over?"

"I think it makes people angry to see her with her head covered. It tells a story about *La Joconde* that makes them uncomfortable. But this means they have not looked closely at the original painting. She *is* wearing a headscarf."

I closed my eyes and searched my memory of the *Mona Lisa* painting. "But you can see her hair."

Noor took her phone back, searched, and handed it to me again. I had to enlarge the image before I saw the scarf, so transparent it was almost invisible.

"I saw it when my class visited the Louvre the year I was thirteen," Noor continued. "I was so excited because the woman in the most famous painting in France is wearing a headscarf, and it is not popular to wear one here. We are forbidden to wear them at school. To see one on *La Joconde* felt so important. As if the artist had seen me. Seen who I am." Her face hardened. "When I showed it to the professeur, she said I was wrong. She said there was no scarf."

"That's awful."

"It was as if the painting was only for people who looked

like my prof. She made me feel like I did not exist. After I painted arms on the Venus, though, I decided that people need to see *La Joconde* as I saw her. The scarf is there—it is real, and if people saw it, perhaps they would be less frightened of people who look like me." She did the "pff" thing with her mouth that in French means, *But of course, I was deluded.* "But my version, she was painted over the next day. So I painted her again. I keep repainting her. Something that makes people so uncomfortable they have to destroy it is worth keeping alive."

I loved her fierceness. "Do you only paint girls wearing headscarves?" I asked. I took another drink of Champagne. I felt warm and slightly fuzzy at the edges.

"Mostly. Like Le Bec mostly does pigeons and Uno only does his Venus stencils. You can work very quickly if you have a character you always paint, and working quickly means the police are less likely to catch you." She gave me a conspiratorial smile.

"Are you showing off your little things, Noor?" Le Bec leaned down between us and took the phone out of my hands. I was going to say I wasn't done looking yet, but he turned a dazzling smile on me. "You like art?"

I nodded. "Noor's been showing me her work. It's amazing."

He put his hand on her shoulder. "It is too bad she will never be chosen for Le Mur." He took his own phone out. "Would you like to see some of *my* work?"

I shrugged. "Sure." I wanted to see more of Noor's art, but I was happy to look at his stuff, too. On the screen of his phone, five giant pigeons slouched against a wall, smoking. "I love it," I said, laughing almost in spite of myself. "It reminds me of my old school."

Nick looked over my shoulder. "Is this the one that's on Le Mur?" he asked.

"Yes." Le Bec grabbed a Champagne bottle and topped off my glass. He made to fill Noor's already-full glass, but she put a hand over it. "If you had listened to me, ma cocotte," he told her, "you could have been on Le Mur, too."

She shook her head. "If I had listened to you, I would be helping you to paint your pigeons instead of doing my own work."

"You would have recognition."

"I would be 'team.' Le Bec and his team." Noor said "team," but the subtitle read "servant." She gave a one-shoulder shrug. "In any case, I already have recognition. People know Headscarf Girl."

"They do not invite her to paint Le Mur Oberkampf."

Noor moved her eyes away from Le Bec, silently considering the wall hung with gates. Le Bec stared at her like he was trying to will her to meet his gaze. Laughing people stumbled by our table; I gulped more Champagne, nervous at the tension that hung in the air, and felt Nick give my hand a quick *It's okay* squeeze. It didn't feel like it was okay, though.

"I am happy for you," Noor said at last, her eyes still on the gates. There was no sarcasm in her voice, but Le Bec glowered at her anyway.

I butted in, hoping to defuse the tension. "So why pigeons, Le Bec? Why not penguins? Or parrots?"

He turned to me, pleased by my attention. "A pigeon is

like an artist. Dirty, unappreciated, small, always with its eyes down searching for crumbs. It is not pleasant to feel like this, so one day I decided to make a pigeon that was big and strong and did not need crumbs from anyone. People liked it, so I made more. And now I do not have to eat the crumbs that others drop." He smiled at me and Nick and threw a glance at Noor. "You should come to see my wall. I am inviting all of you."

"Great," Nick said. I nodded.

"I am sorry; it is not possible for me," Noor said. "I will be working."

Le Bec rolled his eyes. "Drawing portraits of idiot tourists on the Pont des Arts? Wasting your skills?"

She shrugged. "I am not wasting my skills; I am adding to them. And earning money. *I* do not have to steal my supplies."

He shrugged, like, *stealing, schmealing*, as my phone barked with my curfew alarm.

"Whoops," I said. "I have to leave now, or I'll turn into a pumpkin, and I won't ever see Nick again. Which would be tragic." I grinned at him, warm and loose and happy.

"It would indeed, mademoiselle." He smiled, and we both stood up.

Le Bec grabbed my hand. "No, you must stay longer."

"Alas, we can't," I said, pulling out of his grasp. But of course we couldn't just leave; we had to do our farewells, kiss-kiss-kissing our way around the tables. Le Bec lingered so long as he kissed my cheek that I pulled away, giggling uncomfortably. "Okay, bye," I said, stumbling against Nick, who slipped his arm around me as we left and kept me tucked close all the way to the Métro station. As we waited for the train, I said, "This is like a magic carpet ride."

"This?" Nick's gesture encompassed the sulfurous lighting, grimy tilework, and low-level hum of despair surrounding us.

"I mean, not the decor. But getting on in one place and hurtling through the darkness and then emerging in a completely different world—yeah. Portland's pretty monochrome, but here, I feel like I'm meeting the world every day. It's magic." I grinned like a complete goof. But I loved the Métro, grit and all.

He laughed. "You've had a little too much Champagne, mademoiselle."

"Au contrary," I said. "I've had exactly enough."

He looked at me. "*You're* the magic. You turn an ordinary Métro ride into an adventure. You're brave enough to own your 'meh' over the *Mona Lisa*—"

"Meh, meh, meh," I singsonged. "The *Mona Lisa* is meh and I have spoken. Did you know she's wearing a headscarf? That's an un-meh thing about her."

He nodded. "It is."

We smiled at each other. "I'm magic, huh?" I said, fishing a little. Okay, a lot.

"Absolutely. You're smart and funny. You think *I'm* funny. You're nice to my baby sister. And you have hair the color of an autumn sunset."

My brain went *Ding-ding-ding; correct answer!* But I just said, "Those are lovely things to say about me, but none of that's really magic."

He rubbed his eyebrow. "So one of my dad's US colleagues

brought his family here on vacation last year. His daughter's our age, and Dad volunteered me to show her around. She had a list of things she wanted to see: the Eiffel Tower, Notre-Dame, Montmartre—standard tourist stuff. Notre-Dame was closed because they were still restoring it after the fire, so I offered to take her to Sainte-Chapelle, which is this jewel box of a church with incredible stained glass. She filmed some of the windows and said, 'Okay, next?' She ignored all the incredible carving and blew off seeing the reliquaries, which are gorgeous and weird and well worth seeing. We spent the day like that, going to one-of-a-kind places that she didn't bother to look at with her actual eyes, because she was too busy getting 'content' for her feeds." He made dismissive air quotes. "We stopped at a café for something to drink, and she complained that she only got three ice cubes in her Coke. We were sitting in a famous, beautiful café that everyone wants to see when they visit Paris, and she was counting ice cubes. She wanted to go to a club, so that night, I took her to Le Shopping and introduced her around. She was nice to my friends long enough for a photo op, and then she spent the rest of the evening in her phone, except for dancing with Yann."

"Barbie's dream date Yann?"

He threw his head back and laughed. "Yeah. See what I mean? She didn't even remember his name. Then on the ride home, she said my friends were rude because they spoke French at her all night long. They spoke English. Yes, they have accents, but they were making an effort. They were being friendly. She wasn't. This girl was surrounded by amazing things all day long, and she didn't even see them." I made a sympathetic face. "Whereas you," he continued, smiling at me, "think the Métro is magical."

"I've taken a bunch of photos. And I said the *Mona Lisa* is meh."

"She is meh. And you took photos, but you also looked. You interacted. When we've gone to a café, you haven't counted the ice cubes."

"Because I was in a café in Paris. I was too excited to count ice cubes."

"I show you something amazing and you see how amazing it is, not how trending it'll make you on TikTok or whatever. You were nice to my friends tonight."

"Because they're interesting people. You do not meet many debate nerds out in the wild. And they were really nice to me."

"Because you're magic, mademoiselle."

I felt as effervescent as Champagne fizz.

We were both quiet on the walk home from the Métro. At my apartment door, he seemed suddenly awkward. I smiled at him. "Thanks. I had an amazing time."

"Me too."

We stood there for a minute. The doorstep good-night is always the trickiest part of a first date. Do you kiss? Shake hands? Hug? Wave? Normally I'd be tense and awkward, worried about misreading signals, but I was full of Champagne, Nick had called me magical, and I'd seen how the cool kids did it. I leaned in, kissing him lightly on each cheek.

He grinned. "Good night, mademoiselle."

"Night," I said. I watched him walk down the hall to the elevator. He turned around and waved, and I waved back.

The minute I closed the door behind me, I texted Madame Dupuy, hoping I wasn't waking her.

Her call came back immediately.

"Bonsoir, Madame Dupuy," I said. "I'm home."

"Bonsoir, Mademoiselle Tosh. Please tell me what is in the refrigerator."

"What?" Wow, I really had had too much to drink.

"The refrigerator, mademoiselle. Please open it and tell me what is inside."

"Um, okay." I walked into the kitchen, puzzled, and pulled open the fridge. "What the . . ."

"Ah, you are then truly home. What do you see?"

"I see one of the shoes I was trying on earlier. I don't . . ." And then the light dawned. Madame Dupuy had set it up so that she would know whether I was lying when I called. "Never mind."

"Bon," she said. "I will wish you good night. Fais des beaux rêves."

Sweet dreams. Dad used to tell me that when I was still little enough to want him to tuck me in. I hung up, took the chilly shoe out of the fridge, and carried it to my room, shaking my head in admiration. She knew the tricks, and she'd set an excellent trap. I wondered where she learned to do that.

CHAPTER 5

ELEVEN WEEKS AGO

Madame Dupuy got to our apartment earlier than usual the next morning, rousted me out of bed, poured a cup of coffee into me, stuck a pain au chocolat in my hand, and handed me my backpack. "If I permit you to go to a club, Mademoiselle Tosh, you must repay me by going to class," she said as she herded me toward the door.

"Just a minute, please." I hurried into my room and retrieved her heart necklace. "Thank you so much for lending this to me." I held it out to her, but she pushed my hand back gently.

"It is yours now. Please wear it every day. There was another attack last night, one street from the club where you were, and I would like you to be protected all the time."

Unless the pendant shot stun rays, I didn't see how it could protect me, but her concern felt like a hug. The radio babbled in the background, as it did every day. She'd insisted that we set our sound system up so that it played the same boring news station in every room. You couldn't escape.

"It is very helpful for learning French," she'd told Dad. "France Info repeats the main news stories every hour. By the end of the day, even if you are not truly listening, you will have understood at least one news item. So you will know a little more French and a little more news every day."

Dad embraced total immersion, but he had to listen for only an hour or so in the evenings, because I turned it off the moment Madame Dupuy left. I, on the other hand, had to listen whenever I was home, unless I was doing homework. She'd quiz me on the news stories, too. Some days immersion felt like drowning.

"This attack," I said, slinging my pack onto my shoulder. "What happened?"

Madame Dupuy looked uncomfortable. I was about to ask her again when I recognized a word in the newscast. "Did they just say 'vampire' on the actual news? Like as a possible suspect?"

She nodded grimly. "That is the attack I was telling you about. The victim died."

I winced. "But they don't really think a 'vampire' did it, do they?"

"There are people who do."

I remembered what she'd said about her great-grandma fighting off a vampire with the necklace I wore. "Do *you* think that?"

"I hope it is not true, but it is possible, yes."

"That there's a 'vampire' in Paris?" I made the air quotes with my fingers this time because I couldn't believe I was having this conversation with a certified adult. She nodded. Just, wow. "Listen, I love this necklace, and it's so sweet of you to give it to me, but necklaces don't protect against vampires, because vampires aren't real."

She gave me a look filled with sorrow, then said, very quietly, "Yes, they are."

"No," I scoffed. "I mean, maybe it's someone who's mentally ill, but blood-drinking folklore creatures? That's just . . . stories." How could we be having this conversation? Madame Dupuy lived in the twenty-first century. She was practical; she researched if Le Shopping was safe instead of, like, doing a protective incantation or making me carry garlic in my pockets. "If your great-grandma drove a vampire away with this necklace, it was because she lived in a time when vampires were real *in people's heads*. If everybody believed silver repelled vampires, then the people who thought they were vampires would have believed they were repelled by it. It didn't work because vampires existed; it worked because everybody thought it worked. It's circular logic. And superstition. We know better than that now."

"Where I come from," Madame Dupuy said calmly, "vampires have always been real, and silver has always burned them."

We stood, staring at each other. Then, with an effort I could see, Madame Dupuy hoisted a smile onto her face. "Bon, even if you do not believe me, what harm is there to wear it?" She looked at me almost pleadingly. "Do not ignore any solutions, even ones that seem impossible. You do not have to believe that it has any powers. You do not have to believe that there are vampires. But please believe that it would make me very happy to see you wearing it."

I looked at the necklace in my hand. Her wanting me to wear it showed that I meant something to her. She meant something to me, too. So I could ignore the superstitious stuff and do this just because it made her happy. "Okay," I said, fastening it around my neck.

She sighed, relieved. "It would please me if you would carry these as well." She reached into her apron pocket and pulled out a handful of garlic cloves, still in their papery husks.

Just, no. I shook my head. "I'll wear the necklace, but I'm not doing something out of a Dracula movie. Anyway, I have to go. I'm going to be late for class."

MY SCHOOL looked like a mass conversion event when I got there. Girls wore everything from tiny crucifix pendants to enormous Gothic crosses. Professeur Joubert glowered at us as he walked to the front of the classroom. "Vampires do not exist," he said flatly, enunciating every word in his measured way. "However, evil people do. We all hope that this person will be caught and punished. In the meantime, girls, be careful where you go and do not be alone. And," he snapped, "save the crosses for church. They will not protect you from a predator. Furthermore, they are technically in contravention of the law, and I will not allow them in my classroom." He folded his arms and scowled at us until everyone took them off.

When Nick and I met after he got out of school to go see Le Bec's piece, I was jumpy, worried about the attacks and about staying safe. I told him what Madame Dupuy had said to me. "I wonder if I should tell Dad she thinks vampires exist," I said as we got on the Métro. "What if he fires her, though?" I sighed. "I really like her. And she did let me go clubbing on a school night."

"A sterling characteristic," Nick agreed.

"Maybe I just see how it goes. She's trying to keep me safe."

Nick nodded. "If you think she's okay, then she's okay."

The train rumbled under our feet. Nick threaded his fingers between mine. "So do you have plans for Saturday night?" he said.

"Um. Not really, why?" My skin tingled where he was touching me.

"Let's go see the Eiffel Tower."

I grinned at him. "Yes, please. I've been meaning to go see it so I can share selfies of it with all forty-eight of my Instagram followers." He laughed, throwing his head back. The people in the seats around us eyed him suspiciously. I wondered if I'd missed the sign saying it was forbidden to laugh on the Métro. When we got to Le Mur, Nick's friends were already there. Martine was smoking as she talked to Youssef, carefully blowing the smoke away from him. When we did kiss-kiss, I noticed how the harshness of the smoke balanced the sweetness of her perfume. "Those things'll kill you," Nick said. She did look glamorous, though, with her wrist cocked back, the cigarette held between her languidly curled fingers.

"Maybe you could vape," I suggested.

She shook her head. "It looks like an infant sucking on

its, euhm—" She motioned with her cigarette like, *What's the word?*

"Pacifier?" I said.

"Yes. I prefer not to look like a baby." She blew a stream of smoke out the side of her mouth like some vintage Hollywood actress. "Does it bother you that I smoke?"

"Only because it's bad for you. I don't really mind people smoking outside." It was such a *city* smell, like diesel exhaust or hot asphalt or roasting garlic from a nearby restaurant.

"One day, I will quit. But for now, it is my friend."

"That's an interesting way to describe it."

"I can always rely on smoking to calm me when I am agitated." She pointed to the wall where Le Bec had painted his mural. "I think these birds feel the same way." At fifteen feet tall, they practically exploded onto the street. The first one in line, sleek and fashionable in heeled black boots and a cropped leather jacket, was holding its cigarette with its wing cocked back, blowing smoke out of the side of its beak.

"It looks exactly like you," I told her.

She regarded it critically. "The jacket is very nice. I would wear it."

The pigeon next to it wore a Mediterranean-blue messenger bag slung across its body and clutched an e-cigarette. Martine was right; it did look like it was sucking on a pacifier. The third one cradled its backpack between its checkerboard Vans-clad feet, like penguins do with their chicks. It was lighting up, its wing cupped around the lighter, which cast dramatic shadows onto its bird face. Next to it, a goth bird wearing a black leather bustier and flamboyantly winged eyeliner flicked its cigarette onto the sidewalk. The last pigeon wore a beanie pulled low over its eyes and battered, half-laced boots and was lighting a second cigarette off the end of the first one. It amazed me how Le Bec had made them seem more real than the actual pigeons pecking at the sidewalk below. I loved how he'd given the birds personalities—how he'd changed the curve of the beak slightly to give goth pigeon a sneer, how he'd made vaping pigeon's feathers a little raggedy and its body gaunt, like maybe it had an eating disorder. Each bird had a story you could read in its stance, its expression, even the color of its feathers. I knew how hard it was to do that—to bring life to a painting. I'd struggled to do it in art class, my vision of what my painting should look like always at odds with my technical skill. I'd told myself I should have a little genetic advantage—Mom had been a medical illustrator—but it wasn't until we did a printmaking unit that I found a medium that loved me.

"Waou," Youssef said. "I do not like pigeons, yet I love these."

"Why not?" I asked. "Anything that survives on stale fries and breadcrumbs and still manages to strut around like they own the place deserves respect, if not adoration."

He shook his head. "Do you know how corrosive pigeon shit is? It dissolves stone. They are ruining buildings every day of their lives, like tiny architectural terrorists."

I imagined a cell of anarchist pigeons as Le Bec might paint them, hoodies pulled up over their heads, bandannas covering their beaks, cooing out coordinates for their next bombing run. "You're very concerned about buildings," I said.

"I am going to be an architect. I do not want stupid, dirty birds degrading my work."

"Well at least Le Bec's pigeons won't poop on your buildings," I said. Youssef laughed. People flowed around us, many of them stopping to look at Le Bec's mural. I was watching their reactions when Noor caught my eye. "I like your T-shirt," she said. I was wearing a heathered gray tee, soft from wear, with the word "estrogen" broken into three lines and reversed out of a magenta rectangle:

"Thank you," I said. "My debate team had three whole girls on it, including me, so I made us T-shirts for solidarity. We always wore them on the bus to meets."

"You made this?" she asked. "I am impressed."

I smiled, pleased that an artist as good as Noor liked something I'd made. "Yeah. I really love printmaking."

"So what do you think of my work?" Le Bec's voice murmured in my ear. I squeaked and jumped as he put his hand on the back of my neck. Cole did that, and I hated it. It made me feel small and vulnerable. "Such beautiful hair." Le Bec's voice was low, his mouth still uncomfortably close. "I like redheads."

Ick. "Oh, hi," I said, my voice unnaturally loud as I spun out of his grip. "I didn't know you were here."

"I am everywhere." He smiled at me with his teeth.

"Except when you are nowhere," Youssef said. "We were looking for you for an excursion last month, and it was as if you had disappeared. Again."

"I unplugged. I needed a break."

"Let us know when you're going dark, mec," Nick said.

"It would ruin my air of mystery." He turned back to me and gestured at the wall with a smug half smile. "You have not said what you think."

"I like how they're real, but more than real, but you always know they're just paint on a wall, too. I mean, the way you use strokes of so many colors to make the feathers look real and dimensional, but at the same time the paint strokes are obvious and graphic. Realistic is hard, and this is so real you can almost feel how soft the feathers are. But also it's more than real. It's so huge and impressive." Sometimes when I feel really uncomfortable or surprised, I babble. A year of debating had gotten that mostly under control, but Le Bec just made me that nervous.

He gave me a cool look. "The beautiful girl has opinions about my technique."

"I mean—why wouldn't I?"

His expression was hard and closed, like Cole's when I'd critique one of his arguments. Only I'd said complimentary things. I wasn't sure what he was upset about. "It's amazing," I finished lamely. He smiled, satisfied. Nick and Youssef told him the mural was formidable, and he turned his attention away from me. He told us the names of all the people who'd complimented it, described how he'd scored an endorsement from a spray-paint manufacturer, and bragged about how many thousands of new followers he had. Everyone said, "Waou," and told him how much they liked it, but he seemed to want us to keep telling him how great he was. Cole did that. He was always looking for applause, telling me whom he'd beaten and which colleges were trying to recruit him. He'd pout if I wasn't quick enough with my praise for his wonderfulness. When I did something good, though, he brushed it off like it didn't matter. Finally, Le Bec paused.

"I need a snack," I said quickly, before he could start talking again. "Is anyone besides me hungry?"

"I am always hungry," he replied, eyeing me. I moved closer to Nick, who slipped his arm around me.

"Pâtisseries!" Martine said, her face lighting up. "There is a place not too far away that has the best Paris-Brest in the city."

"Take us there now, please," I said. "Also, what is Paris-Brest?"

"You will love it," she assured me.

Paris-Brest is crisp-on-the-outside-chewy-on-the-inside edible perfection filled with whipped caramel-hazelnut bliss. We all got one, except Le Bec, and crowded around the shop's single available table, losing ourselves in pastry-induced rapture. When I finally glanced up, he was staring at me. I wondered if he was still mad at me for daring to have an opinion on his painting skills. I quickly looked away and gently shoulder-checked Martine. "You have next-level snack-choosing skills. I want to live in this shop." I gestured at the huge display case. "I want to be best friends with the baker and eat a different pastry for every meal."

Martine laughed. "There are many more pâtisseries in Paris."

I raised an eyebrow at her. "Are you challenging me to try every kind of pastry in this city?"

She raised an eyebrow right back. "Are you accepting my challenge?"

We agreed to meet the next day at a tearoom on the Right Bank. According to her, they made mille-feuille the perfection of which caused angels to weep. The boys begged off; they had a football game, and Le Bec dismissed the tearoom as "touristique." Noor's eyes had lit up as brightly as mine, though. I flourished my phone and asked, "What's our strategy? Check reviews and try everything that's three-plus stars? Try to find the best purveyor of each type of pastry? We'll need a master list of all the different pastries to start." I was typing notes as I spoke. I loved this part of research, where you're starting to figure out the parameters and it's fresh and exciting. Martine grinned an excited-little-kid grin, and we mapped out our quest. Noor turned to a fresh page in her sketchbook and drew a quick outline of Paris, asking where we should put our quest boundaries—Paris only, or suburbs, too? Nick and Youssef, realizing we were in research heaven, left us to it and started talking football. Le Bec remained aloof, too superior for us but not willing to leave. I had homework waiting, but I wanted to stay in this moment. I felt like I could see my future from here. Things would happen to me in Paris—big, interesting things—that wouldn't happen in Portland. Paris has gravitational force. It pulls things into its orbit and makes them part of itself, and then that force influences people, events—history. What I did here would ripple farther and faster than anything I could do in Portland. It was an exhilarating revelation.

My phone barked my *Fun time's over* alarm, and I was about to tell Nick that I really had to go do homework when Martine mentioned that Noor's Venus de Milo piece was nearby. Le Bec frowned, but I bounced in my chair, excited. "Oh, I'd love to see it in person," I said.

He made a dismissive sound. "I am sure she showed you the photo. That is sufficient. She is very proud of that thing, and I do not know why." I sucked in a shocked breath. "You should see more of my work instead. I would be happy to take you to it right now."

"Oh, I'm sorry," I said, like I had actual regret. There was a sharp edge to him that I didn't want to make worse. "I'm supposed to be home by six-thirty. I'll just swoop by Noor's piece since it's so close. I want to see your work when I have time to enjoy it." I hated myself the minute the last sentence was out of my mouth. Now he'd think I wanted to see his work. I mean, I would have loved to see more of his work, but not if I had to see it with him.

He seemed pleased, and he stood up. "I must go. Be careful; I have heard the Paris vampire is often in the neighborhood where Noor has her piece." He turned abruptly and left.

Despite the apparent high vampire risk, we found the tiny street where Noor's mural was without getting bitten.

"Waou," Youssef said.

Definitely wow. It was about five feet tall and full of detail that the photo hadn't captured: the determined set of Headscarf Girl's mouth as she sewed Venus's arm back on with spring-green thread; the slow bloom of color from the flat black and white of the stencil to the statue's new arms.

"You should be in a gallery," I told her.

"Or on Le Mur," Martine added.

"You need a signal boost," I said.

"We can do that." Youssef snapped a photo and posted it to his feeds. Nick grinned at me and did the same.

"We should do this for all your pieces," Martine said, taking her own photo.

"I like that," I said. "We can do a grassroots publicity campaign. Maybe an interactive map of where your work is. Let's make you famous. Like even more famous than Le Bec."

"Yes," Noor smiled. "Let us make me more famous than *La Joconde*."

CHAPTER 6

ELEVEN WEEKS AGO

"Bonjour," Madame Dupuy called from the kitchen as I dragged myself through the door on Friday. Since it was our first week, we'd had to go only for the morning session, to give us the rest of the day for all the homework Professeur Joubert assigned. I was starting to understand what Nick meant about torture being a part of French school. I dropped my pack in my room and walked the six paces down the hallway and into the kitchen, thinking, *I don't know if I can do this*. She was peeling carrots. In Portland, we had a walk-in pantry the size of our whole kitchen here, yet she served us three courses for dinner every night, all of it cooked in a kitchen that barely fit two people.

"And how was your first week of classes, Mademoiselle Tosh?" she asked me.

I opened my mouth to say, "It was fine," but instead I started crying. Grammar had been springing traps on me all week—gender, prepositions, irregular verbs—and I wasn't sure I was smart enough to manage an entire year of all my classes taught in French. Professeur Joubert had informed us that next week he would stop saying everything twice, and I despaired of getting through class with a decent grade. I couldn't even think about how hellish it would be in full-time, all-French classes. I'd aced three years of French in Portland, but I was struggling here. I'd need a full-time tutor. Or better, a translator. And now, I was standing in the kitchen bawling like a preschooler. Madame Dupuy didn't say anything; she just folded me into an embrace, holding me until I got myself under control. Then she said we were going out.

The sidewalks swarmed with lunchtime crowds, and the streets were noisy with cars. I clung to her hand like a six-year-old, my bubble-tank deflated. I was sure I'd be swallowed up if I let go. The warm aroma of freshly baked bread wafted reassuringly down the block, and she led me into the dim boulangerie where she always bought our baguettes. With its old-fashioned black-and-white marble checkerboard floor and chrome-and-black-accented pastry cases, it looked like it had been there forever. The tiny counter barely had room for the cash register, the one modern thing in the place. Shoppers packed the space, jostling us.

"Bonjour, madame, mademoiselle," the woman behind the counter sang out.

"Bonjour, tout le monde," Madame Dupuy sang back, getting a chorus of "bonjours" from the other customers.

"Bonjour," I mumbled. I also had yet to master the lilting, singing cadences of French.

When it was our turn to order, Madame Dupuy spoke so

quickly that another wave of hopelessness washed over me. I was never going to speak French fluently enough to talk to people. She put exact change into the change tray, and the woman behind the counter handed her a white paper bag and a baguette wrapped around the middle with a square of paper. Then she scooped the change into the register, sang "Merci" to Madame Dupuy, and turned to the next customer in one practiced, graceful swoop.

In the street, Madame Dupuy handed me the bag. "Vas-y," she said. I let go of her hand and opened it to look inside. "Go on, eat it." I fished out a pain au chocolat and gave her a questioning look. It was lunchtime, and pain au chocolat was for breakfast or an afternoon snack. She smiled. "Sometimes chocolate is the only cure for tears." I took a bite. The chocolate was warm and melty, and the pastry crackled and flaked. It tasted safe. Like home. And love.

We walked slowly as I ate. Pigeons waddled in front of us on the sidewalk, too cynical to fly up out of the way of such slow pedestrians. Madame Dupuy didn't say anything else, just held my hand the whole way home. At the apartment, I said, "Thank you."

She hugged me again. "You are welcome. Come help me with lunch."

After we'd eaten, I felt strong enough to wade into my homework, starting with the assigned chapters in *The Hunchback of Notre Dame*. Nick the lifesaver had given me a bilingual version—French on the left page, English on the right. I needed it. Between the archaic writing style and the literary tense with its confusing conjugations, I kept losing track of the story. The book slid from my hands, flopping onto my lap, and I realized I'd been staring out the window at the Eiffel Tower, thinking about Nick, for several minutes. I picked up my phone and texted him: "Looking at the Eiffel Tower rn instead of reading Hunchback."

He replied immediately, which meant it was afternoon break at his school: "That reminds me. Wear sensible shoes tomorrow night."

Me: Are sensible shoes allowed in France? I wouldn't want to violate a fashion law

Nick: I promise they are. Just wear something you can walk in. No pointy heels, okay?

Me: You are seriously limiting my shoe options here, Nick Wallace Tour Co

Nick: 🙄 Gotta go. Break's over

Smiling, I turned my attention back to the book. Hugo really, really liked to describe stuff. By the time he was done setting the scene, I'd forgotten what was supposed to be happening. Amazingly, the story still managed a hefty amount of drama and action and pathos along with a delectably evil villain. But you had to bushwhack through a jungle of prose to get to the good bits. I realized I was reading the same page over and over, sighed, and closed the book. I told Madame Dupuy I was going out for some fresh air and went straight to Saint Martin's to talk to Mom. I'd discovered the little church the week we moved in, and I'd been super happy that there was a place only two blocks away where I could light candles for her.

I'd been so young when she died that most of my memories of her were from photos and from her funeral. I was six and surrounded by weeping, black-clad people, and Mom's absence was a frightening hole in our family. An enormous hole that threatened to pull both me and Dad into its depths. I remember the photo of her on a stand in the church, surrounded by candles. I'd focused on it, and on the love in her face. On the way she glowed in the candles' light like she was still alive.

After the service, at the cemetery, I'd clutched Dad's hand as they lowered the casket into the damp ground, and that was when I'd really known, with the finality of a slamming door, that she was dead. When Dad had thrown a clotted handful of mud into the grave, I'd started to wail. "You're putting her down into the dark." Dad had picked me up and carried me away, howling. We'd gone back to the church, Dad explaining as he drove that what was down in the grave wasn't Mom, that she was a part of us and would always be, even if we couldn't see her. He'd taken me to the votive stand, and we'd lit candles.

"Wherever Mom is, she's in the light," he'd said, "and that light will never go out. When we're sad because we miss her, we can light a candle to remind us." He'd been crying almost as hard as I was, and he'd had to keep stopping as sobs overwhelmed him. Strangely, that had calmed me down. He hadn't been trying to pretend things were okay when they so clearly weren't.

We'd gone to light candles often that first year, and I'd never stopped. After I'd lit a candle, I'd sit in the last pew and talk to her in my head. Tell her about falling off the swing at school and getting a concussion or admit that I liked our new housekeeper—not as much as her, of course. I'd told her things when I just wanted somebody to listen. I'd told her things that I couldn't tell Dad. I'd told her about falling asleep on the way home from a debate meet and waking up in the dark, silent bus with the bulk of Cole next to me. I told her how heavy his hand felt on my chest and how it squeezed and squeezed, stopping only when I groggily asked him what was going on. I described the edge of anger in his voice when he said, "Nothing happened, okay?" I told her how he hadn't taken the weight of his hand off me until I'd whispered, "Okay."

She'd surrounded me with warmth and love, murmuring how sorry she was that it had happened to me. Her love had given me strength to get through State with Cole and then to make the hard decision that I wouldn't be on the team next year. I loved using my mind and my speaking skills to win rounds, and I loved being on the team with Mina and Lily, but I knew I wouldn't be safe around Cole.

The cool air in Saint Martin's raised goose bumps on my arms. I lit my candle and settled into a rush-bottomed chair in the back row. "Hi, Mom," I murmured. I waited until I could feel a slight stirring of air. "School is so hard—way harder than I thought it would be. I'm worried I won't be able to keep up. I'm worried I'll be 'that dumb American' when classes start at my new school this fall."

The air around me seemed to warm, and I felt her telling me I'd do great if I just kept up the studying. *Learning a language is 70 percent brute-force memorization.* I heard the words in my head as though she were right next to me. *Repeat everything until you want to scream, and then repeat it some more.*

"Ugh."

I know. It gets easier; I promise.

"I like our new housekeeper," I told her. "She's intense, but she's been super nice to me. She helps me with my French, and she worries about my safety and stuff." I thought Mom would appreciate knowing that. I told her about my date with Nick at Le Shopping and the shoe in the fridge when I got home. The air around me eddied, like Mom was chuckling. Smiling, I shifted, trying to find a comfortable spot. If you sat on these church chairs for too long, your butt fell asleep.

"I haven't told Dad about Madame Dupuy's vampire thing," I said abruptly, sliding the pendant back and forth on the chain. The *zing-zing* sounded loud in the silent church.

The important thing is that she wants to keep you safe. The words formed in my head. I sat there a while longer, waiting to see if she'd say anything else, but there was only silence.

"Bye, Mom," I said at last, getting up and shaking out my legs. "Thanks."

I walked out the doors and paused, waiting for my eyes to adjust to the sun. Littles shrieked as they played tag in the park across the street, and a painting on its gate caught my eye. I crossed over for a closer look. A little-kid pigeon, holding its mother's wing, waved at me. Amazing. I'd have to tell Nick that Le Bec had put a piece up in our neighborhood.

CHAPTER 7

ELEVEN WEEKS AGO

Back before Lily and Mina had persuaded me to join them on debate team ("Please," Lily begged, "we are suffering a criminal lack of estrogen on the team. You have to join so we won't be the only girls"), before I spent all my free time on research and practice debates, I used to do a lot of printmaking. I liked it because you don't have to be a great illustrator to make interesting art. We'd learned linocut and silk screen in art class, and then I fell down a YouTube rabbit hole, watching hours of printmaking tutorials. I learned how to do stencils and monotypes, gelli prints, cyanotypes, and drypoint, but collagraphy fascinated me. I liked its immediacy and portability. You could take a piece of cardboard and a glue stick, find some interesting textures and shapes—leaves, window screen, string, cardstock cutouts—glue them to the cardboard, ink it up, and pull prints. Cleanup was minimal, unlike screen printing. Collagraphy was incredibly flexible, too. I could make a plate, pull a print, add more elements to the plate, pull another print, and keep doing it until I got a keeper. With most other forms of printmaking, you had to make a completely new plate if you wanted to change something in the image. I loved how every print was a reflection of a moment and a place. I could be intentional with it, too, cutting out shapes or letters to make posters or T-shirts.

So when I woke up Saturday morning with the image of a croissant surrounded by the words "Epic Pastry Quest" lingering in my head, I decided to make team tees for us. Martine had made a spreadsheet—complete with checkboxes—of pastries and the addresses of their pâtisseries, along with meetup dates and times. Noor had drawn a map of our destinations and illustrated each stop with its corresponding pastry. It was a big, coordinated campaign, and it required T-shirts. We were meeting up later that afternoon, after Noor closed her caricature stand, for the first stop on our quest: the réligieuse. Nick came over after his Saturday-morning school session to help me with homework and ended up helping me with the printing, too, sliding the shirts over a piece of cardboard to prevent wrinkles and print-through. He held each shirt steady while I inked the plate with croissant-colored ink, placed it, and burnished it down. When I pulled the plate off the first one, he looked at me, his mouth open in amazement. "You continue to be magical, mademoiselle. I am awestruck by your hidden skills."

I smiled at him, delighted. "It's not really magic. I just have the knowing of the process."

"The knowing of the process *is* the magic. And the doing of the process." I promised him I'd bring him back a réligieuse. "Two," he said. "One for printmaking help and one for homework help."

"THEY TIED the box up with an actual ribbon," I said, holding up the small white box that contained Nick's pastries. The shopkeeper at Vanille et Chocolat had wound magenta ribbon around it, dividing it into four quadrants, and then secured the bunny-ears bow on top so you could use it for a handle. We were walking to the Métro. The réligieuses had been heavenly, and then it had felt so special when they'd wrapped up my to-go order like a present.

Martine gave me a puzzled look. "Of course they did. That is how you take pastries home."

I laughed. "In Portland, you get an environmentally friendly brown cardboard box, but nobody does it up with ribbon and makes it festive. Portland says, *It's just food—fuel for the next protest march. Make it sustainable, sure, but no need to get fancy.* Paris says, *I beg to differ. Nice things should seem like a celebration.* Paris knows that sometimes the only thing standing between you and the abyss is the pretty ribbon on the pastry box."

Martine laughed. "You sound very French."

"I think I've found where I belong." I looked around at the street crowded with people. "You know, I've always thought Portland was a good place to live—green, close to the ocean, close to nature—so it's a little weird how hard I've fallen for this place. It's so relentlessly urban. But there's a different future here for me than I'd have in Portland. And I think the Paris future is the one I want. Not to get away from people and city life, but to be at the vital center of it. I want to be where things happen. I want to *make* things happen."

"And you want those things to be embellished with a pretty bow, yes?" Noor's mouth quirked with a smile.

"Yes, I do, now that I know it's an option. I feel bad, though." I pointed at the rolled-up T-shirt she was carrying. "I should have put it in a pretty bag or at least tied a ribbon around it. I'll have to remember that presentation standards are higher here."

She laughed. "It is enough that you made them yourself."

"I wish I could draw," Martine said. "You and Noor create beautiful things. I just make boring spreadsheets."

"That spreadsheet is a thing of beauty," I informed her. "And I have seen many a spreadsheet. I love your information hierarchy and how natural it feels. I love the checkboxes. I love the way you use color to group information. I love your font—so elegant and readable. And the hyperlinks to explanations of each pastry are genius." She smiled. "Also? If you want to make fun art, you don't need to draw. This kind of printmaking"—I pointed at her shirt—"is super friendly to all art-skill levels. It doesn't care if you don't draw. You just find some interesting textures, glue them to a piece of cardboard, ink it, and print it. Voilà—art."

"Can you show me?"

"Absolutely."

"I think Youssef would enjoy it also."

"I bet Nick would, too. We could do a workshop. Noor?

Do you want to take a break from making fabulous street art and make fabulous collagraphs?"

"I would love to." The street was getting crowded, and we drew closer together. I concentrated on being a tank.

"Great. When should we—" Suddenly I was grabbed and wrenched sideways. It happened so fast that it took me a couple of seconds to realize a hooded figure was grasping my arm so hard it hurt and pulling me away from my friends. I made a startled little "Oh!" and Noor turned her head.

"Tosh!" she cried, and reached out for me, grabbing my free hand with both of hers. Martine reached for me as well. I stumbled on uneven pavement and fell to my knees, breaking my attacker's grip. Tosh and Martine helped me up.

"What happened?" Noor asked.

"Someone grabbed my arm." I looked around for my attacker, but he'd disappeared.

Martine's face was worried. "Did you see who it was?"

I shook my head. "He was wearing a hoodie with the hood up." I tried to remember any more details, but it had happened so fast. Somebody had grabbed me on the street in broad daylight in front of lots of people and tried to drag me away, and I couldn't even say what the color of his hoodie was. My knees bounced, and adrenaline careened through my body, a few seconds too late to be helpful. "Can we get out of here?" Noor and Martine put me between them and hustled me along the sidewalk to the Métro entrance, through the turnstiles, and onto the platform. They stared around like Secret Service agents as I huddled into myself, still vibrating with fear. They got me onto the train and steered me to the two facing benches in the center of the car.

Besides Mom, Lily and Mina were the only people I'd told about what Cole did to me. After that, they made sure I was never alone with him at meets. They even walked me to rounds, which he hated. When Cole and I won State and he grabbed me in a hug, they swarmed us, looking like they were celebrating, too, but pushing him away from me. And now Martine and Noor were doing much the same thing. Watching. Keeping me safe.

"Are you okay?" Martine asked.

My knees hurt from where I'd hit them on the ground, and the adrenaline was now souring in my stomach. But I hadn't been hurt, only frightened.

"Shaken up, but I'll be okay." I looked down at my hands. "Oh no."

"What?" Noor asked.

I turned my empty hands up. "I dropped Nick's pastries."

CHAPTER 8

ELEVEN WEEKS AGO

Nick rang our buzzer Saturday night just as I'd finished helping Madame Dupuy with the dinner dishes. He inspected my hiking shoes, which were the most sensible ones I owned, and pronounced them date-ready. It wasn't yet dusk when we walked up the street toward the Avenue de Suffren and crossed into the Champ de Mars. The Eiffel Tower, illuminated from top to bottom, glowed like a huge lacy *A* against the fading sunset. Tourists crowded the plaza underneath, taking selfies, gazing up at the enormous steel structure, or staring at their phones. Circusy music floated out from a nearby carousel, which glowed with light. A crêpe stand perfumed the air with chocolate and vanilla.

"Have you been to the observation deck yet?" Nick asked. I shook my head. "You'll love it," he said, taking my hand and leading me toward the stairs.

"Nick," I said as we reached the first landing.

"Yes?"

"The grillwork on the stairs is open. I can see straight down. This does not make me feel safe."

"It's not supposed to make you feel safe; it's supposed to make you feel like you've reached your goal despite treacherous odds," he said. When I whimpered, he added, "Do you want to look out over Paris from inside the Eiffel Tower?"

I nodded. I did. I just wanted the stairway to look way less see-through.

"It's just a few more flights," he reassured me. "We're not going all the way to the top. Keep hold of the handrail"—I was gripping it tightly enough to deform it—"and go as slowly as you need to. Don't look at your feet; look straight ahead. I'm right behind you." He moved to the step below and put his hand lightly onto my back. "Now take a step." I did. Behind me, Nick took a step, too. "Another one," he said. We made it to the observation deck one slow step at a time, Nick at my back, talking me up. Every step felt like a leap of faith, but I trusted him. He'd done this. He knew it was safe. When we arrived and I dared to breathe again, I saw that the floor and balustrades of the deck were *glass*. I whimpered even more, imagining myself plunging through and breaking on the ground far, far below as glass shards rained down on me. I pointed down, shaking.

"See-through," I quavered, grabbing his arm. "Not reassuring."

He put his hand over mine. "It's industrial-grade. It's been here for years, and it hasn't broken. It's safe." Around us, laughing kids were leaning on the glass wall, taking selfies. Nick put his arm around me and stepped me over to it, so, so slowly. I kept my eyes slitted so I couldn't see too much.

When we reached the clear wall, he said, "Okay, we're there." I opened my eyes to a sparkling carpet of lights out of which reared the Montparnasse Tower, three kilometers away. It stuck into the sky, as ugly as a telephone pole. "Excellent view of the city from there," he said, pointing at it. "But you just get on an elevator. No adventure. No feeling of having conquered gravity." He smiled at me. "And it has no poetry; it looks like a smokestack. Who wants to see Paris from a smokestack when they can see it from the one-and-only Eiffel Tower?"

Somehow, I'd climbed into a fairy tale. I could hear the carousel's cheerful music, people calling to one another, the muted rumble of traffic, the occasional shout of a soccer player from one of the impromptu games on the Champ de Mars. Nick got his phone out and took a photo of us. I took one, too, but my hand was shaking with terror and exhilaration, and the shot was blurry. I texted it to Mina and Lily anyway. "The observation deck on the Eiffel Tower is GLASS," I wrote. "I am TERRIFIED."

Mina: Is the blur next to you cute upstairs boy?

Me: Yes

Lily: We need better pics!

"What do you think?" Nick asked with a smile.

I shook my head in awe. "This city just— I don't even have words. And everybody walks around, looking all serious and I-have-to-go-to-work-and-be-an-adult-so-I'll-ignore-all-the-amazingness. If I lived here, I'd be doing an endless dance of joy and eating all the pastries all the time while standing on the observation deck of the Eiffel Tower."

"You do live here," Nick said quietly. "And nothing is stopping you from eating all the pastries all the time."

He was right. I was a Parisienne now. I grinned at him. "Clearly I'm living my best life." Paris stretched before us, glittering and magical and full of surprises. *What would it be like to live here forever?* I wondered. What would it be like to be so familiar with beautiful wrought iron towers, amazing pastry, a zillion different cheeses, and cafés on every block that you could take them for granted? I closed my eyes and made a wish, and then I made a promise. *I want to live here forever*, I wished. *I will never take it for granted*, I promised.

When we finally tore ourselves away from the view, I found that going down the stairs was almost as bad as going up. Nick went ahead of me, and I kept one hand on his shoulder and one on the railing. He distracted me with random facts about the tower as we descended step by slow step. It's held together by 2.5 million rivets. Lots of Parisians hated it while it was being built and called it insulting names. Nick's favorite was "truly tragic streetlamp," which we agreed would be the name of our indie band if we ever formed one. The truly tragic streetlamp was repainted every seven years on average, and the job took eighteen months to three years, depending on the weather. After the tower opened, a baker climbed to the first level on stilts. We speculated about why stilts all the way down the last flight. Once we stood firmly on the ground again and my heart had stopped hammering, I looked up at Nick. "I did it! I am the queen of the Eiffel Tower!" I slung my arm around him and took a picture of us, me grinning like someone who had just ascended the Eiffel Tower for the first time, and Nick smiling archly, like he had an excellent secret. This photo was not blurry, and I sent it to Mina and Lily, who replied with heart-eye emojis and exclamation points. "I can't believe I'm saying this," I told him, "because I am morally opposed to anyone dictating my footwear, but good call on the sensible shoes." He smirked. Then the Nick Wallace Tour Company walked me down the lawns of the Champ de Mars, explaining how they were old military drill grounds, and pointing out the military school, just visible at the far end, where Napoleon had learned the skills he'd used to conquer Europe. We stopped at the road that bisected the park and turned, facing back toward the tower, which glowed in the falling dark. Nick pulled out his phone and checked the time, then gestured at the tower and said, "Voilà."

"Very impressive," I said.

He frowned. "No, wait. It's supposed to . . . hang on a minute." I had no idea what he was talking about, so I just stood there and took it in, its lacy metalwork and graceful curves contrasting with the quickly darkening sky. I marveled at how it could be strong and delicate at the same time. And then the whole tower twinkled as the lights illuminating it flashed in running sequence up and down its outline.

"Ohhhhh . . ." I breathed, captivated.

"Okay, *now* voilà," he said. I leaned against him, hyperaware of the warmth of his skin through his shirt, the movement of his muscles, the in and out of his breathing. Tentatively, I put my arm around his waist. He pulled me closer. The tower blinked out, completely dark, and then relit, the lights shining steadily once again.

"Wow. That was just . . . wow. I don't have words."

"I thought you might like it," he said.

"Thank you," I said softly. "Thank you for this evening." I already knew I would never see the Eiffel Tower again without thinking of Nick. My Nick. "I can't believe I never saw it sparkle from our apartment. I spend half my time staring out the window at it."

"You have to know when to look," he told me as we walked. "It twinkles on the hour."

From a cart, he bought a crêpe for each of us, folded and wrapped in a square of paper, smelling of vanilla and sugar and oozing melted chocolate. I'd had crêpes before, but never wrapped in paper to carry with me as I walked under the Eiffel Tower in the softness of a summer night with a boy who made me happy. The kind of boy—and the kind of night—kisses were made for.

I stood on my tiptoes and kissed him on the cheek. "This was wonderful," I said. "Thank you."

He looked at me, then leaned down and grazed my lips softly with his. I returned the kiss. He tasted of chocolate. I felt him step closer and slide his arms around me, sighing, kissing me soft and slow. Time wound to a stop, and there was only now and Nick's lips and Nick's body against mine and me glowing all over like the Eiffel Tower.

CHAPTER 9

TEN WEEKS AGO

Nick: How do you feel about ice cream?

Me: It would make the perfect religion

Nick: Hahahaha. Do you want to go get some?

Me: Always

Nick: Lobby in 5?

Me: No stop by here first. I want to show you Noor's drawing

I felt a little flutter of unease. I'd said yes to ice cream with Nick without thinking, because Nick. Because ice cream.

And then the memory of almost being dragged away from my friends on a busy street in the middle of the day ran an icy finger down my spine. I thought about texting him back and suggesting we watch a movie or something. But it was beautiful outside. And I didn't want to be scared. I wanted ice cream. I wanted normal. I swooped into the living room. Dad had a notebook on his knee and an Alps trail guide splayed on the couch beside him. He was planning our August vacation. When I told him Nick and I were going out for ice cream, he looked up, frowning. "I don't know. It's getting late."

"Dad, it's eight-thirty. It's not even dark out."

He shook his head. "With this vampire thing, I don't think it's safe for you to be going out."

It felt weird to hear Dad say "vampire" unironically. It felt weird that all of Paris seemed to have chosen to refer to this attacker with the name of a monster from stories instead of calling them what they were—a predator. It felt weird that Dad wouldn't notice this story was being told as "Supernatural creature stymies police efforts" rather than "Police unable to capture perpetrator after multiple attacks." It couldn't be that he actually believed there was a vampire; Dad was a fact-based life-form.

"They keep saying to stick to busy, well-lit places with a lot of people around, and to use the buddy system. That's what we're doing," I assured him. "We're just going up to the place on Avenue de Suffren. It's three blocks away. It'll be like half an hour max if there's a line."

He looked dubious. "I'm just trying to keep you safe."

I remembered Lily's mom saying the same thing to her, and how I knew she loved Lily when she said it. I remembered the times when I thought it would have been nice if Dad had just asked a few more questions about where I was going because he should have been worried. But not tonight. Not up the street for ice cream. Not with Nick.

The door buzzer sounded. "Anyway, Nick's here," I said, and went to let him in.

"What's this about Noor's drawing?" he said as he followed me into the living room.

"Hi, Nick," Dad said.

"Hi, Mr. Reeves," Nick replied. "How was the hike across Paris?"

Earlier in the week, Dad had come home brandishing a worn, dog-eared copy of *Paris . . . à Pied*. The city had three urban hiking trails, so we'd decided to combine our first European hiking trip with exploring our new home and had spent the weekend hiking from the Bois de Boulogne through the city to the Bois de Vincennes. We'd never done an urban hike before. It was crowded and noisy, and it smelled like diesel smoke when a bus passed, but there were also oases of green calm and reminders everywhere that Paris has been a place people want to be since the third century BCE.

"It was fascinating." He stuck his finger into the trail guide to mark his place. "We saw two thousand years of history in six miles; ate a three-course lunch that wasn't sausage, cheese, and chocolate; and didn't do any ascents. Did you know that Paris was originally a Roman city?"

Nick nodded. "As a matter of fact, I did."

"Speaking of history," I said, "after we stopped at the antiquarian booksellers by the Seine, I took Dad to Noor's caricature stand, and we had her draw us." I pointed to the portrait she'd done, which was lying on the coffee table so we could admire it. She'd exaggerated our boots and packs, but instead of making us comical, she'd made us look like superheroes starting off on a life-changing adventure. She'd drawn us at the top of Montmartre gazing out over the city. Dad carried the book he'd just bought. She'd softened the angular lines of his face, making him look uncharacteristically carefree. He stood a few steps behind me, like a guardian. I stood at the front edge of the path, all in oranges and reds, my hair blazing, radiating enough energy for a small sun and ready to step into the future. I loved how brave and strong I seemed.

"I'm getting it framed," Dad told Nick. "It's our first Paris souvenir."

Nick smiled at me. "It looks like you're setting out on an epic quest."

"Right now, my epic quest is for ice cream," I said, making *Please let me go* eyebrows at Dad.

Dad looked from me to Nick. "Okay," he sighed, "but I'm counting on you to keep her safe, Nick." I rolled my eyes. "I'm serious," he said to me. "Be careful. Stay where it's well lit. Don't go off by yourselves, and be aware of what's happening around you."

"We'll be careful," Nick promised.

"SORRY ABOUT that," I said as we walked out into the warm evening.

"I get it." Nick slipped his arm around me. "My parents won't even let Sophie go down to get the mail alone."

"But come on, Dad just told you to protect me. He's never treated my being a girl like a preexisting condition before."

"This guy only attacks women, so it makes sense for your dad to be more worried about you."

"I know," I growled. "But I get tired of everybody telling girls to be so scared of everything all the time that we stop living. 'Don't go there. Don't do that.' It's a fundamental misunderstanding of who the problem actually is. Spoiler alert, it's not girls." That was another reason I'd pushed Dad on this. What happened the other day had scared me—because it was scary but also because I'd been so surprised that I hadn't even tried to protect myself. If I hadn't stumbled— Well. I wanted to go out tonight to show my fear it didn't own me. I wanted to remind myself to be brave. I didn't want to get into the habit of running away or hiding when things scared me.

"I know it feels bad," Nick soothed, "but it's to keep you safe."

I sighed. He looked so worried. "I know. But this guy is locking us all up in Be Safe jail. The only way to really protect yourself is to never do anything—not even leave the house. Why do I have to give up basic freedom in exchange for staying safe? I mean, I can't even fall asleep on a bus—"

I stopped, my heart revving.

"What bus?"

"Nothing," I said, seeing Cole's shadowy face for the zillionth time.

"Did something happen to you?"

I shook my head. "It's nothing. I just hate feeling caged. Look, Dad's never even given me a curfew. He tells me all the time how strong I am. But tonight he wanted to lock me up because of what somebody else is doing." The memory of Cole's hand on me, the feeling of being trapped, almost drowned me. I was glad I'd never told Dad about it. "I'm being punished," I went on, "and I didn't do anything wrong."

"I'm sorry," Nick said. We walked on, passing tourists and normal neighborhood people. We all eyed each other, looking for indications of vampire proclivities. "I didn't think about it that way. It sucks."

"Indeed it does," I said.

He hugged me closer, and I let myself relax into him. I liked that he listened to me. That he tried to see things from my point of view. I also liked that he was strong, and he would protect me. And I kind of hated myself that I did. "There's this place," he said slowly, "where I go when I need to really feel free. Maybe you'd like to go there; it might help."

"Yeah," I said. "Definitely. Where is it?"

"You can't tell anyone."

"How come?"

He paused. "It's kind of . . . illegal."

I pulled away and looked at him. "I think you need to explain."

"Okay, so my first school term here was not great. French education is pretty intense, and one day, I froze outside school. I just stopped. Couldn't make myself go in. Martine and Youssef took one look at me and dragged me off with them. They took me down into the catacombs."

"You mean the place with all the bones?"

He shook his head, explaining that there were no bones in the catacombs he was talking about. Unlike their famous tourist-attraction cousins, these abandoned underground quarries were off-limits to visitors. It didn't stop people from going down into them; urban explorers see a gate or a locked door, and they want to be on the other side. They want to see what ordinary people don't.

"It changed the way I saw things, being down there," Nick explained. "You need to know what you're doing. You need to be resourceful. It's hard work getting in, and it's hard work getting back out again. You need to have technical skills. To be good at solving problems. You need to be good under pressure. Every time I come back up safe, I feel like I can take on anything. And there's a whole community down there. You look out for each other. You help each other."

"That," I said. "That's what I want."

"Okay," he said. "But I'm serious. You can't talk about it to anyone aboveground. It's against the law to explore the catas, and if you talk about it up here, someone could get in trouble. The rule is, nobody lets a fellow cataphile down."

I nodded. When you've spent as many years hiking as Dad and I have, you've gone . . . off-trail is how I'll say it, maybe on posted land so remote and uninhabited no one's ever going to know that you ducked between the fence wires, and you've found some places that are hidden and amazing and unspoiled. Those are the ones you don't talk about with anybody, because the more people who know about them, the less likely those places are to remain amazing. You go to renew your soul, and while you're there you walk lightly. So I understood what Nick was talking about. I told him that he could count on my silence.

He grinned. "Sympa. Meet me in the lobby on Friday at midnight." I reached up and kissed him, right in the middle of the sidewalk. Somebody applauded, because France.

CHAPTER 10

TEN WEEKS AGO

The second stop on our Epic Pastry Quest was Comme les Anglais tea salon for its famous mille-feuille. The three of us simultaneously went silent as we took our first bite of the pastry. I put down my fork. "This is one of those life-changing moments, isn't it?" I asked. Martine grinned. "I mean, the religieuse was amazing, but I have now eaten the perfect mille-feuille, and I can never leave Paris. It would break me forever to part from such perfection."

"It is very good," Noor agreed, "but I think I require a larger sample size before I can determine whether it is perfect."

Martine laughed. "I will make another spreadsheet that addresses only mille-feuille."

"That sounds like months of work." I broke another corner of the pastry off with my fork.

"It is a challenge that I could be persuaded to undertake."

Noor popped another bite of mille-feuille into her mouth as Martine and I nodded. It was a worthy undertaking.

"We should rank them in order of excellence," Martine said.

Noor nodded. "Of course." As we scraped the last crumbs off our plates, she told us that she'd painted a new piece the previous day.

"Did you pin it?" I asked. She nodded. The three of us had been getting together when we had a spare hour to photograph and geolocate all Noor's pieces. We'd also persuaded her to post TikToks of her making drawings in her sketchbook or at her caricature-drawing job on her feeds. She drew constantly, and I never got tired of watching her. She was a natural performer; she'd sketch as we talked, barely glancing at the page, and a drawing would grow under her hand as if by magic. Her followers loved it, too; engagement had gone up since she started posting the videos.

"Is it nearby?" Martine said. We always did field trips to her new pieces.

"Yes," Noor said as her phone chirped. She read the text, then looked up. "I am sorry; we will have to go see it another time. Right now I must go to the print shop of my friend and pay him all the money I earned last week for prints of my *Joconde* so I can paste new ones up where the old ones are painted over. And then I must go to work, so I will have enough money to pay for the posters I will need to buy next week. It is very annoying," she growled.

"There's got to be a better strategy," I said.

"I would love a better strategy." She slipped her messenger bag across her body and picked up her portable easel. "But what?"

We promised to brainstorm ideas for her. She headed to her friend's shop, and Martine and I decided to walk home along the Seine rather than take the Métro. It was just cloudy enough to cool the day off, and we tossed ideas back and forth as we walked. A tourist boat cruised by. I looked at the people aboard and realized that to them I was just another Parisienne, having a promenade with her friend. A sense of belonging bloomed in me. I imagined an ongoing Epic Pastry Quest with Martine and Noor. When we were forty, we would still be meeting at pâtisseries, discussing our jobs and families, laughing, being there for each other.

"What about anti-vandal paint?" Martine said, bringing me back to Noor's problem. It sounded like a great idea, but Google said it was expensive and needed special equipment. Not the best choice for a street artist.

"Maybe we're thinking about this wrong," I mused.

Martine nodded. "Perhaps it is not a question of making it impossible to paint over, but of making it impossible to disappear if it is painted over."

"That's genius," I said. "But how would you do it?" We walked on. A group of tourists on Segways passed us.

"I think I know," she said, stopping just before we entered deep shade under the arch of a bridge. She pointed up. "Do you see that carving? The head of a man? If you painted it black, you would still see the man, yes?"

I nodded, thinking it through. "So if Noor can make Mona 3D, then nobody can erase her, right?"

"Exactly," she said. We texted Noor, and she replied after a minute with a heart and a link to a guy who made huge animal installations out of scavenged trash. She thought she could do something similar, although finding discarded stuff might be a problem.

Me: I love you, but I'm not dumpster diving lol

Martine: Flea market?

Noor: 😍

Martine told her we could swing by les puces de Montreuil for her right now if she sent a list of things she wanted. She said just to get lots of whatever was really cheap and had interesting shapes. So we swept through the market, finding tons of usable castoffs, including dead electronics, broken costume jewelry, worn-out hand tools, and formerly fashionable scarves. Since it was almost closing time, several vendors were happy to offload their unsellables to us for super cheap. We spent less than twenty euros for a sizable haul of interesting-looking junk. I plunked down a few additional euros on things I thought would be good for collagraphs. Noor was thrilled when she saw what we'd bought. "These shapes are perfect. I need to work out how to assemble it all, but I think I can put it up this week—maybe Wednesday afternoon."

"You'd skip school?" I asked. She really was serious about her art.

She shook her head. "We have the afternoon off on Wednesdays." Probably to recover so they could make it to the end of the week if their classes were anything like mine. And I didn't have to go all day, just the mornings.

"Do you want help?" I asked. "We could carry stuff for you."

"Yes, I would love to have some help. We should ask the boys, too. Perhaps Youssef would film it."

"He would like that," Martine said, her thumbs moving over her phone, alerting him that he was now the official videographer of Team Noor.

Noor was poking around in one of the bags. "Oh, this is so good. This will be wonderful. If I make a plan of where everything goes and then paste it up on the wall, will you help me glue these things into place?"

"A plan—like a list?" I wasn't sure how that would work.

"No. Like a map. I will make the composition and put outlines for every object. So if I want to use this flower for her eye"—she held up a silk daisy in front of her left eye—"I would put an outline of the flower where her eye should be, and you would glue the flower there."

"Oh," I breathed, starting to understand how it would take shape. "Yeah, I see." I looked at Martine. "We can totally do that, right?"

She said, "Of course we can," like helping execute a street-art installation was something she did all the time. Noor picked up the bag with my collagraph stuff. "Oh—that's mine," I said. "I found some junk that'll make interesting prints."

"When are you going to show us how to do this?" she asked.

"After we do Noor's piece?" We agreed that Saturday

afternoon would work and turned our attention back to planning Noor's installation. Tuesday, she and Youssef went out reconnoitering and chose a site that combined visibility with what Youssef called "Excellent environmental framing." It was also his idea for us to all wear the ubiquitous workers' blue coveralls and block off the area with portable metal barricades, which one of his cataphile buddies cheerfully delivered from an Électricité de France van on Wednesday just as we arrived to do the installation. Noor pasted up a poster with outlines of where every piece of junk went and handed us each a tube of industrial-strength glue. We got into position with our bags of junk and started attaching items while Youssef filmed. When a section was in place, Noor painted it, working with a can in each hand. I loved how her paint brought Mona to life, how the broken pencils resolved into fingers as she modeled them with her spray cans, how the padlock, along with the watch face glued to the center of a silk daisy, turned into amused-looking eyes under the magic of her art. *La Joconde* morphed into something that was almost alive as we worked. Even though it was Noor's piece, I felt the rush of helping to create something, of breathing life into a mundane assemblage of castoffs. When we finished and stood back to look at what we'd done, I fizzed with happy energy. I'd helped my friend make that beautiful thing. I'd helped her make a mark on the city. We helped the faux EDF guy load the barricades back into his van. Youssef had filmed the whole thing, and he promised he'd have the editing done by the weekend. People were already stopping to stare. One guy asked his friend why *La Joconde* was wearing a headscarf, and Noor nodded like, *That's what I mean*. When

I got home, I was so amped up from having committed art in public that I wanted to tell Dad and Madame Dupuy all about it. I wasn't sure, though, whether they'd think it was art or vandalism, so I didn't say anything. It was hard to keep it to myself. The feeling of working together with my friends to create something beautiful and important illuminated me. I wanted more of it.

I was still glowing when I met Nick in our lobby at midnight on Friday for my first trip to the catacombs. As we made our way to a tired-looking, ill-lit neighborhood of grubby apartment buildings with ground-floor businesses jostling next to each other, my euphoria started to fade. There'd been an attack by the vampire two nights ago. Whoever this guy was, the night was his kingdom, and I felt exposed and vulnerable. Nick broke into my anxieties, telling me to turn right, and I saw Noor, Martine, and Youssef waiting for us outside a shuttered shoe-repair shop at the far end of the street. As we greeted each other with bisous, Nick said, "Le Bec isn't here yet?"

Martine shook her head. "Of course not." We had to wait another fifteen minutes before he strolled up. He embraced everyone, and I swung my backpack in front of me so that he couldn't pull me too close. He gave me an annoyed look. Then he took a can of WD-40 out of his backpack and sprayed the rollers of the metal security grating that covered the front of the store so they wouldn't squeak. He produced a small black case from which he chose two long, thin pieces of metal. He stuck the L-shaped one into the lock, held it with one hand, and inserted the other piece, scrubbing it in and out until there was a click. He rolled the grating up slowly and silently.

"Picking locks," I murmured to myself. "That's a good skill to have."

Martine, who was standing next to me, gestured to herself and then Noor. "We can teach you how to do it," she whispered.

"Really?" I whispered back. "Yeah, I'd love to learn how."

Le Bec raised the grating halfway, ducked under it, and spent a long five minutes with his picks on the front-door lock. I kept my eyes on the street, looking for shadowy figures. Finally, he motioned us in. He rolled the grating down as silently as he'd raised it and followed, directing us to the back room. Unlike the dim front, where a little light filtered in from the street, it was completely dark. He flicked on his headlamp. Battered wooden cubbies filled with shoes covered one wall. A large wood worktable, its top scored and stained, stood in the center, with brown and black leather remnants piled on one end. The room smelled sharply of leather, mingled with the solvent smell of shoe polish and a whiff of old wood and dust.

"There is our access," he said, pointing to a tiny wrought iron spiral staircase lurking in the far corner, near an immense vintage sewing machine. We followed him down the child-sized stairs, whose steps were so narrow my feet barely fit on them. The boys, with their bigger feet, had to descend sideways. At the bottom, our headlamps lit up a medieval wooden door set in a vaulted doorway on the far wall. A heavy iron ring served as its knob. Le Bec grasped it with both hands and, grunting, pulled it open. Inside, pillars made of roughly cut stones supported the arched vaults. The stone floor was uneven, worn down into pathways. Shadows lurked and quivered, and it smelled sour, like clothes left too long in the washer. He made for the darkest corner, and we followed. In the beam of his light, I saw a hole in the floor and rungs disappearing into gloom. "We go down here," he said.

Nick pulled me close. "I'll go ahead of you," he said, his lips next to my ear, his breath warm and reassuring on my skin. "That way I can help if you need it." I nodded, thinking, *Or at least break my fall a little*, closing my eyes as he kissed my ear, then my cheek, then my lips. Le Bec went first, followed by Youssef, Martine, Noor, and Nick. As the light from everyone's headlamps drained into darkness, the shadows flowed closer, until there was just my small light keeping them at bay. The nearer the dark got, the bigger the sounds became. Boots on metal rungs thudded like heartbeats.

When I couldn't see Nick's light any longer, I lowered myself into the shaft, climbing down and down, concentrating on setting each foot firmly onto the metal rungs. If I slipped and fell, I'd take my friends down with me. The farther I descended, the more gravity seemed to pull on me—out, away from the rungs, into nothing. Fortunately, the shaft was only a meter or so in diameter. When I felt like gravity's heavy hand would pull me off the ladder, I'd stop and lean back until my pack rested against the wall behind me. Then, reassured, I'd keep descending. After a while I saw things that couldn't really be there—halos in the gloom, glowing shapes and moving squiggles of neon lurking at the very edges of my sight. My ears felt muffled; I could hardly hear Nick when he called up to me, "We're almost there. The landing isn't big, so we're doing it one at a time. There's a tunnel just opposite the ladder; you'll have to crawl through it for a few meters; then you can stand up. Take your pack off and push it ahead of you. If you need me, just call, and I'll come help you."

"Got it," I called down.

Light washed up from below, and Nick said, "You can stop there. I'll tell you when to start again." I hung, my feet cramping on the thin rungs, until I heard Nick's "Okay." The ground surprised me when I felt it, reassuringly firm and flat under my feet. I turned, and my headlamp illuminated the tunnel opening scooped out of limestone and about half my height. I took off my pack, got down on my hands and knees, and pushed it in ahead of me. My headlamp threw jerky shadows on the walls and floor, making me seasick, so I switched it off and crawled forward, feeling for obstacles as I went. In the dark, I had a sensation of floating that I recognized from the flight to Paris: the feeling of being suspended between worlds. Finally I saw a pale glow. I emerged into a room hewn out of the rock, about the size of the lobby in our apartment building. The ceiling hung right above Nick's head, and drifts of rubble ringed the perimeter, interrupted by five dark passageways. I smiled at him, then scanned the room, looking for landmarks, starting to build a mental map, like I did with any new trail. "What's next?"

He frowned and motioned at my headlamp. "Did your batteries die?"

I reached up to turn it on again, shaking my head. "The shadows were making me woozy, so I turned it off."

"You crawled through in the dark?" I nodded, and he looked impressed.

Le Bec consulted a hand-drawn map, then pointed to one of the passages. "We go this way."

We followed him, our lamps flashing on pale cut-stone walls supporting an irregular ceiling of raw stone. Nick entered tour-guide mode. "Would mademoiselle like to know more about this fascinating place?"

"Yes, please."

"These catacombs are the city's underground twin. People have been quarrying rock from here to build Paris since at least the Romans," he explained as Le Bec led us into a tidier corridor with smooth walls and an even floor. "And Paris has been building on top of its quarries for hundreds of years, which is a really bad idea. When neighborhoods started collapsing into sinkholes because there were big voids underground that everybody'd forgotten about, the city got official, establishing an inspection and maintenance service—the cataflics. They don't like us coming down here."

"That is what makes it fun!" Youssef whooped into the darkness, his voice bouncing off the walls before it died away. We walked on, the muffled crunch of our feet on the sandy gravel the only counterpoint to a silence so large it almost seemed like a new sound. We passed rooms—Nick called them "squats"—where cataphiles partied and bunked. Some were just caves hacked into the rock; others had been made of well-fitted stacked blocks. Some even had stone-block "furniture" and camp stoves and grocery bags of supplies. In one room, three guys slept, bundled in dusty sleeping bags. Nick said that they were probably planning to spend several days down here, exploring the more remote tunnels.

Everywhere we saw carvings in the soft limestone, including a pale, sinister face dominated by a bulbous, off-center nose that leered suddenly in my headlamp. I squeaked and jerked away.

"It is okay," Noor reassured me. "It is just Benoît. He is not real." I looked closer, my heart still thumping. "Benoît" was a carved imp's head. I exhaled shakily. He had looked alive.

"I know the guy who made him," Youssef said. "He is a stone carver in his other life. He makes little faces like this that jump out and surprise you."

"It gave me a heart attack," I said, my hand on my chest, trying to calm myself.

"I will tell him. It will please him very much."

"Glad my terror could make his day."

Youssef laughed. We continued until the corridor emptied us into a large, low-ceilinged room glowing with paintings so vivid the colors throbbed in the light of our headlamps. A giant black-and-white rat in a suit reading *Charlie Hebdo* caught my eye, then one of Le Bec's pigeons, dressed in a vampire cloak, with blood on its fangs. Nearby, a woman in a scarlet dress with spaghetti for hair appeared unaware that a smirking man behind her was twirling the strands up with his fork.

"What do you think?" Nick asked.

"Wow. Incredible." Stone blocks the size of benches were scattered around the room, and we found a group of three set close together. Everyone except Le Bec pulled food out of their packs. He sat just outside our group, looking bored. Martine opened jars of rillettes and tiny adorable cornichon pickles and set them out. Nick produced a cured beef sausage and sliced it with his pocketknife. "It's the halal one that you like," he told Noor. She smiled, pleased, and unwrapped three small white packages whose distinctive odor had already told me they were cheese. Youssef put a couple of baguettes next to the cheese and stacked five chocolate bars beside them. Nick reached into his pack again and pulled out bottles of 1664 beer and lemonade. "Did everybody bring a cup?" We all rooted around in our packs and produced camp cups. Nick poured them all half full of beer except Noor's. He opened the lemonade and poured her cup full before adding it to the beer in the rest of our cups. I wrinkled my nose. I didn't like beer that much, and I couldn't see how adding lemonade to it would increase its allure. "Santé," he said, raising his cup.

We raised ours. "Santé."

I took a tiny, I'm-doing-this-only-to-be-polite sip, prepared to be disgusted, but it was delicious: fizzy, citrusy, slightly bitter, just barely sweet, and entirely refreshing.

"This is wonderful," I said. "What is it?"

"Panaché," he said. "Welcome to the catacombs, mademoiselle." We attacked the food like we hadn't eaten in a week. I tried everything. The duck rillettes, which were melt-in-your-mouth meat shreds of deliciousness; the sausage topped with a couple of crunchy, vinegary cornichons; the rich, gooey Brie; the hard, supple Morbier cheese with a thin layer of ash in the middle. It tasted of mushrooms and nuts, not last night's firepit, and I thought it would be amazing in grilled cheese sandwiches.

Le Bec didn't eat any of this marvelous food, not even the

chocolate. He just watched as we did, an unreadable expression on his face.

"Aren't you hungry?" I said, when his staring started to seem weird.

"He never eats anything," Youssef explained.

"That is not true," Le Bec said. "I simply prefer other food."

His tone implied that the feast in front of us failed to meet his standards. Nobody seemed to know how to reply to that. Finally, Noor cleared her throat and pointed at one of the walls. "The vampire pigeon is new since the last time, yes?" she said.

"You have not heard? Paris has its very own vampire." He smiled. "The catas needed one, too."

She shook her head. "No. It is a terrible thing, even as a joke. People are dying."

Le Bec flicked her words away like you'd brush away a swarm of gnats. "You should be proud that Paris has a vampire."

"Proud that there's somebody out there attacking women? Why?" I said. "It's appalling."

"Because a vampire has the power to confer immortality."

"His victims die," Noor countered.

He gave a one-shouldered *So what?* shrug. "Not always. In any case, a vampire is an improved version of a human. He is stronger; he has a better sense of smell and of hearing; he can see in the dark. He is more clever and more resourceful than humans. And like pigeons, he goes everywhere. He does not wait to be invited."

"No," I said flatly. Le Bec looked at me, raised an eyebrow, and turned away, not interested in my response. I got up and stood in front of him. He didn't get to ignore me like that. "Vampires just attack. They don't ask. It doesn't matter how great what they're offering is if they force it on people." I snorted. "And I think what they're offering is just a different sort of death."

He waved his hand dismissively. "You do not understand. People do not know what is best for them. They need someone who does—someone who can *change* them."

I rolled my eyes. "Just, no. Everyone gets to make their own decisions about their lives."

"No, you are—"

"Also? Vampires don't exist."

He gave me a slow grin. "Are you sure about that?"

Before I could tell him he was delusional, he'd grabbed me, forced my chin up, and put his mouth on my neck. I felt his teeth pressing sharply down on my flesh, and I froze. I didn't lift my arms to push him away. I didn't scream.

Nick shouted, "Get off her!" and lunged at him as Le Bec yelped and pushed me away, hard. I landed on my back.

Nick had Le Bec by the jacket. "What the hell were you doing?" he yelled. Noor and Martine helped me to my feet and stood close, asking if I was okay. I was so shaken I couldn't reply.

"It was a joke," Le Bec mumbled, his hand over his mouth, eyeing me like I'd scorched him.

"Not . . . funny," I panted.

"You are so humorless," he scoffed. "Did you truly think I was a vampire?"

Hearing the contempt in his voice was almost worse than being attacked. He was trying to make me think I was the one who'd done something wrong.

Nick glared at him. "You don't do that to people," he growled. "Get out of here right now, and stay away from us."

Le Bec scowled back. "Americans," he scoffed. "You are so sensitive. I made a little joke, and you are offended. You think the entire world must adapt itself to your feelings."

Youssef stepped up beside Nick. "I am also offended," he said.

"You attacked a friend," Martine added.

"'Attacked' is a strong word," Le Bec drawled. "I was being playful."

"You were being vicious," Noor said.

Nick still had hold of Le Bec's jacket. "You need to leave." His tone was calm, but Le Bec's smirk melted. Nick let go and Le Bec stepped back. He flicked his eyes to each of us in turn, calculating what we might do. Finally, he sneered, "As you wish," and disappeared into one of the corridors. Nick turned to me. "Are you okay?" I didn't answer, afraid I'd start crying. I didn't want to cry; I didn't want Le Bec to have made me cry.

Nick put his arms around me. I could feel him shaking. "I'm so sorry. I would never have brought you down here if I'd known this would happen. I would never put you in danger."

"Did he hurt you?" Martine asked again. "It looked like he tried to . . . bite you?"

I nodded. "He tried, but he didn't." I felt his teeth on my neck again, and I put my hand over the spot where they'd touched me.

Nick winced. "That's messed up. Let's get out of here." As

we made our way back to the access hatch, I flinched at every noise and shadow, convinced Le Bec was coming back for me. Even surrounded by friends, I felt vulnerable. When we'd climbed out and were standing on the street aboveground again, I started to shiver. I hugged myself hard and tried to stop. I was fine. I was safe; I was with my friends, not trapped, not alone. Noor noticed me shaking. She zipped open one of her pack's pockets, searched for a minute, then put something small and flat and bumpy into my hand.

"Eat this," she said. "It will help." It was a chocolate bar, the kind with whole hazelnuts. I unwrapped it and took a bite, crunching a nut, and felt tendrils of warmth spread through me.

CHAPTER 11

TEN WEEKS AGO

I love research. I wouldn't have been on debate team if I didn't love that feeling of diving into a topic, learning what it's all about, and then contextualizing it. The world is full of amazing things, and research is one way to discover them. Getting out of your head is another way, which is why I love art, too. It takes you outside yourself. It asks you to do things that might scare you, like dare to put a line down on paper and let it be imperfect. In printmaking, you're always a guaranteed two steps removed from total control. It makes you flexible. It makes you think. It makes you humble. Every time you set up a plate, you need to remember to set it up in reverse so that it'll print right-reading. Seems straightforward, but it's really hard to do it consistently. Ask me how I know. You also don't have complete control over what the ink's going to do. If you roll too much onto the plate, your image will have gloppy edges. If you don't use enough, your image will be a ghost. You can throw out a lot of prints because they don't look the way they looked in your head. My art teacher used to pull my discards out of the trash and ask me why I'd tossed them. When I'd tell her it was because they didn't turn out how they were supposed to, she'd say, "Does the composition work? Objectively, is there movement and balance and interesting positive/negative space? Because if there is, then it works. You have to give up the picture you see in your head and evaluate the picture that exists." I've pulled enough bad prints now that turned out to be good prints after all that I know things can turn out the opposite of how you want them to and still be successful. Except if you forget to reverse letters. Then you really do have a bad print, because nobody wants to have to hold their band poster up to a mirror so they can read it.

Nick had come over Saturday morning to help me set up for the print workshop. Dad had said we could use the dining table; it was the only flat surface in our apartment big enough for five people to work around. We'd put the chairs against the wall and spread plastic sheeting over the table and on the floor. "This is going to be brilliant," Nick said as we smoothed the plastic out. "I found a bunch of stuff I'm going to use." I'd told everyone to bring an assortment of flat shapes and textures to use for their printing plates. I'd also sent them some image links to give them ideas.

"Great," I said, my voice flat. I still felt off-kilter from last night. The couple of hours' sleep I'd gotten had been scarred by bad dreams.

Nick looked at me, his eyes soft. "Are you okay?" He dropped his voice. "I know last night really sucked, and I'm sorry."

"Why are you friends with him?" I set out some tubes of ink. Nick wasn't like Le Bec, and I couldn't understand why he'd want to hang out with him.

He looked down. "I've spent the last few hours wondering that. At first it was because I like his work, and it felt really impressive to know a street artist. He's a cataphile, too. He knows the catas really well, and with him, we've gone places that we wouldn't have known about otherwise. I actually met him because Noor knows him."

I stopped rooting around in my supplies box for the other brayer I knew I had and stared at him. "Okay, but haven't you noticed that she doesn't like him? He's low-key mean to her. He treats her like she's not a good artist."

"He treats everyone that way. She never said it bothered her." He held up a flat, round, handled piece of plastic. "What's this?"

"The fact that he engages in equal opportunity contempt doesn't make it okay. And why wouldn't being patronized about the thing that makes her herself bother her? Just because she doesn't say anything doesn't mean she likes it. Haven't you ever noticed how small she makes herself when he's around? Or how her sketchbook stays in her backpack? Noor's always drawing, except when Le Bec's around." Nick was still holding up the baren, so I told him its name and what it did. He put it down.

"I didn't notice about the drawing." He picked up the

baren again and turned it over in his hands like it held some secret answer.

"So was the VIP catacombs access worth Noor getting her amazing art slammed? Is knowing him better than knowing her? Did you ever notice how Martine goes quiet when he's around? How she kind of puts Youssef between her and Le Bec?"

Nick looked surprised. "She does?"

"He makes her uncomfortable. He makes a lot of people uncomfortable. Haven't you noticed that? Do *you* like him? Like, as a person?"

"Not really."

"But you hang out with him. And people think, *Well, Le Bec's kind of awful, but Nick hangs out with him, so there must be something okay about him.* You've given Le Bec the Nick Wallace stamp of approval."

He took my hand. "I am so sorry, Tosh. Le Bec crossed a line last night. I'll never forgive him for trying to hurt you." I melted a little because Nick so clearly felt bad about what had happened. He still didn't quite get it, though.

I sighed. "He didn't 'cross a line.' Not like, he's a good guy and then he has a bad day or something. He'd already shown you who he was. Every time he was mean to Noor or acted like whatever you all were doing was beneath him, he showed you that he liked to hurt people. And I'm sorry, but staying friends with him told him you were okay with that." He looked like I'd punched him, and I felt terrible. I wanted so badly to tell him it was okay, but I just kept setting out supplies. It wasn't okay, and I couldn't tell him it was, simply to make him feel better. The interphone buzzed, and I picked it up. "We are here, Tosh," Martine's voice sang. "We have supplies." I buzzed them in.

The girls were wearing their Epic Pastry Quest shirts, and I showed them the plate I'd used to print them. "But it is just cardboard," Martine said.

"Yup," I nodded. "Cheap, easy, friendly." Noor examined it like it was beaming ideas directly into her brain. Youssef asked if you could use a plate to print directly onto a wall. I told him it should work, but not to experiment on our walls or Madame Dupuy would kill me. I was happy to see how interested they all were. It made me feel like a contributing member of the group, instead of just Nick's girlfriend.

Everyone put their shapes and textures onto the table, and we chose from the mix of string, leaves, fabric, Bubble Wrap, buttons, and keys. I showed them how to make the plates by gluing the items to the cardboard plates I had ready for them. Then I showed them how to ink, place the paper, and burnish. When I pulled my print off—a quick assembly of leaves—I could tell they saw the magic, too. They got to work. Noor finished first. She'd gone nonrepresentational, building a mazelike composition of buttons and layered string. Martine did an allover pattern of keys covered by leaves that looked like an invitation to the secrets of a forest. Youssef had 3D printed the facades of his favorite buildings in low relief and puzzle-fitted them into a dense architectural pattern. Nick took the longest, carefully shaping and gluing pieces of string to his plate. When he finally pulled the print, he held it up for us to see "I'm sorry" in block capitals filling the page.

"For what?" Youssef asked.

"For hanging out with Le Bec, even though I knew he was an asshole. I paid more attention to how impressive it was to know an artist and to have adventures in the catas than to how he treated us all—especially Noor and Martine. And Tosh. I really screwed up. I'm sorry."

"Thank you," Noor said. Martine nodded.

"I am sorry, too," Youssef said. "And in reality, we know more artists than just Le Bec."

Nick winced. "I'm sorry, Noor."

She gave him an eighth of a smile. "He is very good at reminding people he is an artist. He wears clothes with paint spatters even when he is not painting and fills the conversation with himself and his work. It is easy to forget the other people making art when he is talking."

"He won't be talking to me anymore," Nick told her. "I promise."

CHAPTER 12

TEN WEEKS AGO

"Merde!" I said, scrubbing with the pick into the padlock Noor had fastened to the park bench. I'd been trying for twenty minutes to get all the pins to align along the shear line for just long enough to turn the cylinder and unlock the stupid thing. Noor and Martine had shown me a video of how it looked when the pins lined up. I understood what I was supposed to do. I could see it in my mind; the mechanics were simple, but I still couldn't make it work. "How come this is so easy for you and Martine?" When they'd shown me how to do it, they'd both picked it in about ten seconds, as smoothly as if they'd used a key.

Noor looked up from her sketchbook. "You must fail many times first."

"That's not really useful advice."

She did a one-shoulder shrug, like, *Sorry, that's all I got.*

"You are teaching your hands to think how they must manipulate the pick," Martine clarified. "The more you do the actions, even if they are not successful, the more your hands become comfortable making the motions. Then one day you pick a lock."

"When you're sixty," I grumbled.

"Perhaps sooner," Noor said. "When I started to learn, I watched every lock-picking video I could find. I practiced for hours with my ear against the lock so I could hear how it sounded when the pins move into place."

Martine rolled her eyes. "It doesn't sound like anything."

Noor smiled wryly. "Yes, I learned that. Finally, I asked Youssef to teach me. He is very good at locks, and he is a patient teacher. He would say, 'Do this and do that,' and then tell me a story about someone he knew or one of his teachers while I did what he had said. Then he would say, 'When you do that, try it this way,' and he would tell me another story. It was nice. He did not make me feel stupid, and his stories distracted my brain so that my hands could learn what they needed to do."

"Maybe a story would help me." I said, pulling the pick and wrench out of the lock and shaking out my hands. Noor tipped her head up and stared at the sky through almost-closed eyes. I rolled my head and shoulders to loosen them, then put the wrench back into the lock.

"Okay." She paused, thinking. "I had my first affair of the heart when I was six."

I burst out an incredulous laugh. "That is *such* a French thing to say." I loosened my grip on the pick and kept raking the pins. Noor raised an eyebrow at me, and I said, "Don't tell me: Your eyes met across a crowded playground, and he toasted you with his juice box."

Martine laughed as Noor shook her head. "No no no." She smiled. "He was not real. You know Astérix et Obélix?"

I continued to noodle the lock. "The graphic novels, right? With the smart little Gaulois warrior guy and the little dog and the big strong friend who likes to carry huge rocks around? Nick's little sister loves them."

Noor nodded.

"Don't tell me you had a thing for Astérix."

She shook her head. "Panoramix."

It took me a minute to remember which one he was. There were a zillion characters in the series. "The druid?"

"His beard and mustache are very satisfying to draw. I liked that he made magic potions. I spent many hours teaching myself to draw him and all the others. I would make up stories and draw my own bandes dessinées."

"That's how you got started? Drawing fan-art graphic novels?"

She nodded. "I put people I knew into the stories. I gave Panoramix an apprentice who looked like me—Remix. My friends liked her better than him, so I gave Remix her own adventures." She glanced at my hands, which had stopped scrubbing the cylinders. I gave her a guilty smile and got back to work.

"How did you start doing street art?" I asked, keeping my hands moving.

She sighed. "Some boys from my school pulled the scarf of my friend and called us names when we were walking home.

People saw them do it, but nobody told them to stop. We were so scared. Those boys could have hurt us, and no one would have done anything. It is normal. That summer, I went to a street-art festival, and I saw people making big art about important things. It was a lightning bolt. I thought that if I could make big art about girls in headscarves, we would feel strong instead of scared."

My phone buzzed with a text. When I saw who it was from, I shivered and shoved the phone back into my pocket without reading it.

Martine noticed my shiver. "What is it?"

I made a face. "Le Bec. He keeps texting. He said he was joking, and then he said I hurt his feelings, so of course he lashed out. And then he did a piece on the side of our building and texted me a photo of it and said it was an apology, but it's just . . ." I grimaced. "It's just too much." He'd painted an enormous, cinnamon-colored pigeon version of me. Its eyes were the exact hazel color of mine. Its smile was my selfie smile—slightly aloof, not too wide, with the corners barely turned up. It clutched a phone with my green-and-yellow U of O hard case, and the shoes on its pigeon feet were my favorite platform Vans. I didn't like knowing he'd been observing me so closely. I didn't want to be one of his pigeons. "He keeps asking what I think of it. I know he wants me to say I love it, but it looks just like me, and it feels creepy, not apologetic." I sighed. "I don't know; am I missing some cultural cue—"

"No," Noor said.

"What he did was terrible," Martine agreed. "You were having a discussion, and he attacked you. That is not a joke or a misunderstanding. It is not how you say, 'You hurt my feelings.'"

Noor snorted. "He is not apologizing, Tosh. He never apologizes. He says he is sorry that you have made him apologize to you until you begin to believe that you are the one who has hurt him. And he 'apologized' with a big, public piece that will bring him more publicity. This is not about you. It is about him."

I scrubbed viciously at my lock. "I should block his number." The girls nodded, like, *Wise choice*, just as my lock clicked open. I'd done it. "Look—" I said as Noor's phone buzzed.

She looked up from it, grinning. "Youssef finished the video."

"Show it to us," Martine said. We clustered around her, and she pressed Play. He'd done a beautiful job, interspersing time-lapsed footage of us working—so you saw the image grow in front of your eyes—with lingering shots of some of the pieces that made up the installation. He captured Noor as she was building Mona Lisa's face out of chess pieces, cups, an old handheld video game, and an assortment of scarves. The slow sideways look Noor turned on the camera just before she took out her spray can and made it come alive was a clear challenge to other artists. *Top this*, it said.

We applauded when we saw the closing sequence. We'd finished our sections one after another and stepped back in a kind of extended reveal, leaving the focus on Noor. She made a last pass with the spray paint, putting a glint in Mona's eye. Then she stepped back, took a long look at her creation, nodded to herself, and turned to face the camera. Youssef held the shot for a triumphant moment, then the screen faded to white.

"Formidable!" Martine said.

"So amazing," I agreed as we hugged Noor.

"It looks so big, so important," Noor said, sounding pleased and also stunned. "I did not think it was this powerful."

"It is," I said. "You have to post this right away so everyone can see it." She nodded, already uploading. Then we took her to the nearest pâtisserie to celebrate, treating her to her favorite pastry: a decadent, chocolaty opéra. We watched the video's viewer count climb until we finally had to tear ourselves away and head home for dinner. I didn't realize until I got home that I hadn't given Noor back the lockpicks she'd lent me.

The "Mona Lisa (Headscarf Version)" video went viral Sunday night, racking up several million views. On Monday, *Paris Match* contacted Noor for an interview. Even I knew how big a deal that was. The magazine had a prominent spot on every news kiosk in the city.

"Do you think this interview will help you to get a spot on Le Mur?" I asked. I'd gone to meet Nick after school, and she'd exploded out of the building, waving her phone, so excited she was babbling. It had taken a few minutes before we could get anything comprehensible out of her.

"I think," she said, "that Le Mur is not so important now. I will get more exposure from even a small article in *Paris Match*. But the best thing is that now so many people will know that the most famous painting in France is a portrait of a woman wearing a headscarf. I made a difference. I made people see us." She was laughing and crying, and Nick, Martine, Youssef, and I engulfed her in a huge hug.

The magazine interviewed her Monday, and two days later, she was on the newsstands and the *Paris Match* website. Youssef suggested taking some publicity shots of her in front of the installation for her social feeds. After the success of the video, he was coming up with all sorts of ideas to raise her profile. Noor bounced up and down, delighted by his suggestion. We all wanted to go see the installation again, so we went with them. While Youssef photographed Noor, we stood nearby and watched the reactions of passersby. My favorite reactions were from the girls and women wearing headscarves: their double-takes when they saw it, their squeals and selfies; their smiles; the way they walked a little taller after seeing it.

An image of Le Bec brandishing a Champagne bottle the night he was celebrating his piece on Le Mur swam unwelcome into my mind. It had been fun, being there while he celebrated his triumph, but it was more fun standing here watching people see Noor's piece for the first time. When Youssef finished the shots with her and with the strangers who hugged her because she'd made them feel big, he gestured us in front of the piece. We slung our arms around each other, full of the joy of having helped Noor make this amazing thing.

Someone shouted, "Qu'est-ce qui se passe?" Noor's smile collapsed, and Le Bec stomped up the sidewalk toward us, pale with anger. I felt a sting of guilt, as though my thinking of him had conjured him, and I faded behind Nick, my heart racing.

"What is going on?" he demanded again.

"We are taking photos of the new piece that Noor made," Martine said. "Did you see the article about her in *Paris Match*?"

"Yes," he snapped. "And the video, and all the comments on her TikTok." He glared at Noor. "You now have more followers than I do."

"It is not a competition," she said.

He stuck his finger in her face. "You are not more important than I am. In fact, you are nothing. You would not be an artist without me. I taught you everything you know." His voice rose. "Without me, you would be invisible."

"Yes, you taught me everything *you* know," she said. "You did not teach me everything *I* know." I was amazed at how calm she was.

He inhaled as though she'd slapped him. "The only reason *Paris Match* interviewed you is because you are exotic. That is all. You are a mediocre artist taking attention away from the real artists. Nobody would look at your work if you did not wear that thing." He snatched at her scarf, yanking it askew. Noor gasped and flinched away, and we circled her protectively.

"Do not touch me." Her voice shook with anger.

"Take it down." He pointed at Noor's piece. "Take it down or I will."

"No," she said. He stepped closer, his face reddening.

"I will break you," he said.

Youssef and Nick put their bodies between the two of them. "You need to leave," Youssef said. "Now." Martine and I flanked Noor, and I hoped she didn't feel me trembling. I reached up and took hold of Madame Dupuy's pendant for reassurance. Le Bec scowled back at us. I was afraid he'd turn this into a fight. Finally, he took one step back, then another, his eyes locked on Noor. People jostled him, but he ignored them. Noor stared back at him, confident. When he'd retreated a couple of meters, he turned suddenly and waded into the flow of pedestrians, pushing them aside roughly.

I was still nervously sliding Madame Dupuy's pendant back and forth, but I couldn't hear the zing it made as it rode the chain. I pulled my hand away. On either side of the silver heart I held, the two ends of the chain dangled. My anxious yanking had broken the clasp.

"He did not have to be happy for me," Noor said softly. "I do not expect that. But he did not need to attack me." I felt horrible for her. He'd ruined her moment on purpose. "I think I will go home now," she said. "I have to get ready for work."

As we said goodbye, I whispered, "You did something amazing here today. Don't let Le Bec ruin it."

She just gave me a sad smile.

CHAPTER 13

NINE WEEKS AGO

"I can't believe this," I muttered, pulling everything out of my bathroom cupboard. I was out of tampons. How was that possible? I dumped out my backpack and both my purses, but nothing. I went through my drawers, my coat pockets, even Dad's bathroom. No tampons. I'd have to go to the store. I checked the time. It was seven-thirty p.m., still light in that lovely, glowing way Paris evenings had of spinning out the daylight for as long as possible, the better to enjoy all the delights of the city. I flumped down onto my bed. The store closed at eight. Madame Dupuy had gone home. Dad was at a business dinner, and I wasn't sure when he'd be back. Nick was in the Loire Valley with his family, celebrating the end of his and Sophie's school year by visiting Sleeping Beauty's castle (Sophie), a museum of Gallo-Roman antiquities (Nick, adorable history nerd that he was), and vineyards (their mom and dad). Martine was doing a mandatory family dinner, and

Youssef was at soccer practice. I texted Noor to see if she and her brother could come over to go to the store with me, but she didn't respond. I looked down at the street below. Was it safe to go out alone if I stayed close to people? Every Parisienne had been told so often in the past few months not to go out by herself—and especially at night—that the warning was tattooed onto our brains. But this was an emergency. And it was still daylight. There were plenty of people around. I liked the reassurance of a crowd. If there was a crowd, it was probably safe. People don't congregate where it's dangerous. That's why I didn't like downtown Portland on weekends. It felt deserted and uncanny—almost postapocalyptic—and I was always looking over my shoulder for the threat that had driven everyone away.

I hurried out of the building and joined a group of women walking in the right direction, keeping my eyes open for possible danger. I made it safely to the store, got the tampons, and looked for another clump of pedestrians to follow as I exited. My phone buzzed, and I was so keyed up I jumped and squeaked before realizing it was a text alert from Martine: "Noor has been attacked."

I called Martine, and she picked up immediately. Noor had been attacked and bitten, she told me, on her way home from work. Somebody saw it happen and called the police, and the attacker ran off. The doctors said Noor would recover, but her wound was significant. She'd be in the hospital for a few days. That was all Martine knew. My hand shook as I shoved the phone into my pocket. I couldn't believe Noor had been attacked. It was so awful and unfair. I didn't know what to do with myself. I wanted someone to talk to, someone to listen and to tell me how unfair it was. To hug me and tell me it would be okay. I wanted my mom so bad.

When the group I was following reached the corner, a couple of people peeled off. Saint Martin's was just down the street in the direction they were headed. I'd been gone less than ten minutes, and it was still light outside. I followed them. I could duck into the church for a quick minute and talk to her. I'd be fine.

Inside the church, I went straight to the votive stand and lit a candle. "Hi, Mom," I whispered, staring into the glow. I waited, watching the steady flame until it flickered under a current of warm air that disturbed the old-church chill and embraced me.

Hello, darling girl.

"My friend just got attacked, Mom."

Oh, Tosh, I'm so sorry. Is she okay?

"I think so. She's still in the hospital." I felt distant from my body: lightheaded and shaky. I sank onto a nearby chair and studied the nave, trying to figure out where to start. Honey-colored light washed the pale bricks and warmed the mosaic murals. Even the shadows had a golden tinge. Mom waited, silent, close, and warm.

"I'm so worried about her."

What happened?

A man about Dad's age walked up the aisle, faced the altar, and crossed himself, bobbing as he did, then took a chair in the second row. He sat for a few moments, then lowered himself onto the kneeler, rested his forearms on the chair-back in front of him, clasped his hands together, and bowed his head. He was too far away to hear me, but I dropped my voice to a murmur anyway.

"She was attacked on her way home from work today. Not too long ago." I paused, then forced the words out. "There's this guy who's been attacking women, biting them on the neck. He got Noor."

Oh, sweetie, that's terrible. You must be so worried about her.

The floor seemed to undulate, making the guy who was praying look like he was bobbing in the middle of an ocean of chairs. "I am. And it's not fair, Mom. She'd just gotten interviewed by a magazine everybody reads, and she did a new piece that's been getting tons of attention. She should be enjoying all the love, not lying in a hospital bed because the cops aren't smart enough to catch a guy who's been attacking women for months."

I'm so sorry that happened to her. Warmth swirled around me like a hug, and I relaxed into it.

"I wish you were here to hug me."

I do, too, darling girl. I do, too.

The guy who'd been talking with God stood up briskly, like, *Well, I can cross that off my list.* He walked back down the aisle, throwing me an uninterested glance as he passed. I tensed.

Tell me about that.

"About what?"

You flinched when that man walked by.

"I didn't mean to." I watched him till he left the church. "He looked a little like Cole, though, didn't he?" She didn't say anything. "Maybe not. I'm just so upset about Noor."

I wonder why you would notice him when you're so focused on Noor.

"Oh, you know, Mom. We're always supposed to be alert for danger. And it's worse now, with the 'vampire' out there. That's what everyone calls him. Like they have to turn him into a fictional monster because they can't deal with the fact that he's a real-life one."

I wonder why that man reminded you of Cole.

"I don't know. The suit, probably." I shifted on the chair, trying to find a comfortable position.

Why is Cole still so much on your mind? Didn't you come here to forget about him?

"I mean, he really isn't. He was inappropriate, but he wasn't dangerous. I shouldn't even be thinking about him. My friend is in the hospital with bite wounds. Cole doesn't matter. He was a jerk, but he didn't harm me."

Didn't he?

I shrugged. "Le Bec was the one who tried to harm me. He pretended he was this 'vampire' everyone's scared of and tried to bite me—" Automatically, I reached for Madame Dupuy's pendant, then remembered I'd broken the chain. I'd have to go buy a new chain first thing tomorrow so she didn't know I'd been so careless with it.

"I should go, Mom. I need to get home."

I love you, darling girl.

"I love you, too." I got up and hurried through the big wooden doors into the warm golden evening.

"Bonsoir, Tosh." Le Bec leaned against one of the tall wooden planter boxes in front of the church.

"Oh—" I squeaked. "Hi." What was he doing here? He was smiling at me, but it wasn't a friendly smile. Trying not to show fear, I scanned the street for allies. There was a busy commercial street just around the corner, but here, it was mostly apartment buildings, and residential streets can be eerily unpopulated at certain times of the day. Everyone was probably inside eating dinner. I took a breath. *Be calm*, I told myself. *Think. And keep walking.*

He fell into step beside me. "I did not know that you were religious."

I shrugged, trying to keep it normal. "Oh, it's a pretty church. I like the mosaics."

"You are not worried about the vampire?" He smiled at me, big and insincere and full of teeth.

It made my skin crawl, but I tried to shove some confidence into my voice. "I mean, everybody's worried about the attacks. But my building is super close by." Especially if I cut through our block, between the park and the apartment buildings.

"You have not replied to my texts," he said, "I made you a painting, and you did not even thank me. That was not polite. Do you know what happens to impolite girls?" There was an undertone of malice in his voice that sent adrenaline coursing through me like an electric current. A sick suspicion came over me, and my brain shouted, *Run!*

I ran.

Fear tunneled my senses. I saw only the sidewalk ahead of me. I pushed my legs to reach, to fly. I could feel him closing the gap between us, and I needed to be a few seconds ahead of him so I'd have time to punch in the entry code. I ran, flat out, for my life. Down the sidewalk, past the preschool, the bike rental place. Our park was on my left now, and our building was just ahead. Just a little farther, and I'd be safe. His boots beat the pavement behind me. One word pulsed in my head, over and over, keeping time with my pounding feet and my ragged breathing: *faster.* I was almost there. I heard a change in the tempo of his steps and felt a brief emptiness behind me before the full weight of him struck me to the ground, forcing the air out of my lungs. I gasped like a beached fish, unable to breathe. Pain. Everywhere. I writhed under him, wheezing, afraid I'd be smothered. He rolled me onto my back and straddled me, kneeling on my arms as I labored to pull air into my lungs. I thrashed and tried to throw him off. He hit me. There was a star of pain on my cheek, and then it went nova, engulfing my head in a wave of fire and knives. When it receded enough for me to focus on something besides pain, Le Bec's grinning face hung above me, his teeth shiny in the light from the streetlamps.

"You should have responded to me," he said. "You should have thanked me for the beautiful art I made for you." He leaned closer, and his movement triggered a ripple of nausea. I whimpered, thinking, *Please, no, don't let me throw up.* "Say it," he commanded, shifting his weight on my arms so that I squealed with pain. "Say, 'Thank you, Le Bec, for making me a beautiful painting.'"

"Thank you, Le Bec, for making me a beautiful painting," I croaked, terrified. Somebody would be walking by soon. They had to be. If I cooperated, maybe I'd stay alive long enough for them to see me.

"That is better." He stroked my cheek, and I tried to turn

away. My stomach roiled again. He paused for an endless moment, his eyes playing over my face and throat, his hand on my cheek. "No pretty silver necklace to protect you this time," he said. Then he grabbed my jaw and wrenched my head to the side. His knees drove into my arms, grinding muscle into bone into concrete. It hurt so much, but I couldn't yell. I was trying, but my body was an immobile lump. I couldn't move, couldn't fight back, couldn't even close my eyes. He leaned close, and I felt his breath on my neck. I concentrated on the shadows of the trees against the sky. I tried to remember if I'd told Dad lately that I loved him. I wondered if Mom would meet me when this was all over.

Then pain made thought impossible.

CHAPTER 14

EIGHT WEEKS AGO

I dreamed I was running so fast it felt like flying, like one long leap would send me airborne. Ahead of me was an indistinct figure, also running. I was chasing it, gaining on it. I'd overtake it in a minute, but right now I focused on the joy of the chase. On the way my prey ran away from me like a frightened little mouse. It was fun when people ran. I liked to chase them. I liked the smell of fear streaming off them as I gained on them. I liked the long, weightless moment when I leaped, and I liked the shock of collision when I landed on my prey and forced it to the ground. Best of all, I liked the bright fountain of blood—

My eyes flew open, and I stared around wildly. My body felt heavy, and my mind was full of dark mist. "What happened?" I said, but no sound came out. I tried again, my mouth making the shapes of the words, but not the sounds.

I was alone, immobile and voiceless. Panic slammed into me with enough force to move my hand a few centimeters.

"Shhh," a voice said, startling me. I felt my body attempt to jerk away and fail. "Calme-toi," the voice soothed. It told me not to try to talk or move because I had stitches, and I needed to let them heal. I wanted to ask why I had stitches, but my voice didn't work. Where had it gone? Who'd taken it?

Another voice joined the first. Dad's voice. "Tosh? Are you okay?" Relief broke over me; I didn't know where I was, but Dad was here, too, so I was safe. I tried to turn toward him. My head swam for a second, my stomach lurched, and then everything went away.

When I woke up again, I could move. I was weak, but my body responded when I asked it to. I lay in an unfamiliar bed, covered by a sheet and a thin blanket, in a sparsely furnished room. An IV fed into my arm. *Hospital*, I thought. *Why?* I rolled my head to the side and saw Dad, asleep in a chair near my bed, his head at an uncomfortable angle, his face gray and unshaven. Madame Dupuy sat nearby, reading on her phone. She glanced at me, saw I was awake, and took hold of my hand. I tried to speak, but she shushed me. She told me that I'd been hurt, and I had stitches, and I shouldn't talk.

Where do I have stitches? I wondered. She must have seen the question on my face because she gestured to her neck. I put my hand up and felt the dressing taped there.

"You lost a lot of blood," she said. "We were very worried." She turned to Dad, still asleep, and raised her voice slightly. "Monsieur Reeves." He started straight out of his chair, saw my eyes were open, and gathered me into his arms. I inhaled his familiar smell of cloves and soap, and memories of Mom's funeral washed over me. Then I'd been clinging to him; now it was the other way around.

"I thought I'd lost you," he whispered, choking on tears. "You were—" He broke off.

"You were attacked," Madame Dupuy said softly.

I remembered running, hearing another set of footsteps behind me. Being so scared. The rest of it came back to me like a blow, and I closed my eyes to try to keep myself from seeing Le Bec's face again. I'd been sure he was going to kill me.

"Did you see who did this?" Dad asked when he finally let me go. I nodded. He turned to Madame Dupuy and asked her to call the police officer who'd taken their statements, but she was already tapping the number into her phone. He turned back to me. "Why were you out alone?" he demanded.

I tried to reply, but pain jabbed my throat, leaving me breathless and sweating.

"Well?" Dad said. I pointed at my throat and tried to shake my head, but the motion made me feel like my skin was tearing apart. Madame Dupuy realized what the problem was, reminded Dad I couldn't talk, and left the room to find some paper and a pen. Dad took hold of my hand, and I looked up to see tears slipping down his face. "When the police called . . ." He squeezed my hand. I squeezed back. I remembered the final, dizzy, stomach-dropping feeling of knowing I'd never see him again, and I was so full of gratitude and guilt that I started to cry, too. When Madame Dupuy returned with a pen and a block of sticky notes with "Cordarone" printed across the top in an imposing red font, Dad asked me again why I'd been out by myself. "That could have waited till I got home," he said when I wrote that it was a tampon emergency. I underlined "emergency" and wrote, *Store would have been closed then. It was still light out.* He shook his head. *There were lots of people*, I added.

"You should have waited," he lectured. "Or planned better." I wanted to cry. My period isn't always predictable. And sometimes I forget to buy tampons, just like everybody in the world forgets things. A tampon run shouldn't almost cost me my life.

The police officer Madame Dupuy had called poked her head through the door, and Dad waved her in. It took ages before she was finally done asking questions, ages that turned into centuries because I had to write all my answers out in French. She complimented my grammar, though, so yay summer school and Madame Dupuy. She didn't react when I told her I knew my attacker, but she asked me a lot of questions about where he hung out and who his friends were. When she was done, she assured me they'd find him, which was comforting. She gave me her card and left to chase down Le Bec, I hoped. I slumped back onto my thin pillow and closed my eyes. I was so tired.

"I'm sorry I have to say this, but I can't let you see any of those kids anymore," Dad said.

I reached for the sticky-note pad. *Why?* I scribbled.

"Because they're friends with the guy who attacked you."

They didn't know he was the one doing the attacks. And Nick had apologized for hanging out with Le Bec.

"Are you sure about that?"

What a horrible thing to say. *He attacked Noor. If they were part of it, he wouldn't have done that. Also, they wouldn't do that to me. They're good people.*

"You've only known them a few weeks. How can you be sure what they'd do? And the guy who attacked you apparently was one of your friends, too."

No. He was someone they all knew, but they weren't tight with him. He kind of kept himself aloof.

"At best they sound careless, Tosh. At worst, they're friends with a monster who almost killed you. When you get home, you're going to have to tell them you can't see them anymore. And you won't be leaving the apartment until this guy is caught. Do you understand that? Do you understand that no woman is safe right now? Tosh, I trusted you to be smart, and instead you just waltzed out like the world was full of kittens and rainbows because you couldn't wait overnight to buy tampons."

I started to cry. He was talking to me like I was five. I didn't waltz carelessly out; I had a plan. I was vigilant. And a tampon emergency is a real emergency, not just some minor inconvenience. I wrote that on a sticky note and handed it to him. He just shook his head and put it into the wastebasket.

I went home the following afternoon with a huge dressing on my neck and pain like shaking a tumbler of broken glass whenever I swallowed. I had to drink my meals, and I couldn't talk, but the doctor said it could have been so much worse. Meaning Le Bec could have taken my life instead of just my voice. I crawled into bed full of hurt and grateful to be alive and fell asleep. I woke that evening when Madame Dupuy knocked on my door with a homeopathic infusion to help my throat heal and a small whiteboard and marker so I could "talk." Swallowing was torture, so the tea was cold when I finally drank the last of it. She stayed with me till I finished, then took the cup, felt my forehead, and asked me if I was hungry. I shook my head. She stood there a moment, smiled sadly, and said, "I am sorry about your friends. I believe you." Then she left. I heard her wishing Dad a good evening, and then I heard the front door close.

Dad poked his head in my room. "How you doing?"

I made the seesaw hand motion that meant *Could be worse; could be better*. He nodded. "It's time to tell your friends you can't see them anymore." He stayed in the doorway, leaning on the jamb, until I'd sent the text and held up my phone to show him.

> **Me:** Le Bec attacked me Friday night. It was bad—I just got home from the hospital. He really messed up my neck, and I can't talk. Dad's so angry. He says I can't see any of you anymore because you introduced me to Le Bec. I'm so, so sorry. I'm not mad at you

Then I turned my phone off so I didn't have to hear all their "WTAF" pings.

CHAPTER 15

EIGHT WEEKS AGO

Late the next morning, Madame Dupuy poked her head into my darkened room and told me it was time to get up. She raised the blinds and opened the windows. I rolled away from the bright sunshine, covering my eyes. The warm breeze felt nice, though, and I could hear the shouts of kids playing outside, a chain of warmth and sound that anchored me. Madame Dupuy reached down and felt my forehead and cheeks with the back of her hand, then smiled at me. "Still no fever," she said. "That is a good sign." She left and returned in a few minutes with a melon smoothie. Perfect pearls of condensation beaded the glass, and a tiny sprig of mint made a beautiful green X on the pale orange drink. I wondered if she Instagrammed everything she cooked for us. Maybe in her secret life she was a food influencer, posting photos of gorgeous dishes to make her millions of followers drool. I was definitely drooling—I was so hungry, and the smoothie looked delicious. I took a sip, anticipating the fragrance of ripe melon and the floral sweetness of honey. It tasted every bit as fabulous as a glass of pulped cardboard. And it sent knives of pain down my throat. I grimaced and set the glass on my nightstand.

She shook her head. "That is not enough. Drink some more."

I reached for my whiteboard and wrote that it hurt to swallow.

"I am sorry; you must drink it so you can recover."

I shrugged and wrote that I couldn't taste anything, either. She gave me a look, so I had another sip, wincing as it went down.

"I am sorry about Monsieur Nick and your other friends."

None of this is their fault.

She nodded. "I know."

It made me feel a little less lonely to know that she understood. I drank some more smoothie, sad that I couldn't taste anything and that it hurt this much to do something so basic and necessary as eat. When I'd finished, she changed my dressing, working carefully to loosen the tape, trying not to put pressure on my neck. Even her light touch, though, sent spikes of pain all the way to my toes. She tried to distract me by telling me about her trip to the market that morning, what she'd bought, how many tourists she'd seen blocking shoppers as they photographed themselves in front of the vendors' stands. Then she gasped.

"Where is the necklace I gave you?"

It took me a minute to remember. My life before Le Bec's attack seemed to belong to another person.

I'm so sorry, I scribbled. *I accidentally broke the chain. I was going to get it fixed, but then all this happened.*

She went white. *The pendant is fine*, I wrote, worried that she'd think I'd been careless with her family heirloom. *It's just the chain that broke, and I'll get it fixed or replace it. I'm sorry*, I added, because she looked devastated.

"When?" she breathed. "When did you break it?"

Last week.

"Before you were attacked?" Her voice was tight and urgent.

Yes; before.

She looked like she would cry. "It was supposed to keep you safe from them. Did you— Did he—" She closed her eyes and focused inward, like she was sifting her brain for the right words. She took in a breath, let it out slowly, and looked hard at me. "Did you ever invite him in?"

Like into the apartment?

"Anywhere. Did you ever say to him, 'Enter,' or 'I invite you,' or was there a threshold you told him he could step across?"

No.

She nodded, then turned abruptly and went into my bathroom, returning with my makeup mirror, which she thrust at me. "What do you see?"

I saw a white face surrounded by a rats' nest of unwashed hair. A partially untaped lump of gauze covered my neck from below my jaw to just above my clavicle.

I waved my hand in a circular motion in front of my face, then pointed to the dressing on my neck to tell her I was seeing my face and neck. I looked so wrecked and weak that I wanted to cry. Le Bec had done that to me. She craned around the mirror, and when our eyes met in its reflection, her distraught expression relaxed into a small, cautious smile. I pushed the mirror away. Why had she wanted me to look at myself like this—wounded and vulnerable?

She nodded as though she'd read my thoughts. "*Je sais*; I know," she soothed. "I did not do it to hurt you; I needed to see if the mirror reflected your face."

Why wouldn't it? I wrote.

"It would not if you were a vampire." She said it matter-of-factly.

What?

"I gave you that necklace to keep you safe because silver repels vampires. It burns them if they touch it."

I was about to scoff, but then I remembered in the catas, when Le Bec had "pretended" to bite me, he'd recoiled as soon as he put his mouth onto my neck. Like he'd been hurt. The night he'd attacked me, he'd taunted me about not being protected by my necklace. I remembered because it had been such an odd thing to say.

You can't be telling me that he's a real vampire? That vampires actually exist? I felt distant from myself, like part of me was floating nearby, connected but only barely. It did kind of explain why everyone was using that word instead of something normal, like "attacker" or "predator," though. And Le Bec had torn my neck open with his teeth, like every vampire I'd ever heard about.

She sighed as she sat down on the side of my bed. "My grandparents were vampire hunters," she murmured. "Whenever there was a vampire nearby, they were called. They would stalk, stake, and kill it. They taught my mother, and she taught me. I knew that silver, salt, and garlic repel vampires before I knew how to read. When I was nine, I learned how to kill one."

You were nine? She nodded. I imagined her as a little kid, going off to school, learning about fractions, playing with her friends, and then coming home and getting vampire-killing lessons. *How is that not child abuse?*

She did a sideways nod, like, *I'm not disagreeing*. "I left my family as soon as I was able to."

How do vampires happen? Are they born that way? Is it some sort of genetic thing?

"They are made. Vampirism is a disease that lives in the blood. One is infected by the bite of the vampire."

I went cold. *Le Bec bit me. And you think Le Bec is a vampire.* She nodded. *So that makes me one.* My hand shook as I wrote the words.

She was saying "no" before I'd finished writing. "I cannot see how you could remain infected after a blood transfusion."

I had a transfusion?

She put her hand over mine. "You had lost so much blood."

So I won't become a vampire. I held her gaze.

"I think not."

The skin on the back of my neck prickled. *But you're not sure.*

She took me by the shoulders and stared into my eyes. I felt like she could see my secrets. "You will not. That is all. You did not invite him in. You have new blood. It must protect you."

Why is not inviting him in so important? The transfusion made sense because replacement blood, but it seemed weird that vampires would require hospitality before they could attack someone.

"I do not know." She shrugged. "I was a child when I learned these things. No one explained the why—perhaps they did not know themselves."

What if I do become a vampire, though? An infection might survive a transfusion.

She shook her head. "You will not." Her voice was kind, but it was still a command. Then, so softly I wasn't sure I'd heard right, she murmured, "I cannot kill another one."

After she left, I stared at nothing for a long time, worrying. What if I was a vampire, though? I tried to reassure myself. She thought the transfusion had scoured out any possible vampire infection. I'd also seen my reflection in the mirror. Everyone knew vampires didn't have reflections. So I must be fine, I reasoned. And I didn't feel different. Inconvenient questions kept popping into my head. Why would a transfusion get rid of the infection? They didn't pump out all my blood and replace it; they just topped me off, like a gas tank on empty. The infection could still be there. Would it be diluted? Would I then be only sort of a vampire—and what did sort of a vampire look like? Were some people more resistant to the infection? Questions sleeted through my mind faster than I could process them. I found a notebook and scribbled keywords until my brain calmed down enough to group them into categories. Then I looked at the categories and tried to figure out the main question of each one.

I narrowed my list to my three most important questions: How long does it take after a bite for the infection to become noticeable, what are the symptoms of vampire disease, and is there a cure? Then I dived into Google. No matter how I fine-tuned the search parameters, though, the majority of hits were for fanfic, RPGs and cosplay, and video games. The few medical references I found basically said to see a therapist if you thought you were a vampire, because your brain was broken. So the internet, at least, didn't believe vampires existed.

"Good morning." Dad came into my room and sat down on my bed. "How are you feeling?" I scooted over to make room, sliding my vampire research notebook under my pillows. *Sore*, I wrote.

He nodded. "You really gave us a scare."

I'm sorry.

He sighed. "You've always been a responsible kid, and so maybe I was too lax with you. I let things go because I trusted you to use good judgment. I can understand in a strange country, in a new culture, how it could affect your thinking—how you could trust the wrong people and end up putting yourself in danger."

I started to write that I hadn't put myself in danger, that my friends were good people—that I wasn't to blame for the fact that I'd been attacked, but he took my whiteboard out of my hands. "Listen to me. This isn't Portland. It's a big city with a predator on the loose. You can't just assume that everyone you meet is going to be your friend."

I just stared at him. Dad had met Nick and his parents,

and he'd never said, "That boy is dangerous, Tosh. Stay away from him." A couple of weeks ago, he'd told Nick he trusted him to keep me safe. Madame Dupuy had talked to Nick's mom and interrogated Nick. She hadn't thought he was dangerous or untrustworthy. And it wasn't like bad things didn't happen in Portland. Or on school-sponsored debate trips. I reached for my whiteboard to protest, but Dad set it onto the floor.

"I'm absolutely serious about you staying away from Nick and his friends. And for the foreseeable future, you don't go anywhere without either me or Madame Dupuy. And don't give me that look. I'm doing this because I love you." He pulled me into a hug that sent spikes of pain shooting through my bruised and scraped body.

I pushed away, mouthing, "It hurts." He apologized, kissed me gently on the forehead, and left. I retrieved my whiteboard from the floor and lay back on my pillows. It hurt that Dad had literally silenced me. It more than hurt. It felt like him saying my voice didn't matter.

A few minutes later, Madame Dupuy came in with a steaming mug of throat infusion. She held it out to me. It tasted like hot nothing, but its warmth did sooth my throat a little. "How do you feel?" she asked. I held my hand out flat and rocked it down. Alone is how I felt. Broken is how I felt. She took my hand and squeezed it gently. "You will heal," she assured me. "It will take time, but you will heal."

After she left, I turned my phone on. Lily and Mina had sent a video of themselves visiting some of our favorite Portland places with the sublimely cheesy Eiffel Tower souvenir stuffies Nick and I had picked out for them.

Nick had lit up like—well, like the Eiffel Tower—when I'd self-consciously asked him if he knew any good places to buy souvenirs for my friends. "Bien sûr, mademoiselle. I know the best shops in the city."

"Okay, but I need super-touristy-awful. I promised Mina and Lily that I'd send them the lowest-brow souvenir I could find in the Land of Culture."

He'd grinned at me. "Awful souvenirs are one of the overlooked joys of life."

I'd grinned back. "Take me to the joy." And he had. To a place jammed with Eiffel Tower golf tees, drones, and cake molds; baguette corkscrews; and *Mona Lisa* neckties. "I'm in love," I told him, grabbing Eiffel Tower toothbrushes and baguette pens for both of them. Then I saw the Eiffel Tower stuffies in joyfully garish colors, including a blue-white-red French flag version, and my mouth fell open in awe.

Nick followed my gaze. "Mademoiselle, your souvenir-picking skills are unparalleled. These things"—he held one of the plush Eiffel Towers up—"plumb the very depths of cheesy. Your friends will be horrified and delighted, as I am." Then he kissed me, soft and sweet.

"We miss you, Tosh," Lily's and Mina's stuffies trilled from Mystic Coffee, our favorite hangout. Pierre, Mina's stuffie—now sporting a Sharpied Monsieur Poirot mustache—did bisous with our favorite barista. Then he accompanied Mina, Lily, and Lily's stuffie, Madeline, to Lily's job at the animal shelter. Madeline lost her tiny beret and suffered a split seam and stuffing loss when an adorable German shepherd puppy bounced up and grabbed her. "Banjo—no!" Lily cried.

I missed them so much. Why was I even here when I could be back home, safe, with my friends?

They waved their stuffies and yelled, "Merci buttercups for Pierre and Madeline," over the yapping of the disappointed puppy. Lily looked down at Banjo, then back at the camera. "Tosh, I loooooovve Madeline, thank you, she's adorable. But Banjo is so sad. He needs her more than I do." If I could have talked, I would have already been telling her to give the toy to the puppy—I'd send her another one. As soon as I felt better, I'd go buy one. Which she'd probably also give to Banjo. She melted for puppy eyes. I'd show Nick the video, and he could go with me to get a replacement for Madeline. Except I couldn't show it to him. Or buy souvenirs with him. Mina and Lily grinned at me from my phone. They'd been my friends since middle school, and now they were eight time zones away.

"I miss you two so much," I texted, my tears blurring the words. Because eight time zones. I told them about my attack, about how I couldn't talk. I told them about Dad forbidding me to hang out with my Paris friends and about how he took my whiteboard out of my hands and literally silenced me. "I feel like I'm disappearing," I wrote.

I felt weak, too. The doctor had said that because of the transfusion, it might take months before I was back to full strength. I wondered if I'd be able to go back to class. I looked at the schoolbooks sitting on my desk. At least I could get a jump on my homework. It wasn't like I had anything else going on. I picked up *Hunchback* rather than my grammar workbook, though. I felt that recovering from a vampire attack had earned me a little reprieve from the subjunctive in all its tenses. Although Hugo's book was just as arduous in its own way. I mean, I get that he was a nineteenth-century guy, so the misogyny, racism, and ableism that hung like a fog over the story would just have seemed like character development to his readers. But they must have wondered, after the third or fourth 180-degree plot twist, if Hugo was going to keep the twists coming until all his characters died of plot whiplash. I did love his descriptions of the Notre-Dame cathedral, though. I wondered if it had kept that sense of mystery, awe, and sanctuary after its recent restoration. The Nick Wallace Tour Company would know. I put the book onto my nightstand. Nick had opened the city to me. *Including Le Bec*, Dad's voice said in my head. *Oh, shut up*, I thought. Nick hadn't known Le Bec was the one doing the attacks. Nobody had. He'd made Noor and Martine nervous, though, so why had they still hung out with him? I shifted uncomfortably, remembering how I'd gutted out the year on debate team. Why had I stayed partners with Cole? Why hadn't I asked to change? Because I didn't want to make things weird. Because I didn't want to seem weak. Because I wanted to win State. Because I wasn't sure if Mr. Donnelly would believe me.

I listened to the sounds of the city and thought about my friends. Madame Dupuy brought me another beautiful smoothie—mango this time—that I couldn't taste. I drank it all, though. I wondered what Nick was doing. The sunlight on my walls faded to shadow. Madame Dupuy brought me more throat tea. It tasted bitter this time. Why could I taste bitter, but nothing else? The shadows faded to darkness. Dad came in and wished me good night, and I made a production out of writing *Good night* on my whiteboard to show him I still had a voice. I wondered if Noor felt as broken as I did. The daytime roar of Paris diminished to a rumble. Our apartment took on a sleeping silence. I picked up my phone.

Me: How are you?

Noor: I have been better. They gave me blood in the hospital, and now I am very weak

Me: Same. I miss you

Noor: I am so happy to hear from you. Did your father change his mind?

Me: No. That's why I'm texting so late—Dad doesn't need to know about what happens when he's asleep

Noor: 👋 I was awake in any case

We told each other about our attacks. She'd been walking home from work at about six p.m. Le Bec had attacked her on a side street. Fortunately, someone had seen him, and he ran away. I said he'd been waiting for me outside our neighborhood church.

Noor: I think he planned this. Attacking both of us. I am so sorry

Me: For what?

Noor: It is my fault. I knew he was not a good guy

Me: You didn't make him attack us

Noor: He would not have known you if I had had the courage to break with him. But I knew that he would make things very difficult for me on the street. I had seen him do that to others

Me: Madame Dupuy says he's a vampire

Me: Sorry for the whiplash

Noor: Like 🤷‍♀️?

Me: Like that

Noor: She is joking?

Me: She says her grandparents were professional vampire killers in Croatia

Noor: I do not know what to say

Me: Agree. It's kind of a conversation killer. She said she learned to kill a vampire when she was 9. Who does that to a kid?

Noor: . . .

Me: She said Le Bec could have infected me, but she didn't think so, because I had a transfusion. She made me look in a mirror to make sure I can see my reflection

Noor: Is she okay in her head?

Me: I think so. She also told me that silver burns vampires. That night in the catas when Le Bec "pretended" to attack me, when he touched the silver necklace I was wearing, he pulled away quick. He acted like it burned him

Noor: I do not know what to say. It sounds so strange

Me: I know; it's a lot. You don't have to believe or take a side or anything. But Mme D thinks he's an extra-bad guy, which he definitely is. So maybe she has some insight here?

Noor: I just looked in the mirror. I am human. And now I feel silly

Me: Same. I know. Mme D actually breathed a big sigh of relief, though

Me: Are we okay? I need you to know that I don't agree with my dad. You're not responsible for any of this

Noor: We are okay. ❤

Noor: And we are not vampires

Me: 👆

Me: Do you think Martine or the guys are awake?

They were. I got a little weepy when I read their "We missed you!" texts. I'd missed them, too. Not being able to talk to them had felt like losing a part of myself. Noor and I told them what Madame Dupuy had said about vampires. Nick had the best response: "Just say the word and I'll bring you ice cream with blood sauce anytime."

CHAPTER 16

SEVEN WEEKS AGO

"@Tosh check outside your apartment door," Nick said on our group thread late Friday night. I slipped out of my room and quietly opened the front door. On the hall floor sat a two-foot-tall Eiffel Tower illuminated with tiny twinkling lights.

"I love it," I texted when I was in my room again. "It's perfect! Thank you ❤❤❤" I sent a selfie with it and got a cascade of hearts. Martine texted that I was looking more like myself.

Me: I'm feeling a lot better. Maybe I can get out of my room before I turn 30. Still can't talk, though

Youssef: I thought the transfusion made you weak for a long time

Me: That's what the doctor said. Mme D thinks it's weird that I feel so good, but I'll take it. It's so nice not to feel flimsy and scared all the time. Dad keeps telling me to get more rest, but I am so sick of resting. I want to get out of this apartment.

Martine: @Noor how do you feel?

Noor: Like I should be out painting

Noor: Like I am in jail

Me: Le Bec should be in jail, not us

Noor: Exactly. Why is a predator walking free while we cannot leave our apartments?

The next day our TikTok feeds were full of pics of "#LibérezNosh" chalked all over Paris. On sidewalks, on doors, on walls. The way they'd smushed "Noor" and "Tosh" together to make "Nosh" made my heart smile. Nick had taken it even farther, stopping random people and photographing them holding a handmade sign with the hashtag on it. A group of giggling kids, an old guy outside a tabac, the fishmonger at the market, bemused German tourists at the Arc de Triomphe, and so many others all held up the sign saying to free us. It was amazing. We felt seen and heard.

I was up texting every night with my friends, including Mina and Lily in a separate thread, and I still had extra energy during the day. I kept asking Madame Dupuy to let me help her with the housework or something, but she insisted I needed to rest. Dad chimed in, supporting her. "Do some grammar exercises if you need a project." He was the one who needed a project, though. He hadn't changed out of his elderly U of O tee and basketball shorts in days. His stubble was beyond *It's the weekend and I'm not shaving* but not all the way to *This is an intentional beard*. He looked camping-trip scruffy but not camping-trip happy. He stuck his head into my room constantly to check on me like he thought I might disappear. It was really annoying.

Madame Dupuy did a mirror check every morning, relaxing a bit more each time my reflection looked back at us. My wound, still red and ugly, was healing. Every night as a joke, I'd send my friends a mirror selfie hashtagged #StillNotAVampire. They'd started to reply with their own mirror selfies, making #StillNotAVampire the trendingest tag in our chat. And that gave me something to look forward to when the afternoons dragged. Everyone also posted photos they'd taken while they did the normal things Noor and I still couldn't do but longed to. Youssef's pics ran to architectural details, and they were gorgeous—beautifully composed and lit and often in black and white, which made them seem ageless. I found myself returning to them during the day, when my brain was leaking out my ears because too much grammar. I liked how his photos were simple and complicated at the same time, and I thought I could make some interesting prints based on them. When I posted a pic of my first attempt, Youssef said I'd seen the heart of his photo.

A couple of days later, I was cutting out shapes for another print when Dad checked on me for like the eightieth time that day. "You're looking a little pale," he said. "Why don't you stop for the day, maybe take a nap?"

"*I feel fine,*" I whispered. My voice was coming back, but thin and raspy and soft and easily extinguished. Still, it was amazing to be able to talk, to not have to spend so much time writing my thoughts only to have them skimmed or ignored.

"Just for thirty minutes," he insisted. "I don't like that pallor."

"Pallor is my resting state." Because redhead. I managed not to roll my eyes.

"You should be resting your voice, too. Use your whiteboard."

I did roll my eyes then. "You literally just silenced me."

He shot me an impatient, exasperated look. "You need rest. You need to let yourself heal. I don't want your understandable desire to get back to normal affect your recovery. I don't want you to strain your voice now and risk having problems later. I don't want you to be so active that you have a relapse. You're still weak. You're not back to normal, whatever you think."

What if this was my normal now? I already knew I wouldn't look the same. The wound on my neck would leave a "pronounced" scar, the doctor had said, meaning "ugly." Every time I looked in the mirror, I'd see what Le Bec had done to me. "Dad, please just—" But my voice cut out.

He raised his eyebrows at me. "This is what I was talking about." Madame Dupuy came in with an afternoon snack. I'd graduated from a smoothies-only diet to boiled mashed food, which for some reason had a weird chemical taste that I wasn't loving. Dad seemed to think I looked better after I'd eaten, but he still told me to take a nap. He went off to do work stuff, and I turned my attention back to printmaking. The incessant Paris traffic grumble drifted through my window, louder than usual. I was learning a lot from Youssef's photos, because debate brain wouldn't just let me focus on the art elements; I also had to ask him what things were called and then research them. Sometimes I fell down a rabbit hole, like with zellige or types of vaulting. I liked having context for his images, and it also helped pass the time. I was drawing a detail of receding horseshoe arches when the page went swimmy and a wave of queasiness washed over me. Maybe Dad had been right about needing to rest. I lay down and closed my eyes, which brought on another wave of nausea. I opened them and stared at the ceiling. Traffic was definitely getting louder. I could pick out the voices of individual vehicles, from the mosquito whine of scooters to the bass thrum of delivery trucks. I noticed nap marks in the ceiling from the paint roller, as well as hairline cracks and little round dimples. Rather than the flat plain I'd thought it was, the ceiling was a landscape full of details I hadn't seen before. As I was following the meander of a crack, a ribbon of smell slid by my nose, then another, then another, until I was surrounded by a tangle of scents that were so detailed they were almost palpable: food, asphalt, grass, stone, river. Human. I lingered on that one, so intrigued that I got up and leaned out the window, sniffing as currents of scent from the passers below wafted up. Smells, sights, and sounds bombarded me. A babel of conversations came at me from every direction, like my room was full of people talking. I couldn't tune anything out; I heard every word, saw every detail, inhaled every scent all at once until my head started to ache. I closed the window, which didn't help as much as it should have, flopped onto my bed, and put a pillow over my head. When I woke up just before dinner, I felt normal.

BECAUSE I'D slept the afternoon away, I was still wide awake long after our nightly chat had faded as my friends fell asleep one by one. I wasn't sleepy; I was six-shots-of-espresso awake and vibrating with restless energy. My room felt too small to contain me. I needed to get out of the apartment, even if it was only to go down to the lobby, I felt the familiar flash of frustration with Dad. Why was it impossible for him to see that I just needed a little change of scenery? And then I laughed. I didn't need him to understand anything. It was the middle of the night. He was asleep; he'd never hear me leave.

I let myself out of the apartment, my heart racing with excitement as the door clicked shut. Eager to stretch my legs, I took the stairs instead of the elevator, marveling at all the sounds a sleeping building makes. Water shushed through pipes. Beds creaked as sleepers turned over. Refrigerators sighed open, yielding up their leftovers to nocturnal predators. I stepped into the empty lobby as though I was stepping onto a stage. I should have felt exposed; the front and back walls were glass, and anybody passing on the street could see me. Instead I felt confident. Confident enough to walk out into the soft dark of sleeping Paris. I strode toward the door, and my gaze snagged on the bank of mailboxes, each with a keyed lock. Martine had told me to practice picking locks whenever I could, and in between grammar exercises and printmaking I'd been practicing with an old padlock until I could open it in seconds. Here was a new challenge: a whole wall of locks. I reached into my pocket; the picks were still there. It took me a long time to get the first mailbox open, but I wasn't frustrated or nervous about the possibility of being caught. Instead, I focused on the tiny sounds each lock made as I worked it. The moment the pins lined up and the cylinder turned, I could hear it all click into place. When the little door swung open, I rode a sweet golden surge of confidence.

I moved on to the next one and opened it. Then I opened another one. I continued like that until every mailbox gaped at me. I reached into one and pulled out its contents, flipping through the ad flyers and magazines—nothing interesting—and stuffing them back into the nearest empty spot. I stared at my handiwork, restlessness itching under my skin. I felt powerful. So if I could do anything, I wondered, what would I do?

I pulled the front door open and stepped out into the night, which welcomed me with its shadows and mysteries and stories. The city's heartbeat, strong and steady, thrummed through the pavement. I sniffed a watery mix of mud and old fish with notes of diesel—the Seine. Stronger aromas—vanilla, sugar, chocolate, and crushed grass overlaid with the metallic scent of iron—said the Eiffel Tower and the

Champ de Mars. And underlying all the other scents, the faint sour odor of limestone—the bones of Paris. How had I never noticed all these smells before? They made a mural of bright aromas and dark, as clear and colorful as a painting and more enticing.

Then a sublime scent brushed my nose—malt, salt, and butter—and without hesitating or even thinking I turned and followed its path, my mouth watering. The smell pooled and concentrated just as I stumbled over something on the sidewalk. I looked down, annoyed, and saw our neighborhood unhoused guy, asleep with one arm flung out—that's what I'd tripped over. He groaned and shifted, tucking the arm next to his chest, but he didn't wake.

During the day, he walked the main streets of the neighborhood. "You wouldn't have a euro or two to spare?" he'd ask as people passed. Dad had told me never to open my pocketbook on the street, so I tried to remember to keep a euro coin in my pocket in case I saw him. I felt bad when I gave him money—the odor of alcohol enveloping him told me he wouldn't spend it on food—but I felt worse when I didn't.

I bent and tucked a coin into his loosely cupped hand. His fingers curled around it automatically, but he didn't wake. I moved on, my belly growling. I hoped the smell I was following led to a late-night café or a food truck, because I was starving. Did they do food trucks in Paris? If Dad hadn't locked me up, I'd know. The scent was fading, though, so I reversed my steps until I found it again. It was definitely near where the unhoused man was sleeping. It filled the street like the aroma of roasting meat fills a house. But I saw nothing that could be the source of the delicious odor—no café, no lighted kitchen window where an insomniac whiled away the restless night with cooking. There was only the empty street and the sleeping man. The man who, I suddenly realized, smelled so very . . . edible.

I stared hungrily at his vulnerable throat. His stained beard. His scabbed and crusted face. I wanted to fling myself on him, tear his neck open with my teeth, and slurp up his warm blood as it pumped out of his body. But I hesitated. If I wanted to feed, I'd have to touch him. I'd have to put my mouth onto his filthy skin. The thought repulsed me, yet I was so ravenous I was drooling. My hunger warred with pity and disgust. I knew I shouldn't attack him. I knew how wrong it was. But I was famished. I dropped to my knees next to him. As I reached out to push his beard aside, I heard the soft squish of sneakers on a sidewalk not all that far away. I smelled cigarette smoke, and in the time it took me to wonder whether the late-night smoker would turn down this street and see me crouched over a defenseless man and what they would do if they did, my vision shifted: Outlines softened, the night got darker, and I had to concentrate to see things that'd been clear moments ago. My sense of smell changed, too, coarsening and retreating so that all I could now smell was a boozy outhouse odor, strong enough to make me cover my nose and back away. The marvelous, delicious food odor was completely gone.

I stared at the sleeping man. I'd looked at him and thought *food*. I'd imagined the way his bright blood would spray out, warm and delicious, from his neck when I tore it open. I'd felt powerful and ruthless. How could I have thought something so horrible, so inhuman, especially after what had happened to me and Noor? I backed away, shaking.

"Coward," said a voice directly behind me. I yelped in surprise and whirled, knowing even before I saw the voice's owner who it was.

"What are you doing here, Le Bec?" I whispered. I tried to stand tall and take up space. I didn't want him to know how terrified I was. He could probably smell it on me, though.

He barked a laugh. "I have been waiting for you to come out into the night. To join me."

"No." I shook my head, trying to get rid of the image of him lurking every night in the shadows on my street.

He scoffed. "I made you. Do you think I cannot smell your hunger?"

"I don't know what you're talking about." My voice was scratchy and ragged. I wondered where that delicious feeling of power had gone. I cursed myself for walking out into the nighttime city like it was my backyard, for not even considering the danger that I knew was here. I'd felt so powerful, though—invulnerable. But that feeling was gone now, and I just felt insubstantial and human.

"I. Made. You." He spoke deliberately slowly, and there was an edge of contempt in his voice. "I bit you; I drank your blood; I made you a vampire."

"I'm not a vampire." This much I knew. Madame Dupuy checked every day.

"You are. I smell it on you. Your senses are heightened. You have lost your fear. You feel powerful. Predatory. You long for blood." Shame burned over me. It was true; I *had* felt like that. I wouldn't have left our apartment if I hadn't. Had Madame Dupuy had been wrong about the transfusion? Had it not kept me human? I felt human enough now—scared and vulnerable and trying not to relive Le Bec's attack. What if he bit me again? What if this time he killed me? He circled me, sniffing. I turned with him, keeping my eyes on him, watching every movement, every shift of expression. "Do you know what else I smell?" He breathed me in like I was perfume. I flinched. "Ambition. You want to be important."

"Everyone wants to be important." I needed to keep him talking. Every minute he spent yapping about vampires was another minute for me to figure out how to save myself.

He laughed. "*I* was already important. I created beauty from nothing. But to change someone into a dangerous and elemental creature—that is real art."

"That's not art; that's assault. You 'change' people without their consent—and sometimes you just plain kill them. You've left a body trail across Paris."

He grinned. He was proud that he was a predator. "Those lives were not important."

"You don't get to make that decision." I slid one foot back half a step, moving slowly, hoping he wouldn't notice.

"Oh, but I do. My power gives me the right." He stared down at the unhoused man, still asleep. "Do you think *he* should decide? He's barely human."

"Yes, he should. You aren't the arbiter of who's human enough. Nobody is. Nobody should violate someone else's autonomy."

"And yet it is done all the time, with laws, with prisons, with schools."

I relaxed a little. He wanted to argue with me, and that put him in my world. "You're going off topic. Let's reestablish the parameters of the discussion."

He sighed dramatically. "Let us not. I do not care about your parameters. There is a meal in front of us. Join me."

"I don't want to be like you." I edged back a little more.

"Of course you do. You want power, self-assurance. You want to punish your enemies. You can do that and more. You can be a goddess." He poked the sleeping man with his boot, hard. The man grunted and rolled over. "Go on—bite him. Feed on him. He is food; he has no other value."

I shook my head. "He's a human being."

"What difference does that make?"

"It makes all the difference. I don't want the kind of power that lets me hurt people or punish them. I'm not that person."

"You could be, though." His voice was soft and persuasive. "Do you think this man's life is precious to him? Do you think he wouldn't trade it for the peace of oblivion? You can help him. Bite him. Feast on his blood. Join me." His cadence was hypnotic and alluring, and for a moment, I did consider joining him. He must have seen something in my expression, because he smiled—a winner's smile—and went down on his knees beside the man, then plunged his teeth into the man's neck. The man convulsed, and I didn't wait to see more. I turned and ran. This time, Le Bec was too busy to chase me.

CHAPTER 17

SEVEN WEEKS AGO

Noor: I cannot draw

Noor was always drawing. She was always looking, always putting lines onto paper. She sketched everything: people, buildings, landscapes, laying down gestures and shapes with clean, fast lines that captured the essence of what she observed.

Noor: I am not me if I cannot draw

Noor: And that is not all

Today, she'd cut her finger. She stuck it into her mouth like you do, and the blood seeping from the wound had tasted so delicious that she'd started gnawing on it. She finally forced herself to stop, but her finger looked like hamburger. My heart froze.

Noor: I am afraid that there is something wrong with me

She was really asking if I thought Le Bec had infected her, and I didn't know how to answer. Last night, I'd felt an awful, compelling rush of power and narcissism and hunger, and then he'd told me I was a vampire. But that feeling had lasted for only a few minutes. And when I'd gotten home, I'd checked my mirror right away and seen my reflection.

Me: Can you see your reflection?

Noor: Yes

Me: Then you're fine. Maybe it's stress? Or anxiety?

It was probably stress. I thought about telling her what had happened last night with Le Bec, but I was too ashamed. I'd run away instead of trying to help the unhoused man. I'd talked about his humanity, but I'd left him at the mercy of a monster to save myself.

When I posted my mirror selfie in our chat that night and tagged it #StillNotAVampire, I felt like a hypocrite. Like a vampire by proxy. But if I didn't post a #StillNotAVampire pic, I worried that my friends would ask me questions that I wasn't sure how to answer. I tapped out of the chat early, feeling too guilty and horrible for human interaction. And then I lay in bed replaying my convo with Le Bec until I finally fell into a dream.

I was walking down Rue de Rennes, window-shopping, when a passing guy caught my eye. There was something enticing about the way he moved, and I did an abrupt about-face and followed him. Or rather, followed his delicious scent: rain on stone and dried figs. Passersby scrambled out of my way. I liked that. It felt heavenly not to be scared; it was a rush to be the one doing the scaring. I followed my prey leisurely for a couple of blocks, and suddenly we were on an empty street, and it was night. He glanced over his shoulder and saw me. There was fear in his eyes. The fear made him smell more enticing, kind of like bacon, and I realized how hungry I was. He sped up, and I felt a thrill of power as I matched his pace. I liked that he was scared of me. I followed him for another block, enjoying his nervous backward glances and the knowledge that I could do anything I wanted to him because no one would stop me. I wanted to feed on him. I quickened my pace until I was close enough to reach out and grab him. He was terrified, and it felt amazing to have that kind of power over someone. At that moment, I was his world, his god. My whim decided whether he entered another world or stayed in this one. I grabbed his chin and wrenched it up, my teeth bared.

I jerked awake, my heart pounding. For a long, horrifying minute, I wasn't sure where I was. I finally calmed down enough to feel the bed under me, and I reached over and turned on my lamp. I checked my hands for blood, then went into my bathroom and looked in the mirror. There was no blood on my face or my pajamas. It had been a dream. I remembered how real and wonderful the power to stalk someone and change his life had felt, and I shivered. I didn't like how seductive that feeling was. I didn't like how much I enjoyed the rush of power. I got back into bed, but it took a long time before I could fall asleep again.

I woke up the next morning unrested and ravenous and padded down the hall into the kitchen. I'd hoped Dad would still be sleeping, but he was at the table, staring at his laptop. A half-finished cup of black coffee and a plate with croissant shards on it sat forgotten at his elbow.

He looked up. "Morning," I whispered.

He smiled. "Madame Dupuy's infusion is really helping your voice."

I nodded. I got a mug out of the cupboard and focused on coffee. I love the coffee part of the morning. I love the ritual of making it. I love the aroma as it brews, the first frothy sip, and the gratifying jolt of caffeine. Coffee is a daily miracle, driving away the terrors of the night. When things were so bad last year, when I'd wake up from dark dreams where Cole lurked, when I was at my weakest, it warmed and fortified me. I poured milk into a pitcher and heated it, and when it was just starting to steam, I took the pitcher in one hand and the coffee carafe in the other and poured them both at the same time into an oversized mug. It's such a satisfying way to do it—a little flourish to start the day, a little tour de main—but not so complicated you can't accomplish it uncaffeinated.

I cradled my cup, enjoying its warmth. I let the steam brush my face, then took a sip. I almost spat it across the table. It tasted like burnt feathers dissolved in kerosene. A little bit of me wanted to cry. I just wanted the comfort of my café au lait, not another disturbing side effect to deal with. I dribbled the coffee back into the cup, then used my teeth to try to scrape the taste of it off my tongue. I eyed the croissants on the platter in the middle of the table, wondering if they'd taste terrible, too. Probably. My sense of taste had been completely screwed up ever since my attack. But I was hungry. I picked one up and spread Nutella on it. I'll put Nutella on anything, but it's especially wonderful on croissants. I took a small, careful bite. It tasted like sulfur. But I was starving, so I focused on swallowing without gagging. I forced it all down, one horrible bite at a time, because my stomach kept demanding to be fed. Dad looked up from his phone, saw my face, and said, "You look terrible. You need to go back to bed." I didn't argue with him. Instead, I crawled into bed and slept through most of the day. I woke up just before dinner to the sweet, coppery, slightly rotten smell of duck gésiers. Gizzards are one of my "no thank you so much" foods, and Madame Dupuy knew that. But she also insisted that Dad and I learn to eat inexplicable French delicacies. Tonight they smelled enticing. After my experience with breakfast, though, I dreaded even more than usual having to eat them. They taste like meat pureed with blood and sugar: too rich, too sweet, with disturbing metallic overtones.

Madame Dupuy had made a beautiful meal, as usual. We started with salad. The ruffled lettuce leaves, glistening with dressing, cradled crispy chunks of gésiers. I was relieved—and puzzled—when I sampled a tiny bite of one and it tasted delicious. I hoovered up the salad, and Dad commented on how nice it was to see me with an appetite. Sliced sautéed duck breasts followed, covered with a caramel-colored pan sauce and topped with orange medallions. Steamed baby green beans nestled next to them. A baguette sat on the table ready to mop up every drop of sauce. It broke my heart with its beauty, and it tasted like dumpster scrapings. I had a wolf's hunger, though, so I chewed my way through all of it. Dad complimented Madame Dupuy on the meal, and I nodded. She gave him a calculating look. "Even the gésiers?"

"I'm beginning to appreciate gésiers," he said. "As long as there's enough salad and bread surrounding them."

"Both of you are."

I gave her a weak smile. "Maybe we're becoming French," I rasped. Dessert was fromage frais with raspberry coulis, which I normally love but didn't bother to finish because it tasted like used cat litter. I retreated to my room and tried to watch an episode of *Buffy*, but I couldn't focus. Instead, I leaned onto my windowsill, watching late commuters rushing home from the nearby Métro stop. I felt foreign to myself, like I wasn't me anymore. Le Bec had told me I was a vampire. The mirror test said I wasn't. I couldn't get the unhoused man out of my head, though. The way he'd looked so vulnerable lying there, the way my mouth had watered when I saw him. Was I a vampire? Was I broken? Had I lost myself? The questions chased each other around in a tightening spiral until I felt so dizzy I collapsed onto my bed. Right at eye level hung a print I'd made from one of Youssef's photos. It was a rose window—I hadn't known the name until he'd told me—and the print was an enlarged detail of the tracery. *You're not seeing the big picture*, I thought, my eyes moving over the image. *You need to use debate brain.*

I formulated the question: Was I a vampire? I spent several minutes listing reasons I couldn't be one, but each of them had a counterargument. I tried reversing the question and listing the reasons I was most certainly a vampire—sometimes going to the place you don't want to go gives you clarity—but all those reasons had counters, too. Everything centered on Madame Dupuy's test: Could I see my reflection? I could, so I wasn't. But after what Le Bec said, I didn't quite trust it. I wanted a second opinion. I was trying to remember if she'd said anything else about vampires when my eyes fell on her silver pendant, still sitting on my bedside table, the broken chain pooled around it. Silver burns vampires. That's what she'd said when she'd given it to me. I reached for it, then stopped. Did I really, really want to know? If I knew, I'd have to make choices. Hard ones. I sat perfectly still, balancing between the Tosh I had been and the Tosh I might be. I sighed, counted to three, and touched the pendant. Pain sizzled on my skin, and I jerked my hand back, staring at the filigree pattern branded on my finger. I felt like I'd stepped off a cliff.

When Madame Dupuy brought me the throat tea just before she left for the evening, she was smiling. "Your father has agreed that you can return to school tomorrow." I blinked at her, completely unprepared for this development. "What is wrong?" she asked.

"I'm . . . shocked," I whispered. I hadn't thought I'd get out of the apartment until regular school started in September.

"Yes, well, both of you need a change of scenery. And you are healing exceptionally well. Your father understands that it is the logical thing to do."

"Thank you." I was willing to bet that he wouldn't have seen the logic if Madame Dupuy hadn't pointed it out to him.

She waved my thanks away. "It is nothing." There were restrictions, of course. Madame Dupuy had to walk me to and from school. I couldn't go anywhere unless she or Dad went with me. I couldn't hang out with anyone. But it was better than being trapped in this apartment forever. She'd also convinced Dad to return to the office. It would be so excellent for things to get back to normal.

I finished my tea. Madame Dupuy went home. I gathered up my school things and loaded them into my backpack, wondering whether I could trust myself not to do anything . . . vampire-y to my classmates. Dad came in as I zipped my pack up. "Madame Dupuy really advocated for you, Tosh." My heart stuttered. What if I let her down? The burn on my finger throbbed. What if I hurt someone at school? "And she was right," he continued. "It's time for both of us to get out of this apartment. But do not put yourself in harm's way for any reason." He told me the rules again, and I assured him that I would follow them. "We're going to get through this," he said, hugging me. "Now get some sleep."

The city settled down into night. My Paris chat woke up, and I shared the good news. I told Mina and Lily, too, but they were both at work, so they wouldn't see it till they had a break.

Me: I still can't see you all though

Nick: But at least you get out of the apartment. That's huge

Martine: We are so happy for you

Youssef posted some new photos, Nick shared a video Sophie had made for me at her favorite park, and after an hour or so, the chat went silent. I should have gone to sleep since it was a school night, but I was ravenous, so I went to the kitchen and foraged in the cupboards and fridge. Out of habit, I'd gone straight for the Ritter Sport bars Madame Dupuy kept on hand, because chocolate, but the smell nauseated me. I unscrewed the lid on the Nutella jar, retched, and screwed it right back on. There were fresh apricots sitting in a bowl on the counter, and I picked one up. I put it down again. The honey-and-flowers smell made me gag. I opened the fridge and caught a faint, delicious, blood-tinged odor. Raw meat. I checked the meat drawer, but it was empty. Then I checked the garbage can, hoping Madame Dupuy had tossed the trimmings in there. It was empty, and I remembered that she always took the trash down to the dumpsters after dinner. That used to be my job. Back when I was free.

I didn't stop to put my shoes on, just let myself quietly out of the apartment and rode the elevator down to the underground parking garage, where the dumpsters lived. I could smell ripening meat scraps even before the elevator doors opened. I ran to the dumpsters, my bare feet slapping on the cool concrete, and threw open the first lid. It held a feast: blood-slicked butcher paper and meat trimmings in bag after bag. I tore one open, brushed the coffee grounds off a handful of fatty trimmings, and sucked the blood out. They left a greasy, not-unpleasant aftertaste. I poked through the bag and found the butcher paper I knew would be there. I uncrumpled it and methodically licked the blood off. Then I tore into the next bag. I despoiled bag after bag of trash until I'd satisfied my hunger. Only then, as I wiped my mouth for the last time, did the wrongness of what I'd done hit me. I'd just gone through garbage to find blood. I stared at the filigree pattern burned on my finger. There was no way to avoid the conclusion. I really was a vampire. I sat down with my back against a dumpster. How could I trust myself at school? But if I told Madame Dupuy I didn't want to go, she'd wonder why, and that was not a question I wanted her to be asking. Not given her family business. Maybe she wouldn't stake me herself, but she knew people who would. All she'd have to do would be to make a phone call. Unless there was some way to control vampire mode. Or shut it off.

I remembered feeling it ebb away when I had been about to attack the unhoused man, just before Le Bec had crept up on me. What had caused that? I went back up to our apartment, chewing on the question, and washed my face with scalding water to get rid of the smell of garbage. I brushed my teeth for about ten minutes, trying to scrub away every remnant of what I'd just devoured. Then I fell into bed and lay there, wide awake, frightened, and haunted by the smell of . . . minty-fresh toothpaste? It filled my nostrils, so strong I could hardly smell anything else. I got up, went to the kitchen, opened the fridge, and stuck my head into the meat drawer. All I could smell was peppermint. I remembered the Altoids in my pack, left over from debate team, where I'd shared them with Lily and Mina before rounds. "Blow them away with your arguments," Mina would say as she took one out of the tin, "not with your coffee breath."

Maybe the curiously strong mints could keep v mode at bay.

CHAPTER 18

SIX WEEKS AGO

I fiddled with my scarf as Madame Dupuy and I walked, arranging it to better hide the bandage on my neck. She'd given me the scarf so I wouldn't have to walk back into school looking like a victim. It was greeny blue and lighter than a sigh, perfect for summer. And perfect for me; the colors complemented my hair and gave my pale skin a healthy blush. When we reached the school, she told me to call her if I needed to. Then she hugged me. I watched her walk down the street, and I felt suddenly vulnerable. The noise of traffic and the chatter of my classmates as we waited outside the building roared inside my head. Three boys hovered near a group of girls, showing off: punching each other on the arm, dodging and feinting, their laughter so loud it hurt my ears. They smelled young and nervous—and delicious. Like French fries. I popped another Altoid. It didn't entirely eliminate the delicious smell, but it did help remind me that they were people, not snacks.

By midmorning break, I'd gone through almost my entire tin, a headache throbbed behind my eyes from excessive peppermint and sugar, and I was so tense I thought I'd snap from the pressure of trying to be human. And people had been staring at me all morning. Nobody had said anything, but I felt like everyone knew what my scarf hid. I wondered if climbing up on a table and ripping the bandage off my neck so they could see what a vampire bite looked like would be less weird than the covert way everyone was eyeing me now. I drifted behind the tide of students pouring out of the building onto the sidewalk, feeling like an alien, searching for a quiet spot away from the crowd. Somebody called my name, and I looked around to see Nick, Noor, Martine, and Youssef waving at me from under a tree. My heart bloomed with love. I ran to them, and they surrounded me, shielding me from the rest of the world.

"You all are amazing," I whispered, grinning. I couldn't believe Noor's parents had let her come. She was pale and so thin, and her fingertips were wrapped in bandages. But she was here, hugging me like she hadn't seen me in years, enveloping me in a cloud of menthol. "Do you have a cold?" I asked her. Menthol salve was Dad's cure-all for congestion and the curse of every cold and flu season as far back as I could remember. She shook her head. "Text me later." Her voice was as shredded as mine. I wished Dad could see what a healing gift my friends were. Having them there made me feel safe in a way being shut up in our apartment didn't. I felt safe not because I was hiding from something behind a locked door, but because I was facing my fear, with my friends to support me. You can't hide from all the scary things; you need people who will let you face them, who will support you while you do.

"How was school?" Madame Dupuy asked when I met her at noon.

I blew out a sigh. "Harder than I thought. People stared at me."

"Well, of course they did," she said briskly. "They wanted to see how a vampire's victim looks." I flinched at "vampire." She took hold of my hand. "And now they know, and they will stop staring."

I hadn't anticipated how hard it would be to keep my guard up against v mode in a crowd of people. The Altoids had crippled my sense of smell, but I still had had a couple of waves of heightened senses, where colors intensified and sounds became louder and denser. I worried that if I let myself get distracted at all, something would happen. Maybe I should tell Dad that I just wasn't up to it. But then would Madame Dupuy get suspicious? I was furious at Le Bec for doing this to me, for calling me his creation, for expecting me to join his little coven. He didn't get to own me. He didn't get to win. I'd figure out v mode, and I'd go to class, and I'd be a normal person.

As I settled down to do homework after lunch, I remembered Noor's bandaged fingers.

Me: Thank you for coming today. It was AMAZING to see you

Noor: You are welcome. How are you feeling?

Me: It was hard, but I made it

Me: Altoids work pretty well to stop weird cravings

Noor: I am using pommade mentholée. It is very strong, but I am no longer eating my fingers

I remembered her menthol smell. I went into Dad's bathroom and rooted around in the drawers until I found a jar. I dabbed some under my nose. My sinuses felt like they were exploding, but the salve killed all smells and stomped on their lifeless remains for good measure. I tucked the jar into my pocket.

Me: Wow. Way better than Altoids. I may never smell anything again

Me: . . .

Me: I need to tell you something

Noor: I am listening

I told her about leaving the apartment, the unhoused man, meeting Le Bec, and then my dumpster dive of shame. I didn't leave anything out. I told her how Madame Dupuy's silver pendant had burned me. The filigree pattern branded on the pad of my index finger still throbbed.

Noor: Can you see yourself in the mirror?

Me: I don't think the mirror works. I almost bit that guy, and I'm craving blood

Her reply bubble pulsed for a long time, and I wondered if I should have told her.

Noor: Silver burns me, too

Me: Ugh. I'm so sorry

Me: I'm so angry at Le Bec. He acted like what he did to us was some great thing. He stole our lives

Noor: What will we do?

Me: Have you noticed it comes in waves? Like you'll be fine and then you get a wave of vampire mode? If we could prevent those waves, I think we could manage this

If we didn't control it, I couldn't go back to school. I'd have to tell Dad, who'd probably think I had PTSD or something. I'd have to tell Madame Dupuy, too. That was a scary thought.

Noor: The pommade stopped the urge to eat my fingers. Maybe that would help to manage this

Me: I'm going to try it at school. If it works there, I think we could control our cravings and be normal

I'd also need to have a plan for what to do if it failed.

Knowing that Noor and I were in this battle together helped. The menthol pommade helped, thank goodness. And my friends showing up for morning break every day helped, too. I don't know if I could have kept going to class if they hadn't done that. With them I could be the Tosh I wanted to be: human and happy. Or at least human. Happy wasn't always possible with Professeur Joubert. "Help," I croaked Wednesday morning when I met them at break.

"Tough morning?" Nick asked, kissing me.

"Ugh," I rasped. "We had to do oral presentations again. From memory. I forgot an entire paragraph and fumbled around like an idiot, trying to remember what came next. Then my voice gave out. It was disastrous."

"You're not an idiot," he said. "Oral presentations in French officially suck. Even French kids hate them." Everyone nodded.

Martine blew a stream of smoke out the side of her mouth like a beautiful dragon. "I think you need an excursion," she said. "Something to take you outside yourself."

Youssef smiled. "An excursion is always good."

"Yeah," Nick agreed. "We can adventure to the farthest

reaches of Paris, relax on the sunny quays of the Seine, or summit Montmartre. Whatever mademoiselle desires."

I sighed. "It sounds wonderful, but I'm still on house arrest, remember?"

"We'll engineer a jailbreak."

I arched an eyebrow at him. "Intriguing. Tell me more."

The plan was simple and brilliant. I'd bring a note to school the following day from Dad saying I had a medical appointment Friday. "Tu sais, it is not really from your father," Youssef said, giving me an exaggerated wink.

"Really?" I replied, deadpan, and returned his wink.

Friday morning, Madame Dupuy would walk me to school as usual. I'd wait until she was out of sight, and then, rather than going into the building, I'd casually join the morning pedestrian stream headed toward the Pont de l'Alma and meet everyone at Princess Diana's shrine. We'd head out from there. It sounded wonderful: a whole morning with my friends. I hesitated, though. If I got caught, Dad would yank me out of school and not let me out of my room till I was eighty. But I liked that tickle of risk. It made me feel alive. "Okay," I whispered.

Nick did a fist pump. "Where do you want to go?"

"Notre-Dame."

Hunchback was still living in my head. Hugo had made the cathedral one of the characters—by far the most real and relatable one. "I want to see where Quasimodo swung on the bell ropes and yelled, 'Sanctuary!' I want to see gargoyles."

He smiled at me, his eyes crinkling at the corners. "Your wish is my command."

The next morning, I headed for freedom as soon as

Madame Dupuy had turned the corner. I rode a wave of exhilaration down the street, smiling so big that hardened Parisians, incapable of showing any public emotion but bored aggression, couldn't help curving their lips slightly in reply. It felt like I was in a movie, one of those golden Paris rom-coms where everyone is gorgeous and there's a retro-cute accordion soundtrack for the kissing scenes. As I crossed the bridge, I saw my friends already waiting by the golden sculpted flame where people left bouquets and tributes to the princess. Nick dashed across the busy street when he spotted me, earning a chorus of impatient honking. He caught me up in his arms and swung me around. I laughed and kissed him. This time the honks sounded approving.

WHEN WE reached the cathedral, he went into tour-guide mode. It had taken roughly a hundred years to build and rebuild into its current form, not including, of course, all the reconstruction work that had been done after the fire in 2019, he informed me as we waited in the long line to get into the tower. I wondered how a city stayed focused on anything for an entire century. Once built, it had lasted for almost eight hundred years, through wars, famines, and a revolution. Although a fire had ravaged it a few years ago, it had been rebuilt, and it looked strong enough to go another eight hundred.

"After the French Revolution, when religion was not popular, it became a wine warehouse," Youssef added, the suggestion of a smile dimpling one of his cheeks. "Perhaps the most beautiful wine warehouse in the world, and certainly the most useful church." Nick laughed.

I held my phone up and started filming Youssef like I was making a documentary. "Aside from its wine-storage capacity, Monsieur Rachedi, what's the best architecture thing about Notre-Dame?" I asked.

He didn't hesitate. "The flying buttresses." He pointed out the stone supports embracing the cathedral, flanking it along its back perimeter. They looked like a series of half bridges attached at right angles to the exterior wall. Some of them were double-deckers. "I love them because buildings that soar up to the sky would not exist without them." He explained that walls carried a lot of weight that needed to be distributed so they didn't fall over or break as they got taller and weighed more, putting more pressure on their foundations. He talked about the ways builders and architects had solved this fundamental problem over the centuries. "Now," he said, his eyes dancing with excitement, "we know how to make walls that rise to incredible heights without external bracing. So in one sense, this building is a failure because its walls cannot rise up without external supports. But it is a beautiful failure. It led to better methods."

"Is it a failure, though?" I said. "I mean, I don't think it's a failure to need support. It's like having friends: You hold each other up."

He nodded his head sideways, considering. "Saying the buttresses are like friends makes a nice way to think about it." I smiled. Youssef was the one I was having the hardest time getting to know. He was guarded unless you got him talking about architecture. Then you could start to see who he really was. That was one of the reasons I'd made so many prints from his photos. That, and the fact that he had a great eye. I was about to ask him another question, but his phone warbled, and he pulled it out of his pocket to see what it wanted.

The line moved forward two steps. Martine lit a cigarette, snapped her old-school lighter shut, and exhaled a plume of smoke that floated lazily around us in the hot, still air. I loved her chunky silver Zippo. I loved the scratch of the flint sparking. I loved the satisfying metallic *snick* it made when she closed the lid. I loved the way the end of her cigarette glowed red and then faded back to gray when she took a drag. I loved the way I felt calm and centered and completely myself when she smoked near me. I knew smoking was bad, but still. I'd spent so much time lately feeling odd and irritable, and standing next to Martine as she smoked made me feel peaceful.

Nick, on the other hand, was no fan of secondhand smoke. He waved it away, his motions exaggerated to make his point. She smiled ruefully. "One day, Nick, I promise I will quit." He gave her *I've heard that song before* side-eye, and she shrugged.

"Check it, Nick." Youssef held out his phone so Nick could see, and I caught a glimpse of guys on bicycles. Nick and Youssef huddled over the screen.

I looked a question at Noor and Martine. "The Tour de France," Noor explained.

"Oh," I said, glancing back at the boys. "We've lost them, haven't we?" They nodded, laughing.

"It is almost a patriotic duty to watch the Tour," Noor said.

"And yet you aren't glued to your phone," I observed.

"I will see it tonight at home. My family is very patriotic." She smiled.

Martine stubbed her cigarette out and tossed it into a nearby trash receptacle. "I hope my smoking does not bother you both too much."

Noor shrugged. "My brother smokes."

"I mean, insert health disclaimer here," I said, "but I'm not judging. I kind of enjoy the smell. It's weird, but it seems to make me feel calmer."

She nodded. "That is why I do it."

"Would you mind if I tried one?"

She handed me the pack and her lighter. I lit up, inhaled, and coughed. It felt like swallowing a campfire, but the persistent background pulse of anxiety I'd had since I got home from the hospital flatlined in seconds. I blew out a ragged plume of smoke, coughed again, and said, "Oh my God, this is magic."

"Yes, it is. The magic has a price, as Nick continues to remind me, but sometimes it is worth paying." I nodded, took a few more puffs, then stubbed the cigarette out. I was starting to get lightheaded. I tried to give the pack back to Martine, but she shook her head. "Keep it."

As I slipped the cigarettes into my backpack, she looked from me to Noor. "You know, if either of you ever want to talk about anything, I also am not judging." We thanked her, avoiding each other's eyes. Some things you couldn't help but judge.

When we stepped into the cool stone room at the base of the tower stair, I felt presences, as though everyone who'd worn the stone steps down over the centuries, including all of us today, had left a bit of themselves behind. I liked Paris's feeling of being joined to history, of the past touching the present. Portland has history, too—of course—but it was so recent. It felt like a teenager compared with grown-up Paris. We wound our way slowly up the spiral of stairs to an open-air gallery filled with monstrous stone beasts sitting and leaning on the balustrades.

"Gargoyles!" I squealed. In front of me a winged, horned imp studying a grimoire crouched on a ledge. Near Martine, the offspring of Gollum and a goat stared viciously at the city as though trying to work out which neighborhood to swoop down and eat first. A monkey-bat with body-image issues moped at its elbow. Beside it, Noor eyed a flock of birdlike creatures whose bad temper ranged from "peck you on the hand" to "peck your eyes out while you're still using them" and took out her sketchbook.

"Chimeras," Nick corrected me.

I made a face. "I expected gargoyles, Nick Wallace Tour Company."

He smiled. "And gargoyles you shall have, mademoiselle."

I melted at the way his voice caressed "mademoiselle." I'd missed that so much. It didn't sound the same over text. He took my hand and walked me to the balustrade, then pointed down. Six feet below us, a stony herd of elongated figures—birds, lizards, monks, dragons, and even squirrels—jutted from the building. I focused on a long-necked dragon with a channel carved down the length of its back and an obscenely gaping mouth. Nearby, a miserable-looking monk wore the expression of someone for whom all the ale quaffing was about to turn into ale spewing.

I turned to him. "Are they all supposed to look like they're throwing up?"

"That's how the original stone masons carved them. They're downspouts for the rain gutters. It rains, water collects and runs down the channels in their backs and out their mouths."

I gave him *You're joking* eyebrows. "You're telling me a bunch of stone carvers spent ages making these things so that when it rained it would look like the whole church was puking?"

Nick nodded happily. "You gotta love the medieval sense of humor."

I shook my head, but I was laughing. I'd thought that a cathedral would be all churchy splendor—as unapproachable as God. How great that there were parts of it that made you know it was meant for people.

We lingered in the gallery for a long time, searching for the most bizarre chimeras and seeing how many different gargoyles we could find. Then, finally, we climbed up through the bell tower to the very top of the cathedral. We stood on the narrow walkway and looked at Paris far below, a pattern of dirty-beige, slate-gray, copper-green, and terracotta rectangles. Sun glinted off the Seine, and I picked out the landmarks I knew: the Louvre, the Montparnasse Tower, the Eiffel Tower. I thought of Quasimodo, yelling, "Sanctuary!" as he rushed Esmeralda to safety inside the cathedral. For me, it wasn't the cathedral that felt like sanctuary; it was Paris itself. The city at my feet was home. I could see my future from up here.

CHAPTER 19

SIX WEEKS AGO

I made it back to school, giddy with the secret of my unauthorized field trip, just in time to meet Madame Dupuy for the walk home. She asked me how school was, and I told her I'd learned a lot of fascinating stuff about Notre-Dame. Officially not a lie. I also said how much better I felt since Dad had let me come back to class. Just getting out of the apartment made me feel hopeful. It made me feel like I wasn't being punished for what had happened.

"You do know that is not your fault, yes, Mademoiselle Tosh?"

I shrugged. "Perhaps not my fault, but who needs a chaperone everywhere she goes, and who's walking around free?" She muttered something about the cops, and I felt enough like normal Tosh that I let myself believe for a few minutes that they'd find Le Bec. I hadn't felt this hopeful since before the attack. Smoking changed the game for me. It calmed my clamoring senses, soothed my sparking brain, and quieted my craving for blood without ruining my sense of smell forever. It let me relax my vigilance against v mode a little and be more like my old self. When we stopped at the butcher shop on the way home, I didn't stare longingly at the slabs of raw meat on display. I didn't imagine how satisfying it would be to tear into one of those lumps of flesh. I didn't spiral into a feeding frenzy from the smell of blood hanging in the air. I just waited, looking at my phone, while the butcher sectioned a rabbit for her. I felt a tickle of hope. *I can do this*, I thought. *I can control v mode and keep my life. It's going to be okay.* It could be a chronic condition, treatable with the right combination of nicotine and vigilance. As long as I took regular smoke breaks, I'd be safe around people. I could live the life I was meant to. Five hours later, over dinner, Dad blew everything up.

"I asked work to transfer me back to my old position," he said, putting his knife and fork down.

"What?" I thought I hadn't heard right.

"You're not safe here, so we're moving back to Oregon."

I stared at him, horrified. He didn't mean it. He *couldn't* mean it.

"I told the company what happened to you and how it's affected you. They were very accommodating. I'm pushing for us to leave as soon as possible—a week, two at most."

I was shaking my head. "I don't want to leave. I love Paris."

"Tosh, you almost died. You've been moping around the apartment; you picked at your dinner; you're not taking an interest in anything. You need a safe space. You need counseling."

"I ate all my dinner." I was outraged. It had tasted like nuclear waste, but I'd choked down every bite, because keeping my stomach full felt like a way to keep some of the v mode cravings at bay. How dare he not notice that? "And they have counseling here, although I wouldn't need it if you hadn't locked me up in this apartment and kept my friends away."

He gave an *I'm trying to be patient with you* sigh. "Your friends aren't safe. They aren't good for you. And we're living in a city with a predator on the loose. Did you know he attacked someone else last week? I worried every day this week that something would happen to you while you were at school. I just can't live this way."

"You could have worried about that last year, too." I wanted to shout it at him, but my voice was still recovering, so I kept it soft and even. Plus, if he had to work a little to hear me, he'd really pay attention. Cole had taught me that trick.

His eyes went wide in surprise. "I— Last year?"

"Yeah." My voice didn't waver. Soft and steady. "I wasn't safe in Portland, either."

"What do you mean? You never said anything. What happened?"

"I fell asleep on the bus after a tournament. I woke up because Cole was . . . He was grabbing me."

"Cole?"

I nodded.

"That's definitely not okay, and I'm sure it felt terrible. But you're in actual physical danger here. We need to take action."

My pulse pounded in my temples. My senses went into

overdrive. Shapes got sharper; smells got brighter. "He touched me without my permission, Dad. He did it on purpose when I was asleep so I couldn't say no. I woke up, and he told me nothing happened. It really messed with my head, because every time I was with him—every prep session, every tournament, every bus trip—I didn't feel safe. But then I felt like I was being unfair to him. Do you know how messed up that is?"

"Why didn't you tell me?"

"Because it took a while to realize I hadn't dreamed it. And then it would have sounded stupid to say, 'This happened, but it took me till now to realize it was real.' Who'd believe that? Anyway, what could you have done? Cole doesn't act like a predator. He's funny and smart. No one would have believed that he could do anything bad. And then you told me we were moving to France. It was just easier to leave it behind and start over here."

He got up, came around to my chair, and put his arm around me. "I'm so sorry that happened. But think of going back as a reset. A chance to change things that didn't work before. We can find you a different school if you'd rather not run into Cole."

Dad's arm felt heavy, and I shifted uncomfortably. "If I'm going to reset, I want to do it here. I love it here."

"You're in danger here."

"Okay, say I go back to Portland. Where do I run away to the next time a guy does something to me?"

"There won't be a next time."

I just shook my head. "Statistics say otherwise, so you should probably pick your backup safe cities now."

"You're being stubborn." His voice had an edge of impatience. "I'm doing this for you."

"No, you're doing this *to* me. You haven't asked what I want, what would make me feel safe."

He sighed. "You're overreacting. You don't see how bad Paris is for you. I'm only thinking of you, of your happiness."

"Why can't you see how good Paris has been for me? I mean, I'm getting really good in French. And there's Madame Dupuy. Leaving her would be so hard."

He softened for a minute. He liked Madame Dupuy, too.

"I know it's hard. I know it's unfair, but we live in a dangerous world. I have to make the best decisions I can when it comes to your well-being."

"*You* know it's unfair? How? You were walking home from the Métro by yourself the night I got attacked, but you're not under house arrest for walking without a chaperone."

He waved my anger away. "That's not the point."

"No; that's the whole point. You're making this my fault. You're restricting my freedom, and you don't even see how hypocritical it is. You want to take me away from a place I love and back to a place that has bad memories for me because staying here causes you too much anxiety. None of this is about what's best for me."

He narrowed his eyes, frowning, and I knew he was about to lose his temper. "This conversation is over. We're moving back to Portland."

Inside my head, the arguments roared. Why did he get to ignore my reasons for staying? Why did his fear outweigh my autonomy? I saw him through a red haze, and I wanted to hurt him, to punish him for keeping me from my friends, for tearing me away from here, for trying to protect me by imprisoning me. I could protect myself. I didn't need him. I glanced at his neck and heard the artery throbbing there, under his skin, filled with delicious blood.

I stood up from the table so fast my chair fell over backward, banging on the floor and startling me. Dad had jumped up, too. "Go to your room," he shouted as I ran down the hall. I locked myself in, then scrabbled in my backpack for Martine's cigarettes, my hands shaking. I finally found them, fumbled one out, and got it lit. I drew in a lungful of smoke and felt myself begin to uncoil. "I will not be a vampire," I told myself. "Le Bec doesn't win."

I leaned out the window, blowing pale gray plumes into the evening air, lighting a second cigarette off the end of the first one, desperate to kill the rage and hunger that filled me. When I was calm enough to think rationally, I realized that even with all my safeguards in place, I couldn't guarantee my reaction if I got really angry. I'd barely avoided attacking Dad just now. He'd always be a little in danger around me. And I was in danger, too, if Madame Dupuy figured out that I was a vampire. I didn't see a choice. I had to disappear. I had to go someplace neither of them would look for me. I stuffed some things into my pack: money, passport, a change of clothes, and a jacket. I changed into my hiking pants and shoes and distributed my phone, cigarettes and matches, and lockpicks among their pockets.

I looked around my room. Amid all the prints taped to the walls were a couple of photos right by my bed: me and Nick and the Eiffel Tower, and all of us in front of Noor's *Mona Lisa* installation. I took them down and slipped them into my pack. I looked around one last time. Should I leave a note? It seemed cruel not to at least say goodbye; Dad would lose his mind when he discovered I was gone. On the other hand, it was cruel of him to rip me away from the life I wanted and the people who cared about me and drag me back to Portland. We'd had so many big plans for our Paris life, and they were all ruined. I slumped on the edge of my bed. Finally, I got my notebook and opened it to a clean sheet. *Dear Dad*, I wrote. *I have to go away. I'm not safe to be around. I'm sorry. I love you. Tosh.* I slipped it under the light-up Eiffel Tower from Nick sitting on my desk.

I waited until Dad was asleep, and then I slipped out for the last time. When I was outside, I texted Nick: "Dad's moving us back to Portland. Can you meet me by the park gate rn?" He said he'd be there in five, and I smoked a cigarette as I waited, just to be sure I wouldn't go into v mode on him.

When Nick saw me, his face lit up. I hurried into his arms, craving his comfort. He leaned down and kissed me. I kissed him back softly, and everything faded away but the two of us. We were on our own planet, spinning so swiftly that it made me dizzy. I held on to him, and we spun and spun together like the beginning of a new world.

"Is your dad serious about leaving?" he asked when we finally stopped kissing.

I sighed. I wanted to keep the moment, to make it last forever, so that I'd always be in Nick's arms and he'd always be looking at me like I was a miracle. So I kissed him again and pushed reality back for a few more minutes. Finally, we looked at each other.

"Yeah," I said.

"He can't. You just got here. We haven't done all the things. You haven't eaten all the pastries. You haven't kissed me nearly enough."

I smiled at that. "I'm not leaving."

"You think you can make him change his mind?"

I shook my head. "I've never seen him like this. He keeps talking about how dangerous it is for me here. But he can't make me go back to Portland."

He cleared his throat. "Well, he's right; it is dangerous here. Aren't you afraid of Le Bec?"

"Le Bec can't hurt me."

"Tosh. He almost killed you. He's still—" He squeezed his eyes shut and took a breath. "*I'm* afraid of him. What if he found you again?"

"He already has."

"What?"

I took a breath. Paused. Then plunged. "I'm a vampire."

He shook his head. "What are you talking about? This vampire thing is out of control. You know it's just a word that people use because it gets clicks, right? Something bad happened to you, but it didn't turn you into a monster."

"Nick, I— The other night, late, I had to get out of the apartment. I was going crazy. So I went out for a walk. Out in the city."

"What? Why? That's dangerous."

I shushed him. "Le Bec found me. Tracked me, I guess. He told me he was a vampire and that he'd made me one, too, when he attacked me." Nick scoffed. "That's not the only thing. I almost—" I stopped. I didn't want to tell him about the unhoused man. I didn't want that to be how he saw me.

"Remember the necklace I was wearing when we went to Le Shopping?" He shook his head. "Well, it was a silver heart, and Madame Dupuy had told me that silver burns vampires, so I touched it. To see if what Le Bec said was true." I held up my index finger with the filigree pattern branded onto it. "The silver burned me. I'm a vampire." He stared at my finger. "It's real, Nick. I've been fighting urges for days now. I almost attacked my dad tonight. I can control it when everything's going okay, and I thought that would be enough. But it's not. If there's too much stress, I'm not really safe to be around." He didn't reply, just started walking. "Nick?" I said, hurrying to catch up. He stared straight ahead, his jaw set. I couldn't catch his eye. We left our neighborhood and turned onto Boulevard de Grenelle. I felt shaky and headachy and irritable. And panicky. I took out a cigarette, fast. Nick tutted when he saw the pack. "What?" I said, unable to hide the irritation in my voice.

"I can't believe you're smoking. Just because Martine does it doesn't mean it's not disgusting."

"I know." I lit the cigarette and inhaled. The headache vanished, and my mood evened out.

"Then why?"

I blew a stream of smoke away from him and made a flapping, futile movement with the hand holding the cigarette. "It's the only thing that really controls my . . . episodes." He looked skeptical.

"It's a lot, I know, but I'm telling you the truth."

"Noor? Is she one, too?"

"Yeah," I sighed.

"What's she going to do?"

"I don't know. We thought we had more time to figure it out." The worries of the past couple of weeks climbed onto my back, their weight pressing me down. I imagined them as the chimeras from Notre-Dame: the despondent elephant, whose sad ears brushed the back of my head; the anxious monkey-bat who couldn't settle but swung itself from shoulder to shoulder; and the murderous heron, who drove its bill obsessively into me. Nick looked at me, waiting for an explanation. I felt so tired. "Can we sit somewhere?"

I followed him down a quiet street lined with apartment buildings. One of them had a sort of entry alcove, with three wide steps leading to chipped green double doors. We settled on the second step. I shrugged out of my backpack and put it on the step below, between my knees, then leaned forward, cradling my head in my hands. How did I even start to explain this?

He put his hand on my back between my shoulder blades, right where I could feel the weight of the chimeras, and rubbed slow circles. I relaxed into his touch, focusing on the moment. We sat in silence until I could tell him how close I'd come to attacking Dad tonight. "There's more," I said softly. His hand kept moving over my back, warm and steady. "Madame Dupuy's family are vampire killers." His hand stopped moving. "I know. It's like something in a novel—a really horrible one. I can hardly believe it's happening. Except I've felt things, Nick—things that aren't normal. And I've seen things that I can't unsee, and—" I squeezed my eyes shut, but the tears leaked out anyway. "Madame Dupuy basically said she'd kill me if I was a vampire." I drew in a ragged breath. "I can't go back home. I don't want to hurt anyone. I don't want to die."

He was silent for a long time. "That's . . . a lot," he said. I leaned my head onto his shoulder. "Vampires are real?" I nodded. "And you're really one?"

I nodded again. "Because Le Bec bit me. It's like an infection, I think."

He put his arm around me. "Is there a cure?"

I squeegeed the tears off my face with my hands. "I don't know. I hit it with all my research skills and didn't find anything useful."

"What will we do?" he asked after a minute.

"I have to disappear." He shook his head. "What choice do I have?"

He looked so sad. "Where will you disappear to?"

"The catacombs, I guess. I don't know where else to go. Maybe I can figure this out down there, away from everyone."

"I'll visit you."

"I'd like that." I took a breath. "But it's not safe."

"Tosh—"

I leaned into him, brushing his lips lightly with mine to distract him, to distract me, choosing this moment, this sweet ache, as something I could remember forever if I needed to. An endless, intimate now that my worst secret couldn't pollute. I kissed him like I didn't know if I'd see him again. I felt like we were riding on a carousel in a war zone.

Someone pushed me. I caught the scent of hot asphalt, and an angry male voice snapped, "Hé, les gosses. Bougez." Another shove. He wanted us to get out of the way. He muttered something about blocking the door and pushed me again, like he wanted us to scuttle off, out of his street. Like we were an insult to him. He could have gotten around us;

we weren't hogging the whole step, and I'd squished up tight against Nick at his first push. He seemed angry that we were there at all. Nick and I scrambled up to give him more room, and he mounted the steps, saying something I didn't catch. Nick did, though, and he spat back in fast, slangy, pissed-off French. The guy took a menacing step toward us, then another, keeping up a stream of abuse. I heard his heartbeat. Then the world went red. I was surprised by how easily he went down. I tasted his delicious fear and felt as powerful as God. I was riding a wave of euphoria when Nick grabbed me. I saw his horrified face. I looked down at my blood-spattered shirt. Shocked, I put my hands to my mouth. When I pulled them away, they were covered in blood. I hung in that horrible moment for a lifetime, searching for a crumb of excuse or explanation.

Then I ran.

CHAPTER 20

SIX WEEKS AGO

I ran without thought or plan, focused only on getting away. On escaping Nick's horrified expression and the body collapsed in front of that chipped green door. I ran till I couldn't breathe, ducking into shadowy doorways to catch my breath, and then running again. Unlike the other times, there was no warning. V mode had consumed me instantaneously. One second I was me; the next I was a monster.

I could feel cobbles under my feet, and the streets were narrower. I must have been in one of the older sections of the city. I jogged on, too frightened to stop and rest, hoping for some kind of sign that would tell me what to do next. I felt shaky from running and leftover adrenaline, and that was when a set of steps rose straight from the sidewalk to trip me, sending me sprawling. As I pulled myself to my knees, I saw that they belonged to a ratty, dismal-looking little church. An image of Quasimodo swinging from Notre-Dame's bell rope shouting, "Sanctuary!" swam into my head. A church is a place where the law can't touch you. If I was inside a church, I'd be safe, and other people would be safe from me. For a while, anyway. I got to my feet, eyeing the medieval iron lock. I couldn't believe it hadn't been updated. Martine had shown me how these old locks worked, and for a few moments I just stood there, my hand on the door, clinging to the memory of her disassembling one that we'd bought at the flea market as she explained its mechanics. All I wanted was to go back to that time. The time when I was normal.

Finally, I forced myself back to the present and picked the lock, sending her a silent thanks. I let myself into the church, shutting the old wooden door with a squeak of hinges that made me freeze. After a few minutes, when no one came to investigate, I let myself relax and look around. Although the grimy stained glass held the dark in, my heightened senses let me see the bare, neglected interior clearly. I walked over to the votive stand at the back of the nave. Dust puffed up at every step, tickling my nose. The stand was small and rusty and empty of candles, although there were several discs of melted wax with blackened wicks too short to light. People had sought comfort here, but that was a long time ago. I sighed and moved into the nave, where the few remaining chairs were scattered, as though the congregation had fled in panic. I sat down on the closest one, raising another cloud of dust. When I stopped sneezing, I took out my matches and lit one. Staring into the flame, I said, "Hi, Mom," like always, and waited to feel her presence. Nothing happened. No sense of warmth enveloped me. No *Hello, my darling daughter* sounded in my head. I waited, straining to hear her voice, but it wasn't there, not even a whisper. I tried again. "Mom, I need you." My voice quavered. She'd always answered when I'd called. Always. I waited. Maybe she hadn't heard me. I tried again, louder. "Mom? Please?" The church remained empty and cold. I sagged in my chair, feeling the weight of her absence like a judgment. I'd thought she'd love me no matter what. I'd thought she'd always come when I needed her. But I was no longer human enough for her to answer me. Despair wrapped its bony arms around me.

I stared at the dust-covered altar, trying to erase the image of what I'd done from my mind, but I'd never be able to unsee it. I should have just told Madame Dupuy the truth. I should have let her end me. That man would still be alive if I had. To the right of the altar, a statue of Saint Jude eyed me. "This is beyond even your powers," I told him. He agreed. Behind him, a set of stairs descended into the crypt. I wanted to hide in its shadows. To put myself as far away from the world as I could. I set my feet on the worn steps and descended to a low, empty room whose vaulted ceiling was supported by columns. Flat gray gravestones tiled the floor, so old that the carvings had been worn away by generations of feet. The stones in the corners, though, away from the foot traffic, retained their inscriptions and skeleton-reaper carvings, which grinned at me like old friends. Across the room, an open doorway showed another set of stairs going down. I made my way carefully between the stones to the stairway and descended another level. The staircase continued down into the dark, but I stopped. The room I'd entered was full of old broken things: chairs, panels, railings. I was broken, too; I belonged there. I sank onto the cold stone floor and put my head on my knees. I was so tired. I wanted to go to sleep and never wake up, but every time I closed my eyes, I saw the man I'd attacked, his blood glistening under the streetlight. My clothes and hair were stiff with his blood. I rubbed my face, and dried blood fell off in tiny flakes, like gory dandruff. Worse even than that, though, was the memory of Nick's horrified face. He'd remember me forever like that: feral, bloody, monstrous.

This wasn't supposed to be my life, in a junky cellar under a forgotten church. I was supposed to hang out with my friends and kiss Nick and eat pastries. And grow up and get a job and make a difference. I let myself imagine the future I could have had. I could see my apartment. The kids were in bed and the dishes were done and it was just the two of us, sitting together on the couch with our stocking feet up on the coffee table watching the eight o'clock news and maybe having one more glass of wine. I wanted that. I wanted it so hard—the job and the urgency of family and the stress of being pulled in too many directions. The glow of a successful day at work and the painful throb of a bad day. I wanted to grow up and take my place in the world. Tears slid down my face and dripped off my chin. Le Bec had made me a monster against my will. He had taken away my future. I couldn't live my life preying on people like he did, though. It would be so much better if I didn't exist at all.

The worst part was that I couldn't explain why to my friends. Nick would tell them what I'd done, and they'd hate me. Noor would understand, but what could she do? How would she survive this? I thought that I needed to stop being alive—or whatever it is that vampires are. I didn't want to leave this world without leaving some kind of mark, though—something to say I'd been here, even if not for long enough. I leaned my head back against the stone wall. Limestone feels so hard, but it's a soft stone, easy to carve. I'd learned that on my trip to the catas. I'd noticed street names chiseled into the walls and wondered why anyone would go to all the work of carving them when they could have painted them more easily. Youssef had grinned at me and then carved his initials into the wall with the edge of a euro coin. It had taken less than a minute, and his initials would still be there in two hundred years.

I took one of my lockpicks and scratched *NW* into the stone. Nick Wallace. The boy who gave me Paris. Under it, I carved *NS*, Noor Sidi, who knew my pain because it was hers, too. Next, I wrote *MS*. Martine Sardou's Epic Pastry Quest would remain unfulfilled. *YR* followed. Youssef Rachedi's video clips of my friends sharing their favorite Paris places made me feel connected when I couldn't be with them in person. At the base of the stack, side by side like foundation blocks, I incised *MT* and *LP*. Mina Tran and Lily Parish, best friends since forever, who'd believed me about Cole. I stood back and looked at the letters. Then I enclosed them with a heart. They'd shared themselves with me. They'd buoyed me up. They were my people, my note to the world, my explanation.

I knew what I had to do. I squared my shoulders and started prowling through the junk, picking up busted chair legs and then discarding them (not pointy enough), eyeing sections of wrought iron (good pointy bits; too unwieldy), and covering myself in grime and cobwebs. I climbed over bent railings and shoved panels of wood aside. A two-legged chair blocked my path. I picked it up and found a tumble of spikes and saucers underneath. I pulled one out and saw that it was a flat, shallow dish pierced through the center by a two-ended spike. Maybe some kind of candleholder? The end that poked up into the saucer was just long enough to stick a candle on. The end below the saucer was five or six inches long with a sharp point that looked made to jab into something, maybe a bowl of sand. I shrugged. It didn't matter how it was meant to be used. All that mattered was that it would do what I needed it to. I found a spot between my ribs and tried a poke. It hurt, and my arm pulled back involuntarily. Maybe I should find a place to wedge it and just fling myself onto the point. I was looking around for a suitable crevice when my phone played Madame Dupuy's ringtone. I yelped, dropping the makeshift stake. I saw a bunch of texts from Nick as I picked up the call.

"Where are you?" she snapped before I could say anything.

"I'm a vampire," I said, and started crying.

"Yes. Nick told me."

"He told you what I did?"

"Yes."

"I tried so hard to suppress it." Tears rolled down my face and dripped off my chin. "I really thought smoking would work."

"Smoking helps?" She sounded interested now, not just angry.

"Yeah. If you're not caught off guard and get really angry really fast."

She made a "hmm" noise. "Where are you?"

"I'm not sure." I looked around the room of broken things. "It doesn't matter. I found something I can use for a stake. That's how you do it, right? A stake in the heart?" My voice broke.

There was a long pause. "Yes."

"And if I do it that way, will I stay dead?"

"Mademoiselle Tosh." Her voice was sharp. "What do you intend to do?"

"Stake myself so I can't hurt anyone."

"No no no. Absolument pas."

"Are you saying you'll do it? Because I don't—"

"No! I would not harm you. Why do you think I would?"

"You said you would. You kind of whispered it after you had me do the mirror check the first time. Which is useless, by the way."

"I did not say that."

"You said I couldn't be a vampire, because you couldn't stand to kill another one. That's why I need to know how to do the stake right. I don't want you to be the one who does it."

She didn't say anything for several seconds. "I am very sorry you heard me say that. But it did not mean I intended to kill you if you were a vampire. I did that once, and I will never do it again if there is a way to prevent it. Wait—if the mirror test is useless, how do you know you are a vampire?"

My knees were trembling, and my legs felt ready to give out. I sat down on the floor. "Well, the attack tonight is kind of a giveaway, but a couple of days ago, I touched your silver necklace, and it burned me."

"That was courageous."

I shrugged. "Not really. I just had to know."

"Alors, in theory, it is possible to cure vampirism. I do not know anyone who has ever tried, though."

"Now seems like a really good time to test the theory. What do I need to do?"

"There are three things. They are not easy. One must rub oneself with the vampire's blood. One must eat the ashes of his heart. One must eat the earth from his grave."

"So is that three different ways to cure it, or do you have to do all of them for it to work?"

"I do not know."

"And you need a vampire to do them. Ugh. Why is this so hard?" A text came in, making my phone vibrate. "Hold on," I told her, and swiped to the text screen.

Noor: Something bad has happened

Noor: I need help

Her conversation bubble pulsed for moment, then went dead. I was tapping a panicked "Where are you?" when she sent a pin.

"Madame Dupuy? I have to go," I said. "Something's happened to Noor." I clicked off before she could reply and switched back to the text screen. "I'm coming," I wrote as I ran to the stairs.

CHAPTER 21

SIX WEEKS AGO

I found Noor tucked behind a trash bin holding her backpack in front of her like a shield. She was so still in the shadows that I wouldn't have seen her if I'd been relying on my eyes. Instead, I'd followed the sweet solvent smell of her paints for several blocks. I'd caught the first whiff in front of an unfinished mural. It was a shaky composition of lines and shapes too pictorial to be a tag and too unresolved to be a painting. The line stuttered out, however, as though she'd been interrupted.

"Noor?" I said softly. I didn't want to startle her. "It's me, Tosh."

She peered at me, then got slowly to her feet. "I was thinking perhaps you would not come." Her face was as pale as a cloud, and her dark clothing blended into the night so that I felt like I was talking to a ghost. She kept her head down as though she didn't have the strength to raise it.

"I had to walk," I explained.

She looked up, surprised. I could see her question forming: Why hadn't I taken the night bus? Then her eyes widened as she took me in. "Tosh, you are covered in blood. Are you hurt? What happened?" Her hands fluttered toward me like she wanted to offer first aid but didn't know where to start.

It was my turn to look down. "I'm fine," I muttered. "But it's been a bad night." I stared at her shoes.

"You are not fine. Did somebody hurt you?"

The question stung. "It's not my blood." I sounded sharp, defensive. I wasn't sure why I was so reluctant to tell her what happened. If anyone would understand, it would be her. "Anyway, what happened to you?"

She didn't explain right away, and I looked up to see her feeling around in her backpack. "Here," she said, pulling out a roll of paper towels and handing them to me along with a bottle of water. "Clean yourself up."

I wetted a paper towel and scrubbed at my face. "Seriously," I said, dropping the bloody towel into the bin and wetting another. "Your text said you needed help. What's going on?" She just hugged her backpack and looked miserable. "Okay." I threw away another reddened towel. "You were out working on a piece, right? I'm pretty sure I passed it." She nodded, and I waited for her to pick up the story. After a long, silent minute, I prompted, "Then something interrupted you?"

"I was just trying to paint, you know?" Her voice shook. "I thought maybe on a wall, maybe big, I could find my line again. This guy walks up and starts to talk to me: 'Bonsoir, what are you doing, have you done this before, did you know it is very late and this is not a good neighborhood, maybe you should go home.' And I am trying to paint and also to not look like someone he needs to pay attention to, so I am polite, and I say thank you, I have friends nearby, I will be careful. And then he says, 'No, you are not listening to me, this is a dangerous place.' And again I say thank you, but I am fine. I make sure I am holding a fresh can of paint because I know things will soon become difficult." She paused, and I saw the shape of what was going to happen. I reached out and took hold of her hand. She swallowed, then continued. "Then he says it again: 'You are not listening to me.' And he grabs me and pulls me around to face him. So I spray him in the eyes with my paint. This is when I should run. This is when I always run. To stay safe. But this time I do not, because"—she took a deep breath—"because I am just finished, you know? I am finished being bothered when I am not bothering anyone. I am finished being told where I can be and when I can be there. And then I—" I squeezed her hand.

"It is as if I become a fire. I am so angry. I want to hurt him. My teeth are on his neck, and I don't know how it has happened. He is afraid of me, and it is wonderful. I want to bite him—I am hungry, you know? But I want more to drink his fear. I have never felt so powerful like that." I nodded. I knew exactly how she felt. "So maybe I am not holding on to him tightly enough, because he pulls out of my grip and runs away." She sighed raggedly and scrubbed her face with her hands. "But now what do I do? I have shown that I am not a safe person. I cannot be with people. When my brother makes me angry, will I attack him? I cannot trust myself. I cannot go home." She wasn't crying, but there were tears in her voice. She held up her backpack, shaking it so I could hear the rattle of the spray cans. "I only have my painting things and my phone. Where will I go?"

I gave her a smile that wasn't a smile at all. "I know a place. C'mon." As we walked back, I told her my story. I wondered if she'd hate me when I told her how I got blood all over me, but instead she hugged me, whispering, "That must have been so horrible for you."

"I mean, it was worse for him. But obviously I can't go home, either." We didn't say anything more until we were standing in the basement of broken chairs. "We're safe here for a while—"

"Or everyone is safe from *us*." She looked around. "But what happens next? We can't stay here forever. We'll get hungry"—I winced—"or someone will come to check on the church." I lifted a brow and glanced meaningfully at the dust that coated everything. "Okay, perhaps not that. But we will get hungry, or restless, and eventually v mode will happen."

"So I was talking to Madame Dupuy when you texted. I asked her to—to give me some pointers on how to stake my-self. Because what else was I going to do?"

"Did you tell her where you are?"

I shook my head. "She told me there were cures."

"There are?" Hope lit up Noor's face.

"The problem is, all of them require a vampire. You need its heart and its blood or its grave dirt."

"We know a vampire," she said matter-of-factly.

"Do you think we could actually do it—stake him?"

"I could. He has taken my art away from me."

"But you were working on a piece tonight."

"Did you look at it?" she snapped. "It is terrible. When I paint, my hands see what is in my head. It is the most beautiful feeling. It is as though the image is coming alive as I lay down the lines. But what I did tonight? It was— He broke the connection between my hand and my mind. I cannot live if it stays broken. It is who I am. If I do not have it, I no longer exist."

"But that means we have to go out looking for him. And what if Nick called the cops after I ran away? They might be looking for me. Or if he didn't—" I couldn't imagine Nick leaving the man, running away like I had. He'd call an ambulance at least. "Even if the cops aren't looking for me, there's no guarantee that I won't hurt someone else while we're looking for Le Bec. If we can even find him. The cops sure can't, so how would we even start?"

"We do not go looking for him. We wait for him to come to us."

"Here? How?"

She shook her head. "He is often in the catas. If we can find a way in, then we can simply wait for him there."

It was an intriguing possibility. "But there are miles of passages. We could spend years looking for him."

"So we use what we have—our eyes, our ears, our noses. He likes the catas. He is comfortable there. We will find him, and his blood will cure us. He owes us this."

I thought about it. "You're right. Let's do it."

She held up her index finger. "There is a small problem."

"How small?" I said, thinking, *Of course there's a problem*.

"I do not know any entrances to the catas. Le Bec was always the one who knew where to get in."

I pointed to the stairs. "There's at least one more subbasement down there. I'm thinking that a place with subbasements might also have a way into the catas."

She nodded. "It cannot hurt to look. I know that there is at a minimum one church in Paris with an access."

"Give me just a minute," I said, pulling my phone out. It had been vibrating nonstop with calls and texts from Nick and Madame Dupuy. I shot a quick "I am so sorry" off to Nick. I had no idea how to even begin to apologize to him. Then I called Madame Dupuy. "Noor's okay," I said when she picked up, "and she thinks she knows where to find a vampire."

"Very well. But whatever happens, call me. I will help you if I can." I thanked her. "Mademoiselle Tosh," she said as I was about to hang up, "be sure to put the stake into his heart. Otherwise he will return." She told me how to find his heart, and we ended the call. I led Noor down the stairs to a room hacked out of the limestone. It looked catacomb-ish because of the bare rock, but it wasn't far enough belowground, and it was self-contained: No tunnels or passages branched off from it. I looked at her, defeated. "Well, it was worth a try."

"Look for a grating or a plate in the floor," she instructed. We separated to scan the room. After a minute, she called me over and pointed to a rusty grille set into the floor. I shone my phone on it, and we saw a shaft with iron rungs descending into the darkness. Our way in. Together we managed to drag the grille off the opening, and Noor sat down on the edge, dangling her feet into the dark. "Are we ready?" she asked.

"I think so— No, wait." I trotted back upstairs to the room of broken things and returned with two stakes—one for her and one for me. "For Le Bec," I said. She nodded. I tied them to her pack, and then she lowered herself into the hole. When I could no longer see her, I followed. Like my first descent, it was achingly long, but unaccompanied this time by the fizzy euphoria of being with Nick on a forbidden adventure. This time it was just work.

We arrived in a small chamber that led to a larger tunnel, which we followed until Noor got her bearings. "I am sorry," she said as we retraced our steps for the second time. "I do not have maps. I know where things are in general, but this will take time. I am very sure we will have to turn around several times." She frowned at a street marker over our heads. It didn't seem to be the one she expected.

I shrugged. "I don't have anyplace else to be." She huffed out something like a laugh, and we continued until we came to a branching tunnel, which we took. We walked through a grayscale world that reminded me of being out at night when the moon is new. It was as though the darkness had levels of darkness I'd never been able to discern before, and everything—every pebble, every wall, every chisel mark—was high-def. I'd expected to grope my way through the catacombs, but instead I saw more, and more clearly, than I'd seen with Nick when we were all wearing headlamps. V mode had some advantages.

"What was it like?" Noor said. We'd been walking for a while, and I'd fallen into an ambulatory trance. It took me a minute to understand what she meant. "If you would rather not say," she continued, "I will understand."

"No, it's okay." Nothing I said would shock her. That was comforting. "It kind of felt great, actually. Which is awful but true. Right before I bit him, this amazing power just surged through me. I felt like I was in control for the first time in ever. I felt—" I paused, struggling to convey the enormity of the feeling. "I could feel myself taking up all the space, instead of being small and fitting in, like I usually do. I felt consequential."

She stopped. "I envy that. I always feel small. Well, when I finish a piece, I feel big for a few minutes. When I step back and look at the whole thing and see what I saw in my head has come out through my hands. It never lasts long enough, though. I want it to go on forever, but it fades so fast. And then I am just me again. Le Bec took that feeling of bigness from me. He made me to be always small now."

"To be honest, if I could get that feeling all the time without, you know, killing people, I'd totally sign up for v mode. It was so amazing. But it came from me ripping someone's neck open. And liking it." I shivered at the memory. "And then later, I tried to talk to my mom, and she didn't answer. She always answers." I told her about Mom and lighting candles and her voice in my head when I needed her. "She was gone, Noor. I did something she can't forgive."

She didn't tell me it was okay. Instead, she said, "I chased that guy. I thought, *You are not getting away; I am hungry.* I would have sucked him dry if I had caught him. I do not think that I can be forgiven, either." We walked on. The catas were full of scents: the rock, of course, but also water. I was sure we were close to a spring or an underground stream; the air smelled wet. There were other smells. The scent of chocolate, which hovered everywhere, along with beer, wine, tobacco, and weed, told me what fueled the explorations of most cataphiles. I also smelled laundry soap and shampoo and, fainter still, clothing: the bland vegetal scent of cotton, the chemical sharpness of polyester and nylon, and the earthy, animal whiff of leather and wool. It was disorienting and wonderful. And horrifying. I realized, as I sniffed the air, that I was tracking. Like a predator. Noor pointed to the tunnel on the left, and we started down it. "This section has at least one cat-hole, probably more." She sighed. "I do not like cat-holes."

There were two, and each one took maybe twenty minutes of wriggling on our bellies through a tunnel only inches larger in diameter than we were. About halfway through the second one, as I dug the toes of my shoes into the floor and wriggled a couple of centimeters forward, I had a sudden, sick understanding that there were tons of rock above me. Tons of rock, and then buildings on top of that, with their own terrifying weight. Parts of the catas had collapsed before, and I was seized by the fear that this tunnel would give way, burying us. My breath came out in staccato huffs. I started counting to calm myself: *Un, deux, trois, quatre, cinq.* By the time I'd counted to cinquante, my breathing had evened out. By the time I'd counted to mille trois cent quarante-deux, I could feel the cat-hole widening. I alligator-crawled out and stood up, panting and sweaty, and stretched, my fingers brushing the ceiling overhead. Then I noticed Noor sitting on the floor, huddled into herself, her head down on her knees. I sat next to her. "Are you okay?"

"I hate cat-holes." She didn't lift her head. I scooted closer, until our shoulders touched.

“Yeah.” I remembered how quickly the claustrophobia overtook me. “I thought I was okay in small spaces, but half-way through . . .” I shivered.

“I know that if I go into a cat-hole and it gets too small, I can back out. It is not fun, but it is possible. I have done it. But always when I am in one I begin to believe that I will be stuck. The worst thing is to panic in a cat-hole, but that is what I want to do—to shout for help and to drag myself out fast, even though I can only move a centimeter at a time. It is terrible.”

We were both silent, considering the particular hell of cat-holes. I felt ragged, and Noor was shaking. “Can we just stay here for a while?” I said. Abrasions from my chin to my knees throbbed and stung, and I wished that I’d grabbed my pack when I ran away from Nick. My trail first aid kit was in it.

“What if we fail?” she whispered.

I wanted to say we wouldn’t, but I felt small and raw and scared. I leaned my head onto her shoulder. “If we fail, we fail. And then we try something else. As long as we keep trying, he doesn’t win.”

CHAPTER 22

FIVE WEEKS AGO

It took us a couple of days to find the part of the catacombs where Le Bec's scent was strongest. We would have gone faster if it hadn't been for the cat-holes. We both wanted so badly to avoid them that we wasted time trying to find ways around them, ignoring the fact that they were there because there was no other way around. And once through, we always felt too shredded to continue immediately. We needed a couple of hours huddled silently together to recharge. But Le Bec's scent pulled us onward. We followed its faint tendrils—the metallic whiff of blood, the chemical-sweet smell of spray paint—hoping for a freshening that would lead us to him. Finally, we entered a heavily tagged corridor, and Noor turned to me, her nose twitching. I smelled it, too. His scent was stronger there. Not fresh, but it filled the corridor, telling us he'd come here many times. It intensified near the doorway of a squat the size of my living room. It looked like a subterranean apartment rather than the usual bare, dirty shelter of necessity. Dressed stone blocks formed the walls, as professional a job as any building I'd seen aboveground. A smooth mortar joint tied the masonry into the raw stone ceiling. The opening we'd come through was framed in wood, and a door hung on it. I swung it closed, and it latched with a neat little *snick*.

A rumpled sleeping bag lay on a stone bench along one side of the room. On the opposite wall, a handsome bookcase in dark wood sat next to a matching cabinet. The bookcase held black sketchbooks numbered sequentially in red on the spines. Noor pulled one of them out—number thirty-three. She flipped through it as I looked over her shoulder. It was filled with drawings in black marker, recording everything Le Bec saw, from a street crammed with cars to the group of us crowded together at Le Shopping. I recognized Nick, Martine, and Youssef, looking animated. I was there, too, looking as overwhelmed as I remembered feeling, and Noor sat beside me, watchful and wary. I didn't like how vulnerable he'd made me look. "I hate what a good artist he is," Noor murmured. "Look at that. He captures everyone—their essence—in just a few lines." She replaced the sketchbook and opened the cabinet, which was filled with spray paint, masks, and gloves.

"I think there are lots of good artists," I said, watching her go through the cabinet, "who haven't killed people."

She stopped, then turned around and looked at me. "It is difficult to understand how he can be such a good artist and yet such a terrible person."

"I think that's a false equivalence. Great artist doesn't equal great person."

"But the way he captures people—their essence, their humanity—how can he be so sensitive to that, so capable of making one feel what his subjects are feeling, and nevertheless be a monster? His work is truly excellent. I admire it, and because I do, I also feel that in a certain sense I approve of the monster who makes it. I do not like feeling like this."

How *did* you reconcile bad people who did good things? I hated Cole because that night on the bus, as he gave me one last squeeze before he got up and went back to his seat, I realized that to him I wasn't a person. I was a thing. Yet I used the skills he'd taught me all the time. He was good at research and argumentation, and it felt self-defeating not to take lessons where I found them, even if assault had been the price I paid for them. Still, in the back of my head there was always his voice whispering that I wouldn't be anything without him. His casual dismissal of my humanity and my intelligence was like a fire in a coal seam. It might smolder for years before it broke into the open and exploded into flames.

"I knew this guy," I said. "He . . . hurt me. It wasn't the worst thing he could have done, but it wasn't good. Until then, I'd liked him. Learned stuff from him. So when he did what he did, maybe I felt like—like it wasn't okay, but on the other hand, I did owe him something for spending time and effort on me. I hate thinking about him every time I use something he taught me. I hate feeling like he made me pay for what I learned when I didn't even know there was a cost for it. There shouldn't have been." I grimaced. "I'm not saying this right. I don't really know how to live with skills I only have because a bad person taught them to me."

She gave me an ironic half smile. "Yes. Me too. That is

the problem." She turned back to the cabinet, which looked expensive. Not like some IKEA thing he could bring down in pieces and assemble here. It looked like something that would need movers. "Perhaps I should steal some of his equipment."

I did a conspiratorial half shrug, my left shoulder rising halfway to my ear. "I mean, I wouldn't call the cops if you did." She smiled and stuck her head back into the cabinet. I turned my attention to a tall wing-back chair on a heavily patterned Persian rug in the center of the room.

"Tosh," she said. I turned back to see her holding up a hunting knife.

I grimaced. "Why would a vampire need a hunting knife?"

"I do not want even to think about the possibilities." She shivered, replaced it, and continued rummaging.

I sat down on the chair. Oversized and regal-looking, it had eggplant-colored velvet upholstery, gold-embellished tufting, and a back so tall it almost met the low ceiling. The gilded arms were gouged, though, and buttons were missing from the tufting. The stained upholstery was ripped and bald in spots. I wondered how he'd gotten the chair down here. It would have taken a lot of work. But then, the whole room was a lot of work. Aside from the improbable furniture, its walls and ceiling were covered in drawings of pigeons. They blanketed the limestone so densely that initially I'd thought they were some kind of enormous abstract doodle. It was only after I was sitting in Le Bec's chair, staring idly at the wall near the doorway, that I started to pick individual images out of the snarl of wings, beaks, and feathers. I had the same sensation I had the first week I was in Paris: a barrage of people doing things both mundane and spectacular, but so quickly and so constantly that all I could process was a face here, a gesture there. The room was a microcosm of Paris, a Paris of pigeons. They rode the Métro, played on their phones, staged a screaming sidewalk argument, kissed on a park bench, filled a canvas tote in an open-air market, hurried down the street clutching a briefcase. It looked like Le Bec just kept drawing on top of older drawings, so that in some sections I could pick out only a wing or a beak. He tucked tiny illustrations wherever there was a centimeter of free space, creating a restless, itchy-scratchy avian mass. The walls seethed so hard I had to stare at the carpet to avoid feeling seasick. "Noor, did you notice the walls?" I said. She tucked a box of supplies into her pack and looked up, running her gaze slowly over the drawings. I could see her shoulders hunch up. "You feel it, too, right?" I asked. "I'm not just making it up that it's super amazing and super creepy at the same time?"

She shook her head. "You are not making it up."

I got up from the chair and joined her. "It's like he thinks he's a king," I mused. "Look at that chair; it's a throne."

"King of the vampires," she said sarcastically.

"This is why the police haven't found him. He disappears down here."

"*We* found him, though." She smiled a grim little smile.

"We did, didn't we?"

"We tracked him through the dark without any resources but ourselves."

"We're kind of badass."

She nodded briskly. "Of course we are." She undid the stakes from her pack and handed me one. I made a couple of test thrusts into the air, feeling silly. "Is there a method we follow for this?" she asked, trying to find the best grip on hers. "We will need to conserve his blood, yes? So how do we do it?"

"Madame Dupuy said be sure to stab him in the heart." I showed her where to find the heart, running my fingers over the left side of my rib cage until I felt its steady thump.

Noor frowned. "It is not a large target, and it is well protected."

"Yeah. Maybe one of us can distract him while the other one stakes him?"

"Or we knock him out first. That will make the staking easier."

We looked for something that we could use as a club, but there was nothing. She reached into the cabinet, pulled out a can of spray paint, and tossed it to me. "Spray it in his eyes. It is not as good as knocking him out, but it will put him at a disadvantage."

I pointed to the sleeping bag. "Then toss this over his head. If one of us holds him, the other can stake him."

CHAPTER 23

FIVE WEEKS AGO

A slaughterhouse smell invaded the squat. Noor and I looked at each other. "That's him," I said, tightening my grip on my stake.

She nodded, holding my gaze. "We can do this." The door opened, flooding the room with the smell of blood and terror, and I knew there was another body on the streets of Paris for the police to find.

"Bonjour, les filles," Le Bec said as he entered. "I see you have finally come to join me." We just stared at him. "Of course, you have done it the wrong way around. You cannot enter my home without my permission. But here you are, so I will invite you in retroactively."

I snorted. "We are not here to join you," Noor told him.

"But of course you are." He sat down in the purple throne chair and surveyed us like a king would a couple of particularly useful peasants—pleased and not a little surprised that we showed any ability at all. "How do you like my home?"

"You live in a squat underground," I said. "It's hardly *Amazing Interiors*."

He laughed dismissively. "I own the catacombs. All of it is my home—my kingdom."

I did a slow nod. "Your kingdom is a bunch of rocks and dirt in a hole in the ground. I can see why you'd be proud." That explained why the police couldn't find him, though, if he lived down here full-time. I wondered if he'd taken any victims from the cataphiles who played down here, in his "kingdom."

"My kingdom is not just the catacombs," he said, sitting up straight in his absurd chair. "My kingdom is the night."

Noor and I looked at each other in slack-jawed disbelief. "Did he just use the most hackneyed vampire phrase in the whole history of bloodsucking monsters?" I asked her.

She nodded. "I find it difficult to believe, but yes." She turned back to him. "Does drinking blood damage your brain?"

He looked shocked for a moment. "No," he snapped, recovering. "It makes me powerful."

"How?" I asked, genuinely curious. "How does being a bloodsucking predator make you powerful?"

He held up a pedantic index finger. "In fact, I am not a predator."

"You stalk people. You attack them. You kill them or turn them into monsters. That's the definition of predator."

The finger rocked side to side, chiding me. "I do not kill

people. I bite them and they change. Sometimes they change into beautiful predators, like you two. Sometimes they change into corpses." He smiled, the snotty little superior smirk that debaters are really good at because it provokes an opponent so effectively. And an angry opponent is a careless opponent.

I matched his smile. "You bite people against their will and without their consent. You feed on their blood."

Noor backstopped me as smoothly as if we'd been debate partners since middle school. "You do not ask; you just attack. You—"

"I do not need to ask. Who would not want to be like me?" Noor and I both raised our hands, and he seemed genuinely surprised. "Écoutez, les filles; there are two sorts of people in the world: victors and victims. I made you victors. You have power now; you can do whatever you want."

"You made me your *victim*," Noor said. "Your unprovoked, uninvited attack took away my ability to draw. It—"

Le Bec laughed. "You were not a good artist in any case. It is hardly a loss."

She looked stricken, and a sickening thought came to me. "Did you bite her because you were afraid her art would be more popular than yours?"

He folded his arms. "Of course not. She is not good enough to be competition." But in the moment between my question and his reply, before he'd controlled himself, he'd recoiled, and I knew I was right. He settled himself in his pretend throne and steepled his fingers. "Bon, you have invaded my home without my invitation; you have insulted and accused me; and you say you do not intend to join me. Why are you here?"

I grasped my candleholder tightly. "Because in order to cure ourselves of the disease you gave us, we need your blood," I told him.

He started to laugh. I struck with the stake, hitting him as hard as I could. I felt it pierce his flesh, then rebound off bone. Noor attacked from the other side, but he'd recovered from his surprise and jumped up, dancing away from us. We went after him in a fury, stabbing and slashing. He fought back. He was strong, and his hits landed hard. I knew our blows were landing, too, because I saw the blood. But he just kept hitting, and we were defending ourselves instead of attacking him. We careened around the room, slashing and thrusting with our stakes but unable to slow the momentum of his attack. I was panting and sweaty, aching from his blows and ashamed of my weakness, of my inability even to hurt him as much as he was hurting me. He was trying to wear us down, and I realized he'd kill us if we didn't stake him soon. "You . . . don't . . . win," I grunted as I slashed at him, but I knew we couldn't overcome his strength advantage. If we could incapacitate him somehow, though—I remembered Noor's instructions about the spray paint, and I threw a quick glance back at the sleeping bench, looking for my can. He elbowed me in the chest, knocking me backward. Noor was still all over him. I tried to catch my breath. He grabbed her by the shoulders and slammed her against the wall, leaving his left side—his heart side—open. I plunged the stake into him. A second later, my face exploded. I howled as the pain of his punch pulsed through me, blowing me apart in an explosion of agony.

I came to lying on my back, feeling shattered. I wasn't sure where I was. Moving my head sent white-hot knives slashing, so I held still. Then Noor cried out, and everything came crashing back. I rolled slowly up to sitting, the pain throbbing so hard I retched, which made the pain worse. I forced myself to my knees, and then to my feet, wishing my head would just split in two and get it over with. Noor was making small urgent gasping noises that sounded worse than screaming. They sounded like the end of something. I swallowed my nausea and tried to focus.

Le Bec had her pinned against the wall, his forearm across her throat. "I created you," he growled. "I own you. I can do anything I want with you." He leaned harder on her neck, and she gurgled weakly. My heart turned to stone. I took an unsteady step toward him, raising my arm, ready to drive the stake through him and send him to hell. But my hand was empty. I cast my eyes desperately around, but I didn't see my stake. Noor gurgled again, a wave of panic hit me, and I snatched up the closest thing—his sleeping bag. Noor's lips were blue. I staggered across the room and flung the bag over him. *Please work*, I thought, gathering it to me. I stepped back, yanking as hard as I could, and pulled him over backward. I scrambled to find the zipper, my head screaming, and zipped it quickly as he struggled, turning him into a vampire burrito. He flailed his legs, starting to work his way out the bottom, and I wanted to cry. I kicked him as hard as I could. While he writhed and wheezed, I dragged him to the rug and rolled him up in it. It was all I could think to do.

I turned to Noor, who was slumped against the wall, eyes closed. She was still breathing. Tears spilled down my face, relief and pain together. I heard a noise behind me and turned to see the carpet moving. He was trying to unroll it. "Just stop!" I screamed at him, but he kept rolling, a tail of carpet expanding behind him. I leaned over and rolled him back up, and he immediately started unrolling again. I needed him to stop. Just for a minute, so I could think. I grabbed one end of the roll and dragged it in front of the cabinet, sobbing in frustration and fighting him the whole time. I wedged myself between the cabinet and the wall, pushed desperately, and felt it lean forward, then crash down, driving an animal wail from him. I scrambled back to Noor, who was coughing, and knelt beside her. "Are you okay?" I touched her shoulder like she might break. She nodded, and I hugged her, sobbing.

"Is he dead?" she rasped.

I shook my head. "No. I rolled him up in the carpet and pushed the cabinet on top of him. He wouldn't stop moving."

"We have to stake him."

I nodded. "I lost mine. Where's yours?"

She felt around and found it. I reached out for it, but she shook her head. She didn't look strong enough to stand up, but she levered herself to her feet with me helping. The overturned cabinet still heaved every so often as Le Bec continued to struggle. I picked up the spray can I was supposed to use when we rushed him. Noor took a breath, wheezed, and nodded. We wrestled the cabinet upright and unrolled the rug. He twitched as I unzipped the sleeping bag. Freed from his bindings, he pushed himself up and made a rush for us. I blasted him in the eyes with pigeon-feather gray, and he screeched, reeling. We tackled him, piling on as he struggled to get up, pinning him with our bodies. Noor moved her fingers over his ribs, stopping where she felt his heartbeat. He bucked, almost knocking her sideways, while I focused on grinding his shoulders into the ground to keep him still.

"You are worthless," he spat.

"And you are dead," she said. We both grasped the stake.

He started to say something else, but his words gurgled away. His eyes went wide; then they went out. We'd found his heart.

CHAPTER 24

FIVE WEEKS AGO

We looked at each other. "We did it," she said. There was no triumph in her voice, just a weary acknowledgment that we'd completed an unpleasant task.

"We did," I replied flatly. We should have been celebrating. We'd taken down a vampire. We'd won. But I just sat there, empty and exhausted. Wordlessly, Noor dragged her hand through the blood pooling on the ground next to his body and smeared it on her arms, her face, her clothes. *Right*, I remembered, *this was part of the cure*. This was why we staked him. I dipped my hand into the puddle. It was warm. When she asked me if I could rub blood on her back where she couldn't reach, I laughed. She looked at me, wondering what I could possibly find funny right now. "It's like helping a friend put on sunscreen." I giggled. "But vampire version." She started laughing, too. We rubbed each other with blood, laughing until we gasped. Finally, we caught our breath and stared at the body. Noor said, "We have to do this, yes?" I wanted to say no, but we didn't know which cure, if any, would work. We needed to do all three.

I nodded. "Good thing he thoughtfully provided a knife for us." We started giggling again but stopped when I got the knife out of the cabinet. His heart seemed absurdly small for the amount of work it took to get it out. It was slow, squishy going, and when we were done, it sat on the floor, ugly and malevolent and leaking blood. I glanced at the body and looked away quickly. We hadn't exactly done a precision extraction, and I wanted to burn the memory out of my brain with acid and fire. Noor pulled the sleeping bag over him. "Thanks," I said. "Now we just have to ash this thing." I poked it with the toe of my boot, then started to cry.

"Oh, Tosh." She hugged me.

"How do we even do it?" I sobbed. "We don't have any wood. I mean, I have matches." I wasn't completely useless. "But what do we do, singe it into submission, one match at a time? It'll take forever." I slumped down and curled into a ball, weeping so hard I could barely breathe. We'd come all this way, done hard, horrible things, and now we were going to fail.

"It is okay." She rubbed my back, which made me cry harder. I wanted all this to stop: the pain and anger and despair and disgust. I wanted to be a normal girl living her best life in Paris instead of a blood-caked abomination.

"I think— Wait a minute." She walked over to Le Bec's bookcase and took out one of the sketchbooks. She opened it and tore out a page, crumpling it and tossing it onto the ground close to the heart. "We can use these. His 'throne' will burn, too, if we break it up." I dragged a hand across my eyes, got a sketchbook, and started tearing out pages. We built a pyramid of wadded-up drawings and surrounded it with sketchbooks stood on end and fanned open to catch the flame. We laid the broken bones of the chair on top, then lit the loose paper and fed the flames with Le Bec's art until everything had been burned up and the charred lump of his heart sat in their ashes. The squat stank of burnt meat. Noor eyed it grimly. "Why are these cures so disgusting?"

"Right?" I agreed. "There should be a pill or a vaccine, instead of this DIY horror kitchen." When the heart was cool, we used a spray can to bash it into powder. Then we stared at the disgusting pile of gray ashes.

"Maybe if we put them in water, they'll go down easier?" I suggested. Noor got her water bottle, and we mixed the ashes in until we had a toxic-looking slurry. We took turns drinking, one of us gagging while the other one forced down another swallow.

"I think I feel worse," she said when we were done.

I nodded. "If he wasn't already dead, I'd definitely kill him for this."

She held up the empty water bottle. "So what disgusting thing must we do next?"

I made a face. "Eat his grave dirt. Except to do that, he needs a grave." He was dead, and he was still making our lives miserable. "So I guess we'll have to dig him one. With our hands."

"In the cabinet, there is a shovel that folds up." She gave me an ironic half smile. "For one time, he did something useful." The shovel was an aluminum one you use to dig a firepit or trench around a tent. The handle was so short we had to kneel to dig in the packed rubble floor. We worked together, Noor on the shovel and me pulling out the bigger chunks of rock as she loosened them. After a couple of hours we switched, and almost immediately I hit solid rock. I directed a baleful look at the sleeping-bag-covered lump.

"I hope there's a hell," I told it, "and I hope you're frying." The hole we'd made wasn't yet deep enough to hold him, so we started scraping at the rock. We worked mechanically, one of us raking the shovel over the stone and the other scooping the dust out. Noor found some dust masks in the cabinet, so at least we weren't breathing it, but it got into our eyes and coated our clothes and skin until we looked like the ghosts of gravediggers.

Finally, she stopped me. "I think it is deep enough," she said. We were both kneeling waist-deep in the hole, and at the edge there was a pile of rubble and another of fine, pale rock dust that we'd excavated. The shovel blade was worn down to a quarter of its original size.

"We actually did it," I said, only half believing what I saw.

"We did," she agreed, her voice flat.

We dragged Le Bec to the hole and rolled him in. Then we just stood there, too exhausted to start filling the grave. He wasn't a pretty corpse, but my eyes kept darting to him, pulled by a nagging idea that something was missing. Besides his heart, obviously. Noor picked up the sleeping bag that had covered him while we were digging, and I saw her stake on the ground. She was about to toss the bag in on top of him when I stopped her. I picked up the stake and stepped down into the grave. I positioned it over his chest, then drove it in with my remaining strength. I felt it bury itself in the rock beneath him.

Noor nodded. "So he can never get up again. Good."

We filled the grave in, except for one handful of fine dirt, smoothed it even, and then dragged the carpet over it. We examined it from all angles, but unless someone knew what lay under it, they'd never suspect it covered anything but stone and gravel. Noor looked at me. "I guess we eat dirt now," I said.

We'd drunk the last of the water, so we had to swallow the dirt dry. It felt soft at first on my tongue, like powdered sugar. It tasted like dirt, though, and it went down in a choking, clayey lump. I hated Le Bec a little bit more. Noor gulped hers down stone-faced, her eyes watering. "What next?"

I shrugged. "We wait?" We sat down on the sleeping bench. I was beyond exhausted, and I was sure I'd fall asleep the moment I stopped moving. But images from the past hours played a blood-spattered PowerPoint in my head every time I shut my eyes. Finally I just stared at the tangle of pigeons on the wall.

"You know," she said after a while, "I really hate how he has done the walls."

"It's a bit extra," I agreed. "All those staring pigeon eyes." I shivered.

"We should redo it." She got up with a groan and started collecting the spray cans that had spilled out of the cabinet when I pushed it over onto Le Bec. When I realized what she had in mind, I helped her sort the colors. She picked out a small stretch of wall by the door and showed me some basics: what caps are best for what job, how to make fat and thin lines, how to make flat shapes look dimensional. She left me to practice and got to work.

I noodled around with stylized human shapes, drawing with the paint, changing the positions of arms and legs until the figures looked right. I could hear the soft hiss of paint as Noor worked on the other walls. It felt healing to be making art with her. The squat felt different with our marks on the walls—like a sanctuary rather than a graveyard. I lost myself in colors and shapes. Noor had finished the rest of the room by the time I'd gotten my little mural the way I wanted it. I turn to look at what she'd done and gasped.

She'd painted Paris—the monuments and shops, the people and parks. There was Le Shopping, with a swirling crowd of dancers. There was a boulangerie with a line out the door. Chimeras from Notre-Dame promenaded down the Champs-Élysées. Mysterious figures in blue EDF coveralls painted a mural on the side of a building. One of them wore a scarf, and one had a thick red braid hanging down her back. A Métro train on an elevated track careened through a neighborhood with an accordion player riding on top, a trail of notes following him. A cartoony Eiffel Tower leaned inquisitively into my panel, where I'd painted two figures dancing under a fat yellow sun. "They are beautiful, Tosh," she said, looking at my dancers. At the bottom of the mural, she'd written, in friendly block letters, *Paris est à nous*.

"You got your art back," I said, hugging her. "It's amazing."

She grinned. "I am so happy. And so relieved." Then she pointed at my mini-mural. "We are an excellent team."

"We are," I agreed. The squat was littered with cans of spray paint, and I started to pick them up. She joined me.

"We cannot have our beautiful piece surrounded by trash," she said. We put the cans back into the cabinet. I wondered how long we'd have to wait to see if the cures had worked. I wondered what we'd do if they hadn't. When everything was tidy, I took another look at our mural, so alive and vibrant. I squinted at my sun, which had glowed when I'd painted it, but now looked dull and faded. "Is it getting dark in here?"

She looked around the room and then at me, her eyes widening. "I think it worked," she said.

"What worked?" Then I realized. My vision was starting to fade back to human. Those awful cures we'd taken had worked. I sniffed the air, which minutes before had been layered with the overwhelming smell of spray paint, the still-strong tang of blood, and the persistent sour odor of limestone. They were all still there, but muted. "Oh," I said. Then I realized what losing v mode meant down here in the dark. "We need to find a way out of here before our senses revert." She caught up her pack immediately, and we left the squat. No one would know now that it was once Le Bec's. He was gone: dead, buried, and never to rise. Paris belonged to us again, just like Noor had written on her mural.

We hurried while we could still see in the dark and follow a scent trail. We were lucky, in an awful way, that the blood smell Le Bec carried with him was still so strong, because that's what we followed until the trail went cold at a fork, and we found ourselves fully in the dark and merely human once again. I wondered if, after all we'd done, we'd end our lives down here. We had shut our phones off to save battery, but we turned them on and used the flashlights to see where we were. I scanned the two corridors that made a Y there, wondering if it really mattered which one we chose. We could have been working our way farther and farther from an exit and never have known it until we collapsed from exhaustion and dehydration. We were running on fumes as it was.

"Stay with us," Nick had cautioned me when he took me into the catacombs. Was it only a month ago? "People who don't know the catas can get definitively lost down here. Even people who do know them can lose their sense of direction." He'd told me about Philibert Aspairt, who went exploring on his own down here in 1793 and got lost. Cataphiles had found his skeleton eleven years later, and they'd buried him right where he'd died. They put up a monument commemorating his lonely death, which is more than we would get.

Noor interrupted my grim musings. "Look; there is the trail." She pointed up at the black line painted down the center of the ceiling. It was like the one we'd followed my first time in the catas. I'd forgotten all about it. Thank goodness Noor hadn't. We checked our phone batteries, which were so low we could use them only sparingly. We had my matches, though. After an hour or so of groping our way along in complete blackness, we came to another crossroads and lit a match. Noor found a street marker she recognized. "Merde," she said. "We are going the wrong way." I was hungry and thirsty and cold and tired. I didn't want to retrace our steps. All I wanted to do was sit down and cry. "I am so sorry," she said, sounding miserable.

If we stopped, I wasn't sure we'd start again. So I pretended I wasn't exhausted and hopeless. I forced some cheer into my voice. "It's not a crisis. We just have to go back. It's better than having to stake a vampire."

"I just want to go home." Her voice shook.

"Me too." I hugged her. "And we will. I mean, we wouldn't have made it this far without you."

"In the wrong direction."

"Okay, yes, but now we know what the right direction is. And all we have to do is walk. We don't have to kill a vampire or eat his heart. We just have to walk. It'll be easy." I took her hand and tugged it. We needed to keep moving. She fell into step beside me, and we marched into the dark, feeling our way toward freedom. Time didn't feel the same in the catas, so I'm not sure how long we'd been walking when Noor asked to stop for a rest. We sat down right where we were standing, and I scooted as close to her as I could.

"I'm cold," I said. She jostled against me as she rummaged in her pack. I could hear zippers sing as she opened pockets. Then I heard a crinkle. "Voilà," she said.

"Voilà what?"

"Chocolate. I always have some for emergencies." She felt for my hand and put a chunk in it. I remembered our last excursion in the catas, when she'd also saved me with emergency chocolate.

"Oh my God," I moaned, forcing myself to take small bites and chew each one thoroughly. "It tastes like a miracle." I felt a little warmer. After a few minutes of rest, I forced myself to get up. Noor protested but got to her feet, taking point. I followed, my hand on her pack. "Is there water along this route?" We'd need some fairly soon. Once again I regretted not thinking to snatch up my backpack, with its water bottles, as I fled after attacking that man. Dad always said you could go longer without food than you could without water. I used to tease him because he obsessively checked trail maps before we hiked to identify water sources. You can't carry enough water with you on a long hike—it weighs too much—so he'd mark all the sources we could expect to find along the trail. We always hiked with a backup water purification kit, too. He'd had giardia, and his goal was never, ever to have it again. I wished he were here with us now.

"Yes," Noor said. "We will be okay." We walked on, feeling our way through the blackness. After a while, she asked what we were going to do when we got out of the catas. I'd been thinking about that, too.

"Madame Dupuy said she'd help us."

"Do you trust her?"

I hesitated. "She told us about the cures."

"Yes. But her family kills vampires."

"We're not vampires anymore."

"How do we prove that to her?"

"The silver test," I said.

"But we do not have anything silver. And if we ask her to meet us with silver, will she think that we are still vampires and that we are trying to trap her?"

"Good point." I was so tired it was hard to think.

"Nick?" Noor suggested.

I groaned. "Nick saw me rip someone's throat open. Maybe Martine or Youssef?"

"Perhaps." We considered this. "So we call Martine—perhaps Youssef—and they meet us. They will run away when they see we are covered with blood," she pointed out.

"Right. We need somebody we don't have to explain this to. Somebody who won't be shocked when they see what we look like. Madame Dupuy knows about vampires. She said she'd help us." Noor sighed. "What if we call her? Just call her and tell her the cures worked? See what she says?"

Noor was silent for a couple of minutes. "Very well. I cannot think of a better alternative. But if she does not respond well, we cut the call."

"Agreed."

She stopped. "Crossroads." I lit a match and watched without really seeing as she inspected the street names. A smile spread over her face. "The access hatch is just a few meters down that tunnel."

The hatch opened into an underground parking garage, still and dark except for the pale glow of exit signs. I was so grateful to see any light at all after days in the dark that I started to cry. Tears glistened on Noor's face, too. I turned on my phone and texted Madame Dupuy: "The cures worked." She called me immediately, the ringtone sounding like a calamity after all the time we'd spent in the silent dark.

I put her on speaker. "Where are you?" she said.

"Can I trust you?" I countered. She didn't say anything. "Not to kill me?" I clarified.

"They really worked—the cures?"

"Yes."

She inhaled shakily. "Yes, Mademoiselle Tosh, you can trust me."

I looked at Noor, splotched with dried blood and limestone dust. She hesitated, then nodded. Madame Dupuy arrived half an hour later with clothes for us, wipes to clean up with, and cheese, bread, and bottled water. We tore into the food immediately and slurped the water greedily. After we'd eaten every last crumb and finished off a bottle of Vittel each, we cleaned up and changed. When Noor took off her blood-caked headscarf, Madame Dupuy unlooped the scarf from around her neck—because of course she accessorized to come pick up a couple of runaway vampire killers—and gave it to Noor to cover her head. Then she made sure we looked normal, bundled our filthy clothes into a shopping bag, and took us to her apartment, where she put the clothes into her washer. Just like this was a normal housekeeper task: clean up runaway vampire killers, destroy evidence.

"Bon," she said. "Would you like some tea?"

Noor and I looked at each other. "Yes?" I said. She filled the kettle and put it on the stove. "What are we going to do?" I asked.

"You are going to sit down in the living room." She measured tea into an infuser. "We will have tea, and we will talk." Noor gave me an *Is this for real?* look. I shrugged, baffled by Madame Dupuy's matter-of-fact calm. She made a shooing motion at us, and we dutifully went and sat down. I should have been thinking about what we would say, but my brain just wouldn't engage. And then, she was setting a silver tray down in front of us with an old-school silver teapot and sugar bowl with little silver tongs. I remembered how she'd put my shoes in the fridge the night I'd gone dancing with Nick so she'd know that I had kept my curfew, and I tipped an imaginary hat at her cleverness. Silver burns vampires. When she poured the tea for us, I held her eyes as I used the tongs to add a lump of sugar to my cup. Noor put two lumps in hers, stirred, took a polite sip, and then attacked the plate of Petit Écolier cookies. I didn't even bother with the polite sip. I was famished, and the cookies were delicious. Madame Dupuy nodded to herself and started asking questions. Technical questions. Where had we found stakes? She thought using the candleholders had been clever and resourceful. What did we do with the body? She was pleased when Noor told her I'd pinned it to the bottom of the grave with a stake. "That is what a true vampire killer would do," she said, and I felt a tiny spark of pride. Then she asked about the cures. She was impressed that we'd figured out how to burn his heart. "I always imagined that it would be so difficult," she said. We assured her it had been. She wanted to know how we'd known we were cured. We explained how our senses had faded from predator back to normal.

"It was like when you go to see a film," Noor explained, "and the lights in the theater fade to darkness."

"And you were not afraid when this happened?"

"Terrified," I said. "I thought we'd die down there like Philibert Aspairt. But Noor navigated us through the darkness with no maps. She was amazing."

When we'd answered all Madame Dupuy's questions, I had one. "Do you think we're still vampires?"

She shook her head. "That is why I brought food when I came to get you. If you had not wanted to eat it, then I would have suspected." I thought about asking if she'd also taken stakes with her, just in case, but of course she had. I would've. "And of course when you touched the silver tongs and were not burned, I knew. So what do you want to happen now?"

I put my head in my hands. "I want all this to go away."

"I want to go home," Noor added. I nodded. I'd run away because I was angry and scared and literally not myself, but curing my vampirism had scrubbed that away. The anger at Dad about moving back to Portland had been replaced by—well, I was still angry. But the overwhelming rage was gone. I'd thought a lot about him while we were in the catacombs. For one thing, he'd taught me the skills I used down there. Like how to make a fire. How not to panic when you're lost. He'd taught me self-reliance. And I could see why he'd want to protect me. He'd been scared, too. When you're scared, you don't think.

Madame Dupuy pursed her lips, considering. "I think that is possible."

I shook my head. "Maybe for Noor, but I attacked someone when I was with Nick, and I think maybe I . . . killed him."

She shook her head. "He is alive." I wanted to weep with relief. "After you ran, Monsieur Nick stayed. He called an ambulance and did first aid until it arrived, even though he himself was in shock. When the police questioned him, he did not tell them about you. They think it was another Paris vampire attack that he fortunately stopped. You made him responsible for the terrible thing you did, Mademoiselle Tosh. You owe him much."

I texted Nick immediately, apologizing for what I'd done, for leaving him to deal with it, and for not responding to his earlier texts. "I want you to know that I'm not like Le Bec anymore." I didn't want to say "vampire" over text. "Noor and I cured ourselves." He returned a one-word reply that tore a hole in my heart. "Ok." As I wondered if I could ever explain to him what it had been like to be in my body, battling my worst urges, and losing in such a terrible way, another text from him pinged: "Where are you?" I texted back that I was safe and waited for his reply, but none came.

We told Madame Dupuy how we'd gradually realized that we were vampires. "The mirror test is useless," Noor said.

"Just like the invitation thing," I chimed in. "I never invited Le Bec in anywhere. In fact, I kept trying to push him away because he made me uncomfortable. I don't want to be negative, but—does your family really know all that much about vampires?"

"I assure you, they know how to kill them," she said grimly. "But for the other things . . . there is no real science of the vampire. There is only what people say. 'Do not invite them in.' 'They do not have reflections.' 'A victim can cure himself by eating the ashes of the vampire's heart.'" She smiled sadly. "My grandmother told me that anything involving millet seed is useless, even though everyone says to scatter it around. Then she showed me the scar on her neck."

Noor inhaled sharply. "Is that how you know about the cures?" Madame Dupuy nodded. *There should be studies*, I thought. Science-based research. Properly designed experiments. Reality-tested solutions. No one should ever have to face that malevolence like Noor and I had: alone, with just a stake and a handful of folklore to protect us from a deadly predator.

Madame Dupuy was thinking along the same lines. "Tell me everything: what you did, how you felt. We need facts to fight this." She interrogated us about our symptoms, our feelings, how we tried to manage our cravings. She thought the menthol salve and smoking solutions were very good.

"Not good enough, though." I told her how I'd almost attacked Dad, and Noor described how she'd wanted to bite the guy who was harassing her while she painted.

"What did you do then?"

"Ran," I said as Noor said, "Hid." We told her about the church of lost causes, but she stopped us when we started to tell her about its catacombs access.

"No. You stayed in the church. You were frightened and exhausted, and you stayed there because you felt safe. Tosh, you did not want to return to Portland. Noor, you did not want to leave Tosh alone because you were worried that she might run away. Both of you spent three days hiding in the church arguing about what you should do. Finally, Noor, you convinced Tosh not to run away. Tosh, you were afraid your father would be angry with you, so you contacted me."

I just stared at her. "Why are you helping us get our story straight? Why did you come to get us? Why are you giving us snacks? You should be calling the police and Dad. You shouldn't be acting like this is normal and okay. We killed someone."

"Do you want me to call the police?"

"No. But—"

"You killed a vampire. I cannot judge you for that. It is because of vampires that I lost my family." She looked suddenly vulnerable, and I could see the girl she'd been twenty-five years ago, getting off the train in Paris alone, wondering what she'd do next, how she'd survive. "I know what it is like to run away because of vampires, to scratch a new life in a new place. I do not wish that for anyone, and certainly not for girls who were brave enough to hunt one down and battle him to his death. You rid the city of a terror, and you proved the efficacy of three cures for this disease. You did nothing wrong—" I started to shake my head, and she reached out and took my hand. "Nothing. Do you understand me? When you became vampires, you were forced, against your wills, into a world of darkness and brutality. You could have become like your attacker, feeding on others. But you chose not to. You battled your worst selves, and you were clever and strong enough to defeat your attacker and cure yourselves. You prevented him from making more vampires." She held my gaze until I nodded. "I am simply helping you understand how to tell your story so your innocence is obvious. If you do not wish me to do this, however, I will stop."

I looked at Noor. "We did not choose what happened to us," she said. "But we chose to become human again. I think that is important."

Madame Dupuy nodded. "I agree." Together, the three of us built a narrative that was simple, believable, and vampire-free. We didn't have to be told that no one besides us could ever know what had happened in the catas. Then we practiced our story till Madame Dupuy was satisfied that it sounded true. "Now," she told us, "it is time to call your parents."

CHAPTER 25

FIVE WEEKS AGO

Why?

That was the question everyone asked—Dad, Noor's parents, the police (multiple times in multiple lie-spotting configurations). *Why did you run away, Tosh? Why did you girls go out into the night when you knew it was dangerous? Why did you spend three days in an old church without telling anyone where you were?* We stuck to the script. *I was angry. I wasn't thinking straight. I didn't want to leave Paris. Noor was trying to convince me not to run away. She was worried something would happen to me if she left me alone.* I cried when the police officers asked if I'd thought about how much I'd hurt my father. *Yes, I thought about it a lot. It was stupid and thoughtless and I regret it so, so much.*

I apologized to Dad, again, as we waited for the Métro. He was gray with fatigue and stress. "Why, Tosh?"

"I'm sorry I hurt you, but you hurt me, too, Dad."

"I was trying to keep you safe."

"You isolated me. You locked me up in the apartment, you forbade me to see my friends, you ignored my words when I couldn't talk, and now you're taking Paris away from me. Every time you try to keep me safe, you take something important away—my autonomy, my friends, my voice, my new home. It's not my fault Le Bec's a predator, but you're punishing me for being attacked."

"It *is* your fault. You should have been more careful. You have no idea how dangerous it is out there."

I reached up and tore the bandage off my neck. "Yes, I do." The few early-morning passengers stared at us. "I will bear this reminder of the worst night of my life for as long as I live. I will remember how terrified I was, and I will remember how much he enjoyed my terror. If I let my fear decide where I live, what I do, who my friends are, or where I go, it's like reliving that night forever. I don't want to live a fear-based life. And I don't deserve to be punished because you're scared of what could happen to me."

"You aren't being realistic. There will always be bad people out there, and you need to learn to be careful. I'd think your attack would have taught you that."

"You keep saying predators are unavoidable, but you never say they're unacceptable." The train pulled in, and we got on. We had our pick of seats this early.

He huffed, exasperated. "What do you want me to do? As much as I want to, I can't stop them. You need to do the work here. I can't protect you all the time, so you need to be careful to stay safe."

I rubbed my eyes. I was so tired I could barely focus, and I didn't want to have this argument right now, on no sleep and after what Noor and I had been through. But I needed him to hear me. "You can say, 'That's not okay,' when you hear someone say creepy things. You can say, 'I believe you,' when someone tells you what happened to them. You can make it a little less easy for predators to exist. You can keep doing it even if it feels awkward. You can set an example so that other people feel empowered to do it, too."

He sat with that for a minute, looking upset. No, not upset, I realized: uncomfortable. "Okay," he finally said. "I'll try. But I'm your father. I can't stop protecting you; it's my job. And you put me through hell, Tosh. For three days, I imagined the worst possible things—and I couldn't do anything to save you." His voice broke.

He was so distressed, and I wanted to feel sympathy, but instead I seethed with resentment. Noor and I had chosen to save ourselves, and we beat Le Bec because we worked together to overcome him. We didn't need Dad to step in and save us. "Did you ever imagine a good outcome, Dad?" I asked, trying to keep the aggravation out of my voice. "Did you ever think, *I raised a smart, resourceful person, and I can trust her to use her skills if she gets into a bad situation*? Because that's what actually happened. Noor and I kept each other safe."

He looked at me—really looked at me. "I guess—yes. But it's hard to not be scared for you."

I was too exhausted to tell him he was still missing my point. I just said, "I know you love me, Dad. I just wish you knew what it was like to live in my skin."

Neither of us spoke the rest of the way home. When we

got back to the apartment, Dad looked at his watch and sighed. "I'm going to try to catch a couple of hours' sleep before I have to go to work."

"Okay." I turned toward my room. I planned to sleep for a solid week.

"You know," he said, "when I saw you in the hospital after you'd been attacked, that brought it all back—the black time when your mom was sick and I couldn't help her. I had to watch her fade away, and I felt so powerless. Then I almost lost you. I don't think I could have survived that."

"You didn't lose me, Dad."

He folded me into a long hug. "Thank you for coming back."

"MADEMOISELLE TOSH."

I turned my head groggily toward Madame Dupuy's voice. "Mmm?"

"It is time to get up. You are going with me to do shopping in fifteen minutes."

I felt around for my phone and squinted at it. I'd slept nine hours, but it felt like fifteen minutes. I struggled out of the sheets that had twined themselves around me, cleaned up, and joined her in the hall by the door. She pointed to the rolling caddie she used for groceries, and I took the handle.

"Thank you for everything you did for us last night," I said as we waited for the elevator.

She made the "pff" sound that meant, *It was nothing.*

I sighed. "I'll miss you so much. I'll miss everything about Paris." The elevator dinged and opened its doors to reveal Nick and Sophie.

"Tosh!" Sophie exclaimed. I froze. If it had just been Nick and me, I'd have turned around and taken the stairs. But Madame Dupuy put her hand on my back and gently propelled me into the elevator. I bent down to do kiss-kiss-kiss with Sophie and then stole a peek at Nick, but he was staring at the button panel like it held the secrets of the universe. Sophie greeted Madame Dupuy, who returned her greeting and then wished Nick good day. The warm, rich sound of his "Bonjour, Madame Dupuy" was so comforting and at the same time so distant that Sophie had to repeat what she'd just asked me while I blinked back tears. "Where have you been? Have you been sick all this time? Did Nick give you the porte-clés I bought for you with my own money?" He'd left the Astérix keychain outside my door the night before I'd tried to kill someone in front of him. Just a handful of days ago, but it seemed like decades.

"Yes, he did." I pulled my keys out and showed her the little Astérix figure dangling from the ring. "Thank you so much; it's just perfect."

"I kept asking him if you'd gotten it, but he just got sad and wouldn't talk to me. Did you break up?"

"I—" I looked at Nick, who was not looking at me so hard he was generating a heat aura. "I guess we did. I did something bad, and then I ran away. I hurt Nick a lot." My voice shook. "Even though I didn't mean to."

She put her hands on her hips. "Well, are you sorry that you hurt him?"

"So very sorry."

"Tell him." She pointed to her brother, who'd flattened himself against the elevator wall, as far away from me as he could get in the small space. He looked miserable.

I tried to catch his eye, but he wouldn't look at me, so I apologized to his ear. "Nick, I put you in a terrible position and I regret it so much. I know I really hurt you. I hope you'll forgive me." He didn't say anything.

"Nick," Sophie said loudly. "She said she's sorry. Now you have to forgive her." He remained silent. "Nick—"

"It's okay," I interrupted. "He doesn't have to do it right now."

"Yes, he does, because if he doesn't, I'll never see you again."

My heart cracked. "Oh, Soph, that would make me so sad. But sometimes when you hurt people really badly, it takes time for them to recover."

"Are you still friends with me?"

I crouched down and took her hand. "I will always be friends with you. You helped me when I was sad and alone my first day in Paris. In fact, you were my first friend in Paris." Nick glanced at me for a moment, his face soft, like he was remembering our first meeting, too, when he and Sophie had helped me with the building codes. I smiled at him, but he'd already looked away.

"I will always be your friend, too." She was silent for a few moments. "Do you want to have a playdate? Just us, without Nick? Like, tomorrow, if my mom says it's okay?"

Yes, I wanted to say. I wanted to play Barbies or ride scooters or dress up like pirates and princesses with her. But I shook my head. "I'm so sorry; I can't. Dad is moving us back to Portland, and I have to start packing."

"But you just got here."

"I know, and I really want to stay here. Paris feels like home now. But Dad says we have to go back."

Sophie threw her arms around me with such force that I knew I'd stay hugged for a long, long time. "You can stay here. You can live with us."

I held on to her. "Oh, Sophie. I would love that more than anything, but I can't. My dad would worry too much about me if I stayed."

"Tell him to stay here."

"I've tried. He won't listen to my reasons."

She finally let go of me. "Well, can I video chat with you when you're not here? I do that with my grandmas and granddads. It's almost as good as talking in real life."

I nodded. "If your parents say you can. And if it won't make Nick uncomfortable." The elevator dinged and the doors opened.

Nick cleared his throat. "It won't." He didn't look at me.

I followed Madame Dupuy out of the elevator, looking back when Sophie yelled, "Bye." I waved, she waved, and then Nick was leading her away.

Madame Dupuy and I stopped at all her usual vendors: the primeur, who supervised his tween son as he selected scallions, tomatoes, and baby potatoes for us; the poissonière in her chest waders who greeted Madame Dupuy by name and told her that the dorade was freshly caught; the scary fromagière who always glared like she'd prefer to hack a wedge off me instead of the wheel of Brie de Meaux. Our last stop was a tiny stand selling fresh apricots, and then we headed home. As we waited to cross the street, Madame Dupuy turned to me. "How much do you want to stay here, Mademoiselle Tosh?"

"More than anything. When we moved here, it felt like coming home in a way that Portland never made me feel. It felt like Paris was the true home of my heart. It sounds super dramatic, but this feels like the place where I'll make a difference. If I go back to Portland, I know I won't be where I should be, and I'll lose the life I should have had."

The light changed, and we started across the street. "Have you thought that you have already made that difference? With what you did the other night?"

"But it's not finished, is it? I've been thinking about that man—the one I left Nick with. He's probably infected, and he'll probably infect others. I have no idea how to clean that mess up, but it is my mess, and I want to try to fix what I've done."

"So what would you do to stay here?"

I shook my head. "After I ran away like that, Dad's not going to reconsider. I'll have to go back to Portland and follow his rules for another year, until I turn eighteen. Then I'll work my way back here somehow. Take a gap year and get a job and save up. Find a study-abroad program. Get a job here as an au pair. Whatever I can do, because I belong here."

I don't know what Madame Dupuy said to Dad that evening, but when the EU needs a new trade negotiator, it should hire her. She got him to agree to stay in Paris for the school year if I agreed to let him track my phone, maintained an A equivalent in all my classes, hung out with my friends only at school or at our apartment, and saw a counselor. I didn't love the conditions, especially the tracking, but she got me friend time, and in any case, staying here was worth the compromise. When I texted Noor the news, she was packing for her family's August vacation to Turkey.

Noor: I am so happy ♥♥♥♥♥!

Me: I wish you weren't going on vacation. You could come over and we could hang out

Me: Dad could glare suspiciously at you

Noor: Hahaha

Me: Fun times

Me: Actually, I'm glad you're going on vacation. You don't need the dad glare

Noor: Tell that to my father, please. He will be glaring at me for a long time

Noor: I will bring you back a souvenir from Turkey

Me: Oooh, yes please! The gaudiest one you can find

Noor: 😘 Of course

I texted Martine to tell her that Dad had relaxed the friend rules. Slightly. She sent me a beach selfie from the Île de Ré with a string of heart emojis. I knew she'd tell Youssef. I didn't bother texting Nick, because after our encounter in the elevator, it was pretty clear that he didn't want to talk to me. So I was surprised a couple of days later to see a text from him as I was packing for our Alps hiking trip. Dad had forgotten to cancel the reservations when he decided we were moving back to the US. So we were having an August vacation along with the rest of France. I hoped that a couple of weeks of pounding trails would get him back to himself, because he was still acting stiff and strange with me. My heart fluttered as I clicked on Nick's text, and then it fell when I saw the words "Hi from Sophie. She says she hopes you're having fun in Portland" under a photo of her in a kayak. I replied that Dad had changed his mind, and we were staying in Paris. I stared at the screen, hoping Nick would reply, would say something so that I knew he'd forgiven me. Finally, I read, "She says yay." The speech bubble pulsed for a moment, then disappeared.

EPILOGUE

NOW

Dad's walking me to my first day of school at École Jarret. We talk about my classes and the gorgeous early-September weather. He asks me, once again, if I'm sure I can handle this. I don't roll my eyes. I don't tell him I killed a vampire, bathed in his blood, ashed his heart, and ate his grave dirt, so going to school in French holds no terrors for me. Instead, I say yes, I can handle this. And I thank him, again, for letting me stay in Paris.

"Madame Dupuy will meet you right here after school," he says when we get to the school gate. He's told me this like five times.

"Okay," I say. That's also part of our bargain. Madame Dupuy walks me to and from school. And I get to stay in Paris, where I belong.

"Be careful," he says, because he still wants to protect me. I say I will, and he hugs me, then watches me go into the schoolyard. I turn around once I'm inside and wave. He waves back, then starts down the street, and I relax, the weight of his worry slipping off my shoulders.

The school's courtyard is filled with students, their voices bouncing off the stone walls of the buildings in a clamor of shouts and laughter. I see Noor standing near the entry doors, and I hurry over and hug her. What with vacations and getting me reenrolled in school after Dad had unenrolled me, we haven't seen each other since we cured ourselves. "I got you something from Turkey," she singsongs, and pulls a palm-sized box out of her backpack.

"Yay, a souvenir." I clap excitedly. "Is it cheesy? Is it the cheesiest?"

She nods sideways, scrunching her face up. "Maybe not *so* cheesy. But I thought you would like it."

I open the box, and inside, nestled in tissue paper, is a chain with a round, dark blue glass pendant on it. On the pendant are concentric colored circles: white, then pale blue, then black.

"It is a charm against the evil eye," she says, taking it out of my hand and motioning me to turn so she can fasten it around my neck.

"I love it. And on a silver chain, too. So thoughtful. So vampire-resistant." I hand her a packet printed with Swiss flags. "I got something for you, too." She opens it and lifts out a cowbell keychain, the gaudiest one I could find. The bell is painted all over with cows, edelweiss flowers, and Swiss flags and hangs from a wide leather strap with absurd blue, red, green, white, and yellow fringe along its edges.

"It is perfect," she says, holding it up. "I love it. What is it?"

I tell her, and she rings it, producing a *clonk, clonk* that sends us into giggles. She attaches it to her backpack, and every time she moves it clonks and we dissolve into laughter. "Are you ready for this?" she asks when we've finally exhausted the comic possibilities of cowbells.

I do the one-shoulder shrug. "Yeah." We watch the other students as they talk and joke and show each other things on their phones. "Madame Dupuy talked to her family yesterday," I say quietly. "They were really interested in the cures. They want to run some experiments."

Noor looks shocked. "There are enough"—she hesitates, then drops her voice—"vampires to do that where they are?"

I nod. "Not just where they are." The man I bit is still weighing on me. And Le Bec's victims, too—the ones who didn't die.

"I will be interested to know the results of their experiments."

"Imagine if they find a nonhorrible way to cure v mode," I say.

"Oh, that would be so wonderful."

Nick comes through the gate, followed by Martine and Youssef, and we wave, smiling tentatively. He sees us and lifts his chin in a guy wave, without quite making eye contact. Martine waves, and Youssef raises his hand in a half wave, happy to see us, I think, but also following Nick's lead.

"Should we go over?" I ask. "I don't want to make Nick uncomfortable."

Noor gives me a look. "I think it is okay if Nick is a little uncomfortable."

"What do you mean?" I watch a cluster of students smoking under a plane tree. Noor and I would be standing with them now, wary and worried about v mode, if we hadn't gone after Le Bec.

"I know he thinks that you hurt him that night, but he should allow you to make amends."

"I've tried." I shrug helplessly. "I mean, we cured ourselves, and he knows that because I told him. We took responsibility. I'm not sure what else I could do to persuade him how awful I feel about what happened." I glance over at him. He and Youssef are laughing. He looks happy and carefree.

Noor follows my gaze. "He also did something terrible to you without intending to when he introduced you to Le Bec. You accepted his apology. Does he think his pain is worse than yours was?"

"Fair question." I watch a clump of kids approach Nick and Youssef. I recognize them from that night at Le Shopping. I think they're cataphiles.

"I think we should not let his discomfort keep us from our friends. And in any case, cataphiles do not leave each other behind."

Martine glances over at us and smiles, and it seems like a welcome. We cross the schoolyard toward her, and the smile turns to a grin. She embraces us both. "I am so happy to see you," she says.

"Me too," I reply. "I thought I'd never be able to leave our apartment again. I thought I'd have to do school online. But we worked it out, and Dad even agreed to let me do an extracurricular activity." He kind of had to. It's a graduation requirement. "So I'll be doing Model UN with you."

"Super!" Martine hugs me, and I hug her back, hard. I

missed her so much. When I finally let go, she tries to persuade Noor to join the team with us.

Noor shakes her head, smiling. "I am joining the rock-climbing group."

I can tell Martine is as surprised as I am. Noor's never mentioned anything about climbing. "I didn't know you were into that," I say. "Except for, you know." I point at the ground.

Noor nods. "That is a benefit. But if I want to do pieces on big buildings—if I want my work to really be seen—I will need the skills I can learn doing rock climbing."

Martine and I agree that it's a brilliant idea, although I can tell she's a little disappointed that we won't all be doing Model UN together. Noor asks her about her vacation and shows off the cowbell, making Martine laugh. We compare notes about beaches and hiking trails and the street-art scene and food. It feels comforting and happy, and I'm so glad to be exactly where I am at this moment. Exactly where I should be. Youssef asks Martine a question, and she turns to answer. I look around the schoolyard, noticing faces, wondering if I'll see them in my classes.

On one side of the yard, the blank white side of a narrow building rises sixty feet above us. I nudge Noor with my shoulder. "That would be a great place for a piece." She follows my gaze and laughs. "I'm serious," I say. "Nobody could paint over a building-sized Headscarf Girl." She pulls her sketchbook out of her backpack, and I know I've hooked her. I watch as she fills a page with thumbnail sketches, working out the composition. She turns the page and makes a bigger drawing, of two figures. I recognize myself from the nimbus of curls that surrounds the head and spills over the shoulders of the second girl. I look up at the building again, imagining what the sketch would look like big enough to fill the blank space, and I can see it, faint gray outlines emerging from the flat, white expanse. Then color blooms across the figures: Noor's scarf shimmers with the colors of a forest, from the gold-green of new leaves to the dark blue-green of a stand of fir. My hair takes on the tones of a fall forest, all oranges and reds and russets. Our faces come to life, just as I've seen other faces take shape under Noor's spray can. We look happy. We look strong. Our bodies start to resolve. Noor is wearing tones of violet—pale for her jeans, darker for her long-sleeved tee and Chuck Taylor high-tops. Splashes of color are scattered across her shirt, like she's been painting. My clothes are the color of the sea. Greeny tropical blues shimmer and swoop over my loose top and leggings, darkening to cobalt and lightening again as restlessly as waves. On my feet, I recognize my favorite checkerboard Vans. We're standing on a pedestal of block letters that spell out "Nosh."

The mural continues to develop as I gaze awestruck at it. Shapes gain dimension, colors gain depth. Mural Noor is now holding a spray can, its nozzle pointed straight out like she's painting the air in front of her. There's a quirk to her mouth that wasn't there a minute ago. She looks ready to step off the wall and into the world. I look at Mural Tosh and notice she's holding a padlock in the palm of her hand—an old-fashioned one, with the lock on the front. The shackle is open. Her other hand holds a pick.

"It's spectacular," I say. I imagine showing it to Mina and Lily when they come to visit next summer. It almost seems to be breathing. There's a clatter of wings, and a pigeon rises in front of it—just a normal pigeon being itself, plump and gray and real. The sun catches a patch of iridescent feathers on its neck as it wheels and disappears. Noor is still beside me drawing the mural into life, and I know that soon enough, everyone will see what I'm seeing—two badass girls, sixty feet tall and unstoppable.

Author's Note

If you or someone you know is a victim of sexual assault, you can find help and resources at rainn.org or by calling 800-656-4673.

If you or someone you know is having thoughts of suicide, call or text 988 right away.

ACKNOWLEDGMENTS

This book wouldn't exist without my husband, Kevin Gillies. He moved heaven and earth to get us to France for four wonderful years. Thank you, Kevin. I love you.

You never know who's going to believe in your wild ideas. Rio Thomas, nine years old and apparently absorbed in his Game Boy, looked up and asked, "Are you going to write a book?" after his mom and I had been jokingly pitching story ideas to each other. Rio's belief in me made me believe in myself.

Dan Lazar saw possibilities in the manuscript I sent him and worked patiently with me to develop it. I'm so grateful for his calm support, thoughtful questions, and excellent negotiating skills.

The best editors see the big picture when an author can't even see to the end of the chapter. They have a light touch and a skill for asking insightful questions. Jeannie Thomas read multiple ugly drafts and discussed characters, motivations, and themes endlessly with me as I struggled to turn this into a coherent story. Genevieve Gagne-Hawes (Oxford comma forever!) brought unfailing good cheer and wonderful questions to her edits. She helped me tighten an ambling plot and bring more realistic motivations to my characters. She also encouraged me to give Tosh and Noor the ending they deserve. Ali Romig is *The Uninvited*'s most ardent fan and champion. Working with her was pure delight. Her obvious affection for the characters won my heart, and her thought-provoking editorial questions won my gratitude, because they made rewrites a pleasure. I'm so happy this story found a home with her.

Sarah Chassé, Colleen Fellingham, and Alison Kolani double-checked my facts and ensured that my grammar, spelling, and punctuation were correct and consistent. I'm especially grateful to them for helping me understand the nuances of hyphenating compound words. Any mistakes remaining in the text are entirely mine. Trisha Previte designed the cover of my dreams: beautiful, mysterious, and blood-tinged. Michelle Canoni made the interior design of the book as evocative and lovely as the exterior.

My critique group helped me turn an idea about spooky Paris into a story. Jennie Booth loved Madame Dupuy as much as I do. She earned my undying gratitude by laughing at the funny bits. Kim Graff insisted—correctly—that eleven chapters in was way too late for the Inciting Incident to occur. She also lent her considerable skills with query letters when I was writing mine. Niki Lenz modeled excellent plotting skills. In addition, she patiently, kindly flagged all my paragraph-long sentences until I learned to focus on the idea rather than the flourishes. Katherine Settle showed me how to be a generous critique partner and encouraged me to find a way for Tosh to live.

Dorothy and John Banks, my parents, have always believed in me. I was a student in both their classrooms. Dad taught me design; Mom taught me to write. She read an early version of this book, and I wish she had lived to see what it has become. Dad's enthusiasm encouraged me to keep revising when my own enthusiasm flagged. Maddie Youngberg, pigeon fan extraordinaire, reminded me what it was like to see Paris for the first time. Additionally, she answered my many questions about pop culture, having a blood transfusion, and suicidal ideation. Russell Jones kindly read an early chapter and offered great dialog edits. Tam DeRudder Jackson told me about the Pomodoro Technique. Without it, I would still be stuck in drafting hell. Amy Hyde is the kind of smart, funny, resourceful woman I hope Tosh grows up to be. Afsane Rezaeisahraei gave invaluable feedback about Islam and asked questions that made the book better. Tripp Lake and Alexandra Katich provided helpful legal expertise.

It's against the law to explore any of the Parisian catacombs except the officially sanctioned Catacombes de Paris, so I am indebted to all the cataphiles whose websites, photos, and videos helped me understand what it's like to explore the City of Light's forbidden underground spaces. Two books helped me build a realistic subterranean world. *Les Catacombes de Paris* by Delphine Cerf and illustrated by David Babinet first piqued my interest in the catacombs. Alain

Clément and Gilles Thomas's *Atlas de Paris Souterrain* is an excellent guide to their history, geology, and uses.

Anyone who's interested in how vampire legends originated will find Paul Barber's *Vampires, Burial, and Death* a fascinating read. This one-stop explanation of all things v is where I found the cures for vampirism that Tosh and Noor use.

Enfin, j'ai une dette de gratitude immense envers les françaises et français, qui, avec leur patience, gentillesse, et amabilité, ont fait si heureux notre séjour en France.

About the Author

NANCY BANKS has washed buses, worked as a graphic designer and art director, and co-owned a bookstore. She lived in France for several years and still regrets that she never finished her Epic Pastry Quest. Currently, she lives in Denver with her husband and their dog. *The Uninvited* is her debut novel.